Autumn:

A Twist of Fate

Autumn:

A Twist of Fate

Yasauni

www.urbanbooks.net

Urban Books, LLC
300 Farmingdale Road, N.Y.-Route 109
Farmingdale, NY 11735

Autumn: A Twist of Fate
Copyright © 2024 Yasauni

ISBN 13: 978-1-64556-630-4
EBOOK ISBN: 978-1-64556-631-1

First Trade Paperback Printing September 2024
Printed in the United States of America

10 9 8 7 6 5 4 3 2 1

Distributed by Kensington Publishing Corp.
Submit orders to:
Customer Service
400 Hahn Road
Westminster, MD 21157-4627
Phone: 1-800-733-3000
Fax: 1-800-659-2436

Autumn:

A Twist of Fate

by

Yasauni

Part 1:

Charm

Prologue

Charm

May 1999

"How dare you do this to me?"

I heard my mother's voice carry throughout the house to my room. I opened my eyes, letting them adjust to the pitch-black room.

"It wasn't like that. You don't understand," my father pleaded with my mother.

My heart thumped in my chest and echoed in my ears. I was scared. My parents arguing was new to me. Out of my six years on this earth, I had never heard them raise their voices. Even if I had done something terrible, it never resulted in them yelling at me. Our house was quiet unless we were having company.

"Bitch, I told you to leave!" my mom shouted. I had only heard my aunt Sonya use that word, and she told me never to use it when she said it around me. My dad called it profane language, whatever that meant. All I knew was that I was never to say that word.

"You may live here, but you don't pay any bills. William, you have to choose," my aunt Sonya said.

Why was my mother this upset, and what was my dad choosing? I began to feel butterflies swim in my stomach, and my palms began to sweat. I knew whatever was happening on the first floor would be life-changing. I started to cry. I remembered Aunt Sonya telling me, "You are a big girl, so no tears." So, I wiped my face and sat up in bed, letting my chubby legs swing before my little feet hit the plush pink carpet my mom and I picked out.

"I have been with you over nine years, and *this* is what you do to me? I'm your fucking sister. I raised you when Mama was working her ass off to make sure we could eat." My mother's southern twang, which she tried so hard to cover, predominated in her voice. I took one step toward the door and tripped over thin air. I cursed my clumsiness as my mother went on crying and yelling.

"You two can have each other. I'm taking Charm and leaving. You will never find us." My mother's footsteps thumped on the wooden floors on the first floor. I pushed myself off the floor, carefully opened the door, and walked to the top of the stairs. Then I decided to return to my room for my shoes that light up. My mother said we were leaving, and I wanted to be ready to go when she came for me. I had no idea what was happening, but I would go with her if my mother left. I started descending the stairs, making sure I held on to the railing so I wouldn't fall.

"Over my dead body!" my dad's voice bellowed, causing the walls to shake and me to fall face-first.

I screamed at the top of my lungs, knowing I was about to break something on impact. I thrust my hands forward to brace myself, ready for the impact with the floor. My mother turned just in time to catch me from falling on my face. I wrapped my arms around her neck as she held on to me like this would be the last time she would ever hug me. Finally, she put me down, making sure I was steady on my feet. She rubbed her hands over my head down to the tip of the twisted ponytail she had made three days ago.

As I looked around the room, I saw the stress and tension on everyone's faces. The air down here was so thick I could barely breathe. I saw the pain etched on my mother's tear-stained face. My dad wiped his hands down his face like he had the weight of the world on his shoulders, but Aunt Sonya's face is one that I could never forget. She had an expression of devious satisfaction.

"Baby, I love you. Always remember that no matter what happens in the future or what anyone in this house tells you. Are you going to remember that?" Mama questioned. I nodded.

"Say it," she demanded. As tears rolled down my chubby cheeks, my mother wiped them away.

"Always remember that you love me," I repeated. My mother pulled me close to her, hugging me and rubbing my back in small circles.

"That's right. Mommy will be back soon to see you. In the meantime, be a good girl for your dad and auntie Sonya." She choked on her words, then hiccupped.

My mother went to her room on the first floor, packed a small bag, put on a jacket, and walked out the door. I watched out the window as she got into a waiting cab. I sat there for hours, crying at the window as my dad and aunt tried to console me. My mother had never left the house without me; if she did, she would be back before I got home from school.

Even as a child, I knew something wasn't right about this night. Something told me that this moment would forever impact my life, but I didn't know precisely how or why. Weeks passed, and I asked for my mom constantly. Aunt Sonya did everything my mom had done in the house, including caring for me, but everything seemed different. My dad was happier than I had seen him in a while. He would do the same things with Aunt Sonya that he used to do with my mom. Before Aunt Sonya moved in, he was just as happy with my mother. I was confused about what was going on. One day, he came home and kissed Aunt Sonya on the lips. He set some papers on the counter, then whispered something in her ear. Her facial expression changed from happy to sad in a heartbeat.

"When is Mom coming home?" I asked as they stood in the kitchen.

"Baby girl, let's sit down. We need to talk." My dad and aunt Sonya both grabbed my hands, and we walked over to the couch. I could see the sadness in their eyes as my dad pulled me into his lap.

"We need to talk about Mommy," he told me. Aunt Sonya put her hand on my back and rubbed it in small circles. I turned to look at her. Her eyes were full of tears, and so were my father's.

"Mommy had a bad accident when she went away." His voice cracked, and he cleared his throat.

"Where is she? Is she coming home?" I asked, not understanding what he was saying.

"No, baby," Aunt Sonya answered, and my father cut his eyes at her.

"What do you mean, no? She promised she would come to see me. Where is she?" Tears came to my eyes. My mom would never tell me she would do something and not follow through.

"Baby, remember when Greg, the fish, went to heaven, and I told you he was going to be with God and my mom and dad would take care of him?"

I nodded, remembering when my parents stood in the bathroom with me as I flushed my first pet down the toilet. My parents explained that Greg was going to fish heaven, and my grandparents would feed him for me.

"Well, baby, Mommy has gone to heaven with Greg." My little brain couldn't process what my dad and aunt told me. My mother would never leave me. She was just here a couple of weeks ago, and we had talked about her coming back here to see me.

"Daddy, why would Mommy leave me? She promised she would be back." Tears had formed in my eyes and were now running down my face. My dad pulled me close to him, hugging me.

They wasted no time putting a small funeral together that consisted of my dad, aunt, my best friend, Autumn, and me. They told me that my mother would've wanted an intimate funeral without a lot of people crying over her body. My dad let me pick out a pretty white and gold casket and the colors we would wear to put my mother to rest. We stood in the mausoleum with a closed casket and a plot with my mother's name on it. I couldn't stop the tears that continuously came from knowing I would never see my mother again.

"We can share my mother," Autumn whispered, locking her hand in mine.

"Thanks," I whispered back.

After the preacher prayed over the casket, we returned to the limousine and went out to eat. My dad and aunt did everything to make me feel better that day, but nothing worked. The only thing that would have made me happy was seeing my mother enter the restaurant doors.

"I know I'm only your aunt, but I will do everything in my power to make sure you never feel like you don't have a mother. I will be here for you every step of the way."

Her intentions were good, but nothing compared to having my own mother here to care for me.

After my mom's untimely demise, the years flew by. By the time I turned 7, my father and aunt had married. I struggled with the knowledge of my aunt now being my stepmother. When I turned 10, my little brother Donovan was born, and I was the happiest big sister in the world. I was no longer the only child. When I heard his cries in the middle of the night, I would get up to help Aunt Sonya feed him. As soon as I got home from school, the first thing I did was check on him. I would go into his room when everyone was asleep at night to ensure he was still breathing. I loved Donovan so much that I didn't want God to take him away from me like he did with my mom.

Chapter 1

Charm

I sat at the table, nervous as hell. I couldn't believe I was really about to do this. If it weren't for losing a bet I knew I would win against my best friend, Autumn, I would enjoy our girls' night out. I sat at the table, tapping my foot to the girl singing off-key onstage. To everyone else here, it probably seemed like I was enjoying myself, but Autumn knew differently. I could tell from the smile she was wearing on her face that she knew I was about to make a puddle in this seat.

"You're going to be great. Why are you so scared?"

I heard what she said but ignored her until she kicked me under the table. I finally glanced her way, and she gave me a reassuring smile. She knew better than anyone else that I feared singing in public. Singing did something to me. I felt like everything in the world was good when I let the music rhythm pump through my veins, and the lyrics flow from my mouth. The only thing wrong is I would get in front of these people and probably throw up, or worse, fall off the stage. When I get nervous in front of people, serious things happen. Like the first day my boyfriend, Michael, tried to talk to me, I ran into a street pole. Or when my father begged me to sing at his best friend's wedding, one of my heels got caught on the runner, and I fell. I could go on and on about how accident-prone I am when I'm nervous or emotional.

"Don't worry about me; worry about calling the cutie whose number you just got."

She rubbed her hand over her pixie cut and kind of smiled. I would get through this without a hitch. I just wanted my friend to go out on a date for once in her life. Autumn and I had been friends since we were 4. When we turned 18, I went to college, and she joined the marines. Almost three years later, her triplet sister, Winter, died, and Autumn became a mother to her 3-year-old nephew, Storm. Something as tragic as that hit her, her parents, and her sister, Summer, hard, but Autumn felt it differently because she had been away for five years.

"What are you going to sing?"

"I'll figure it out before I get up there," I told her, sitting back in my seat and relaxing.

"You're up next. I already put your name on the list."

I immediately sat up straight. I wasn't ready. I began to bite down on my lip, feeling the rush of butterflies hit my stomach.

"Why would you do that?" I whined, wanting to strangle her.

"I knew you would wait until the last minute and then find a reason not to do it."

She knew me well. Before I could lie to her, saying I wouldn't do that, they announced my name and the spotlight landed on me.

"I picked out a song for you too. Knock 'em dead, girl."

Autumn smiled at me as I got up. I moved around the table, making sure not to bump into anyone. The last thing I wanted was for them to start complaining about the big girl who knocked over their drink or bumped into them. I was so nervous, my hands began to sweat as I ascended the stairs . . . and tripped on the second stair. I closed my eyes as a wave of embarrassment hit me. One of the men from the table I dared Autumn to get a number from came up, giving me his hand as I made it up the last three stairs. I gave him a nod of thanks, and he gave me a dimpled smile that made my heart skip a beat.

I stood before the microphone, and the beginning of Beyoncé's "Halo" filled the speakers. I closed my eyes, and when the music cued me to sing, I opened my eyes, focused on Mr. Dimples, and let the words flow right out of me. When I hit the last note, everyone stood up, clapping, whistling, and yelling for me to sing something else. I took a bow, and Mr. Dimples gave me his hand to help me down the stairs. I returned to the table, where Autumn was jumping up and down with a huge smile.

"Every time I hear you sing, you sound better than the last time. You really should be in someone's studio." She hugged me tightly before we sat down.

"You know she's right. My name is Chase."

Mr. Dimples had come behind me, and I hadn't noticed. He held his hand out to me for the third time this evening, but this time, to introduce himself.

"Nice to meet you, Chase. I'm Charm."

I took his hand in mine, hoping that I wasn't turning red from blushing. This man was the epitome of everything holy and sinful. He is the prettiest man I have seen in my life. I knew I would go straight to hell entertaining him when I had a man, but I couldn't help staring at him. Those hazel bedroom eyes, thick eyebrows, long, thick, black eyelashes, thick black hair that I would love to run my fingers through, scruffy beard and goatee, medium muscular build, tall frame, nice smile, and Lord, those dimples . . . My mouth instantly went dry, and I thought about everything hidden underneath his clothes. I had never in my life dated outside of my race or thought about cheating on Michael, but Chase made me want to do all of the above. I diverted my eyes to the floor, thinking, *Why would he want to date someone like me?*

"Can I buy you a drink?"

Autumn nudged my arm, getting my attention.

"No, thank you. We were just about to leave," I blew him off.

"How about your number?" he asked with so much hope in his eyes.

"I have a boyfriend," I told him, getting up and leaving the bar.

I stood by my car, waiting for Autumn. Suddenly, the door to the bar burst open, and she stood there, gazing around the parking lot until her eyes fell on me.

"What was all that about?" she yelled across the lot, waiting for an answer.

When she approached me, I was looking down at my shoes.

"Look at me, Charm."

I raised my head, looking everywhere except in her eyes. Autumn came home looking for the old Charm, ready to take the world by storm. While growing up, Autumn was my rock. After my mother took off on my dad and me when I was 6, my family was turned upside down. My aunt Sonya began to help out with me, and everything was going smoothly until a year later when she became Stepmother Sonya. After my father put a ring on her finger, she became downright mean and degrading. Autumn and her mother kept my spirits up and told me I was beautiful. I had never been small, even as a child, and they made sure I knew the world wasn't right in their estimation of beauty.

There was so much that Autumn didn't know about me, and I didn't want to get into it right now. I would have told her when she came home, but she had just lost her sister and gained a child. This was our first girls' night out, and we went to a bar. I didn't want to burden her with my insecurities. They don't call it self-esteem for nothing. That means I need to work on it.

"Talk to me, Char." She shortened my name like she had done so many times.

"Why would a beautiful man like him want to talk to me? Out of all the beautiful model-sized women in there, he wanted me. He must have been looking at all this expensive shit Michael wants me to have on when I'm walking out of the door," I blurted out my thoughts without thinking.

I looked down at the matching Saint Laurent pumps, purse, and 5-carat princess-cut tennis bracelet. Everything I had on, people killed for, especially living in Chicago. Hell, they killed for less. All this stuff I had come with was the price of my humanity. Michael feels that keeping me in the most expensive things will keep people from seeing that I'm overweight.

"What do you mean by that? He came to talk to you because you are a beautiful, full-figured woman with the voice of a damn angel. Where is all this coming from? Your evil stepmother or that prick you call your man, Michael?"

"We can talk about this later. I just want to go home and sleep," I told her.

"I had fun tonight. See you later and don't think this discussion is over."

I didn't say anything. I got in my car to drive to my condo on the Lower South Side. Since it was late, my drive from downtown was quick. I couldn't wait to get inside the house and drown my sorrows in some Chunky Monkey ice cream. I kicked off my heels at the door, went right to the kitchen, got my ice cream and a spoon, and then flopped down on the couch. I picked up the remote, found a chick flick, and dug in. The explosion of flavor hitting my taste buds put me in a state of euphoria.

"That's the last thing you need this time of night," he said as I closed my eyes, leaning back on the couch.

He was wrong. The last thing I needed was for him to be at my house while I was trying to eat away my depression. *Why couldn't he stay at his house? Why did I give him a damn key to my house?* I thought.

"You're right, babe," I responded, placing the ice cream back in the freezer, only for him to go behind me and dump it in the garbage disposal.

"You want to talk about the man whose face you were in tonight?"

Here he goes again. For him to be such an intelligent man, he lets his imagination run wild.

"And what man would that be?" I questioned.

"The man at the Lion's Den Bar at the table with you."

"He was no one," I answered, irritated that he was spying on me.

"He didn't look like he was no one. It seemed he knew you well with how close he stood to you and how you were smiling all in his face."

"I'm not about to do this with you tonight—or any other night."

I practically stomped to my room, stripping out of my clothes and pulling out a night tee to sleep in. He stood at the door watching me with his face contorted.

"What?" I raised my voice, annoyed with him.

"You need to lose at least eighty more pounds before you start stripping in front of me."

His words were like a bulldozer to my heart. I shouldn't have been shocked. He has said way worse to me, but tonight, for some reason, it hurt like it was the first time. I looked down at myself, remembering a time I loved everything about me. Years of being with a man who puts me down every chance he gets does this to you.

When I first met Michael, he was so attentive and loving. He stayed that way for about two years before he started doing what he called "critiquing" me. Critiquing turned into criticizing, and criticizing turned into blatantly being disrespectful. Then he began working on my self-esteem, reminding me no one else would want me. He was my first everything. I pray every day that we can return to how it used to be. But as each day passes, I know the chances get slimmer. Other than his little quirks, he's a good man, or at least as good as I can get.

Chapter 2

Chase

"At least you thought about what we talked about and acted on it," my father, Collen, said from the other side of the table.

When I moved back to Chicago several months ago, my father talked with me about my nonexistent dating habits and my ex-girlfriend, Allysa. Allysa and I dated throughout high school and half of college. That girl was the best thing in my entire little world, but she always complained about our long-distance relationship. We would travel back and forth every chance we got. My being in Massachusetts at Harvard and her being in Chicago at UIC took a toll on us and our relationship. She complained about travel and being unable to see me when she wanted until she stopped answering my calls one day.

When I rushed to Chicago to see what was happening, I found her with my childhood best friend at the country club. That was the day I decided to leave Chicago for good. I would spend time with my family over the winter break after college. I chose never to move back here again, but here I am. There's only one thing that could bring a person back to a place that they have sworn off, and that's money . . . and a lot of it. I'm a businessman and a damn good one. I have run some of the most lucrative businesses worldwide, including my own. ChasingLan Inc. is a multimillion-dollar company that I built from the ground up. My specialty is restructuring companies.

After pulling together my money and buying out my first drowning company, people began to notice me. I did the same thing three more times, and then the board of executives from different companies started to contact me, offering me large sums of money to help them with their businesses. I knew my businesses were in good hands, so I took them up on their offers. Since Chicago was a place I didn't want to be in for too long, I refused the offer of a current CEO asking me for help. However, after several calls from him and an eight-figure deal, I agreed to return to the Windy City as acting CEO of a business that had seen more money than I had made in the last four years. I still couldn't believe that this business was on the brink of bankruptcy.

"You're so off your game, you are making women run away." I wanted to punch my friend Dylan in the stomach. He was sitting on his high horse because Charm's friend, Autumn, approached him for his number.

"Screw you, Dylan." I slumped back in my seat, watching Dylan gloat.

He was right. I was off my game. I could smile at any woman, and she would be willing to do anything I wanted for the night, but not Charm. I hadn't dated in quite some time, but I still had women's company every now and then. I had so many one-night stands I didn't even know women still wanted to be wooed.

"She said she has a boyfriend."

"That's what all women say when they don't want to be bothered," Dylan retorted.

I sat back, thinking about the woman named Charm. She was so beautiful in more ways than one. Her cinnamon complexion and big brown eyes lit up when she sang, but her full lips and gorgeous round face are what caught my attention. The fact that she was more than a handful of woman made me want her even more. The heels she wore made her plump, luscious ass sit up high on her back. What I liked most about her was her confidence in how she walked. Even while tripping up the stairs to the stage, she had a way of still standing tall and getting the job done. I could tell she was the type of woman a man like myself needed in my life. Although she stumbled, she could get up with all the confidence she walked through the club with.

"I'm about to head out. I have an early flight in the morning." Dylan and I both stood up, giving each other a back-thumping hug.

"Thanks for coming out here to help me find a place," I told him as he walked out of the bar.

Dylan was a top real estate agent who made a living selling houses to the rich and famous. When I chose to move back to Chicago, I finally bought a place I could call my own. I didn't come here to visit my parents often, but when I did, I would just go back to my childhood home for my stay. Since I planned to be here for a while, I knew I needed my own place. Who would be better to help me with that than someone who knew what I liked? I had made the right choice calling him out here for reinforce-ment. Dylan had found me a penthouse in Lakeshore East close to the water. The floor-to-ceiling windows gave me a great view of the Chicago River and downtown Chicago. I was in the thick of everything I loved about living here: the fast pace of the city and the most beautiful skyline I have ever seen. Plus, it was close to work and the bars. If I had to be here, I would be surrounded by everything I love, including the water.

"It's kind of late. I'm going to follow Dylan's lead." I called for the waitress to close my tab as my father dropped a large cash tip on the table for her.

We left the bar, and my dad got into his car.

"You want me to drop you home?"

"No, it's only around the corner. I'm going to walk."

"Okay, son."

I tapped the top of the hood before he pulled off and began my walk home. I had been in Chicago for a couple of months getting settled in. Tomorrow, I will be starting my job as acting CEO of Forest & Co. Forest Foods has been around my entire life. It began with a few stores in the Chicago area. As time passed, the stores began to pop up throughout the Midwest; now, they are all over the United States. These stores were like Walmart. There isn't anywhere in the States you could go and not find a Forest Foods close. Everything I knew about this company ran through my mind as I walked home. I knew someone was stealing money, but I couldn't pinpoint who that person was.

I walked into my penthouse, took a deep breath, and looked around; it was so quiet.

"I should get a dog," I stated out loud, hearing a brief echo.

I sat on the black Italian leather couch and put my feet up on the table, throwing my head back. If I were being truthful with myself, I was lonely. Over the past year and a half, I have watched my friends, Brenton and Dennis, settle down with the love of their lives. They were happy. Dennis even had a baby. My goddaughter, London, will be turning 2 soon; sadly, she is the only glimpse of happiness I have. Though London has three godfathers, I feel like she loves me the most. Brenton, Dylan, Dennis, and I went to Harvard together. We helped each other there and overcame many things throughout the years we have been friends. We've been through everything from breakups to overbearing family members, death, and abductions. We have always found ways to be there for one another and get ourselves through it.

I closed my eyes, shaking off all these feelings of being alone. Then I sat up and picked up the bag next to me. I pulled out my Mac and all the papers I had tucked neatly into the bag. Powering up my laptop, I began to go through the files for Forest & Co. I knew I was missing something vital. I reviewed the numbers over the last three months and who had access to the company's accounts. I finally decided to close the computer and get some rest. I would figure this out in the morning. Right now, I need some sleep.

I lay in bed tossing and turning, but I couldn't sleep. I placed my hand on the empty side of the bed, feeling the coolness of the sheets. The thought of Charm being next to me crossed my mind, and within seconds, I had a massive hard-on. It had been awhile since I had gotten laid, and moving to Chicago would make this even more challenging because I didn't have a female friend to fix the problem. I wouldn't be able to sleep like this. I groaned, got out of bed, and walked to the bathroom for a shower.

"I guess it's me and you again." I looked down at my left hand. It had been awhile since I had to do this. I shook my head, checked the water temperature, and stepped into the shower. This was going to be a long night.

I woke up looking at the clock before hitting my alarm. It felt like I had only slept a few hours. I needed at least another thirty minutes of sleep. So, I closed my eyes, not wanting to get out of bed. Then I thought better of it. This was my first official day on the job. I opened my eyes. I had to get ready. When I got out of bed, I dragged my feet across the cool wooden floors, going into my walk-in closet. Today would be about getting everything in order. I had a meeting with the board of directors at nine. I pulled out my black Stefano Ricci single-breasted suit and added a navy blue tie and matching shoes. I was a firm believer that your first impression was your best impression. My clothes would show I was about to restore order to this company.

I grabbed everything I would need for the day and headed out the door. The corporate office was a ten-minute walk from my penthouse. Since I was a little early, I casually walked down the street as everyone around me rushed past and pushed through the crowds. I walked up to the office doors and stopped in my tracks. It was *her* carrying so much stuff in her hands. I wasn't sure if she saw me.

Charm.

She ran right into me, dropping everything in her hands, including coffee, on both of us.

Chapter 3

Charm

"I am *so* sorry," I apologized profusely. I couldn't believe this was happening to me. Out of everyone in Chicago I could have run into today, it had to be Chase. Not only did my nervousness make me run into him, but I also wasted all four cups of coffee on us.

"It's okay. At least it was all iced coffee. You can stop apologizing."

Chase looked at me, causing me to look down at myself. Coffee had stained my cream blouse and navy blue pencil skirt. I glanced at him, and his suit was ruined.

"I will pay to have all your things cleaned. I am so sorry."

I took a second to write down my number on one of the napkins I held. I didn't have a lot of time. My shift started in an hour, and I needed to be back by then, or my boss would shit bricks.

"I can take care of it, but I need to go back home and change before work," Chase told me, turning to run in the opposite direction.

I could kick myself in the ass for this. Why did I have to be *that* person who can trip over thin air when I get nervous? Sitting in traffic, I cursed up a storm. Fighting traffic during rush hour was like pulling teeth. When I got to the house, I moved at lightning speed, trying to hurry to get back to work. Just how the day started let me know that today would be the day from hell. I wanted to do nothing more than crawl back into bed and start everything over tomorrow. Playing hooky from work began to sound really good. Then my phone rang. I looked at the screen, rolling my eyes, then answered.

"You are late!" My boss, Joseph, or as he preferred, Mr. Hillard, yelled into my ear.

I glanced at the clock on my nightstand. It was one minute after nine. I could have literally been getting ready to step off the elevator at this moment. I took a deep breath, so I wouldn't say anything that could get me fired.

"I know, Mr. Hillard. I had a little accident right outside the building, and I had to come back home, but I'm on my way now," I explained, stepping into my Jimmy Choos.

"That's no excuse. As soon as you get here, come to the boardroom. We have a meeting. And expect a write-up too."

I pressed the end button on the phone before yelling every explicit word I could think to call him. This was my *first* time being late in my four years working for the company. I made it to work an hour early every day and stayed as late as needed—only for him to write me up for *one* time of being late. Since I was being punished anyway, I took an extra five minutes to make myself a latte. Walking out the door with my caffeine in my hand, I happily made the thirty-minute drive to work.

I stepped off the elevator, ready to speak to my coworkers . . . only to see somber and frightened faces. As I tried to catch any of their eyes, they turned away or looked down.

"What's going on?" I asked one of my coworkers in accounting about it.

"Check your email."

I trotted to my desk, pulled up my email, and read over the document sent to me. Now I understood why Joseph was being an ass. *His* job was on the line. Since I was assistant to the chief financial officer as well as an accountant for the company, what did that mean for me? I jumped up, remembering that he had told me to come to the boardroom once I arrived. I picked up my laptop, jogging the best I could on the four-inch heels I wore. I looked through the windows of the tall glass boardroom to see many pissed-off faces. The new CEO had his back turned, looking out on the street, then he turned around. My eyes landed on his face as I was opening the door . . . only to trip right into his arms.

"I'm so-so sorry," I stuttered, looking down at my feet.

"The third time within two days. I must be one lucky man," he whispered as he helped steady me on my feet.

I was past being embarrassed. I held my head down as I walked to my seat on the other side of my boss. If looks could kill, I would have dropped dead right where I sat as hard as Mr. Hillard was glaring at me. He had a way to look at you when he was displeased, and that made you want to crawl under a rock.

"Charm Linsey, I presume," Chase nodded at me as he spoke. "I'm glad that you could make it. I personally requested that you be here in this meeting today because I have a special job for you." He paused, walking around the room, passing some empty chairs.

Where are Nancy and Philip? I thought as he stood behind the chair in which Philip usually sat. What in the hell is happening in this room? I searched the faces around me and noticed the expressions that I thought were of people being pissed off were actually expressions of utter fear.

"Charm, you are a very intelligent woman. Why are you the assistant to the CFO instead of doing what you went to school for?"

I sat with my mouth open, unsure if I should answer the question. When I started working for Forest four years ago, I was fresh out of college, searching for someone to give me a chance at accounting. Mr. Hillard hired me as his assistant, promising to move me up in the company. He told me as soon as an accounting position became available, I would be the first to get the job. Technically speaking, I had a job in accounting because I did plenty of work in that field. I just didn't have the title to go with it. Working here paid my bills and had its incentives. I made a decent amount of money. I know it should've been more, but why trade my peace of mind for money? I know the ins and outs of this company. Mr. Hillard could be a better person and boss, but it could be way worse.

"I'm waiting for an answer."

I looked from Mr. Hillard to Chase.

"Well, I'm content with my job," I answered, hoping it wasn't wrong. Mr. Hillard smiled, and Chase gave me an expression that made me feel like he knew my deepest, darkest secret.

"Four years of undergrad with a double major in business and accounting. Plus, another two to get your master's in accounting, and you are content with being an *assistant*?"

I swallowed. *Who gave this man my information?* I was nervous and started fidgeting, knocking over Mr. Hillard's cup of coffee. I could see the steam coming out of his ears. Mr. Hillard was pissed, shaking his hand that the cold coffee had spilled on.

"You are an absolute klutz."

My eyes dropped to the floor. "I'm so sorry. Let me get you another." I stood up, but Chase held up a hand to stop me.

"No need to be nervous, and there's no need for you to get Joseph's coffee. Since you have been doing all of his work over the years, you now have it permanently. Joseph, you can go collect your things. You're fired."

I sat in my chair feeling faint. Mr. Hillard jumped out of his chair.

"I have worked here for over fifteen years. You, on the other hand, have been here all of *two hours*, and you're firing *me?* I will sue this company for every damn thing it's worth. You don't know who I am."

Mr. Hillard stomped up to Chase like he was ready to have the fight of his life. Chase nonchalantly wiped imaginary lint off his suit jacket as Mr. Hillard stood before him, cursing with spit flying from his mouth like a rabid dog.

"You have several options. You can stay here and tell me who else has helped you steal money from this company. You could try to fight me, lose, and go to jail for assault. You can pack your things, leave here, and hire a lawyer. Or, you can act an ass and leave here in cuffs for the very reason you are being terminated. You choose."

Mr. Hillard closed his mouth after Chase had spoken. He walked to the table, picked up his belongings, and headed for the door.

"Leave the laptop. That is company property." Mr. Hillard walked to Chase, trying to hand him the laptop. Chase nodded toward the table, and Mr. Hillard set it down.

"Write down the password, please." He scribbled something on a piece of paper and walked out the door. I had never seen that man so compliant since I started here.

"This meeting is adjourned for today. Remember to send me everything I asked for. We will reconvene here again in two days. Charm, please meet me in my office in thirty minutes."

I nodded, picked up my things, and headed to my desk. I needed to take a breather. I guess my day has changed for the better. I sat at my desk, thinking of everything that had happened in the last thirty minutes. I was now the head of an entire department. I wanted to stand up, scream, or jump up and down excited about my promotion. But I knew I couldn't do any of that, so I did the next best thing. I sent out a text to the people I love.

Charm: I just got a promotion! *smiley emoji*

Autumn: Congrats, I'm so proud of you!

Michael: Great. Do you want to talk about your cheating last night?

Autumn: WTF is he talking about?

I slapped myself on the forehead. I had them in a group text. My phone began vibrating in my hand. I wasn't about to let them kill my mood, so I turned off my phone and headed to Chase's office. I knocked on his door and waited for him to respond. When he didn't, I stuck my head in the door. Then I turned to his receptionist.

"Are you sure he's in here?"

"Yes. He wanted you to come straight in," she replied.

I walked into the room to hear him whispering from his private bathroom.

"Can you believe my luck? It's the same woman from last night. She is even more beautiful now. I guess the heels are an everyday thing for her because she has some on now. Yes, and she fell right into my arms. If only I could have one taste of her. I swear she . . . I have to go. Later, Dylan."

I listened to a one-sided conversation until Chase came out of the bathroom. Looking sheepish, he stood in front of me as I narrowed my eyes at him.

"If you think promoting me and giving me a raise is going to get you some ass, think again. I have morals and too much to live for to sell myself short."

His mouth dropped open, and his eyes widened. I turned to open the door to the office. I didn't have to take this shit. I dealt with enough working for Mr. Hillard, and he *never* approached me that way.

"I would never do that. I apologize if anything I said made you feel that way. Please have a seat, and we can talk about this."

I hesitated but backtracked my steps. I decided not to sit. I stood behind the chair, holding my laptop to my chest like a safety net.

"Please, sit. We have a lot to go over."

Chase sat behind his desk. Only then did I sit in the chair facing him. He made a face that caused his dimples to come out. They looked like delicate carvings on his face. I have had many "I can't believe it" moments today, but I think him being my new boss is the most fascinating. As he spoke, I admired his full pink lips as they moved.

"Are we good?"

I blinked several times at his question. "I'm sorry. Can you repeat that?" I asked, trying not to return to a perfect world where he was kissing me all over my body.

"I was saying that I would never compromise myself by doing something so unethical. I promoted you to CFO because you know the ins and outs of the job. It takes too much to hire someone and teach them everything you already know. You have done a job that someone else has been getting paid for, for years, and you have been great at it. It just made sense to give you the job and raise to go with it."

"Did you know who I was last night?"

"No. I didn't even know you were the same Charm I would give the job to until this morning when you dumped your coffee on me." He laughed, but I felt my face turning red from embarrassment.

"I really am sorry about that." I bit my lip, hoping he knew I was telling the truth.

"We're past that. I want to know if you could work with me on getting this company back in order. I know we are attracted to each other, but can you put that to the side?" he questioned.

"That is behind me. I told you last night that I am in a committed relationship." I didn't know how often I had to tell him that I was with someone, but hopefully, he would listen this time.

"Charm, I don't want you to misunderstand anything I'm about to say. Helping this company means more to me than any piece of ass. Mr. Forest is paying me a lot of money to complete the job. This is not a ploy to get into your pants. I need your help finding out who else has their hands on the company's money. Working with you can help me get this information quicker, but I'm willing to find someone else in your department to help me get the job done. Are you willing to help, or should I get someone else?"

I was baffled by his directness. I sat there silent for a minute. Listening to what he said to me showed me that this was not the same man who tried to woo me last night. This was Chase the Businessman.

"What do you need me to do?" I pulled out a pen and pad to take notes.

"First, I need you to know that helping me with this will have you working earlier and later than usual. If this will cause problems in your relationship, please leave now."

He paused, waiting to see if I would head to the door. When I didn't, he continued.

"Second, you need to hire an assistant. There will be times that you will not be in your office. If something important comes up, you can get the message immediately. The position that you are holding now requires you to have some business dinners and sometimes go out of town. Here's your company cell and laptop. You can move into your office. Your new salary has already been uploaded to the system. You can leave early today to celebrate, but be in tomorrow at seven. We have a lot to get done."

I nodded and got up from my seat. "Thank you, Chase."

"By the way, I wrote some info down for you and I will email you everything you need for tomorrow morning. Congratulations, Charm." He smiled at me as I walked out the door.

Chapter 4

Charm

When I walked into my new office, I sat behind the huge cherrywood desk, took a deep breath, and slowly exhaled. I couldn't believe that I'd gotten such a huge promotion. I had to pinch myself to make sure I wasn't dreaming. I picked up the office phone and called my father. If no one else shared my joy, I knew I could count on him and Autumn.

"Hey, Dad," I spoke happily into the phone as soon as he answered it.

"Hey, baby girl. How are you today?" he asked in his deep, soothing voice that I loved to hear.

"I have some great news."

"Hold on. Let me put it on speaker so your mother can hear too." I rolled my eyes as I heard him calling her name, telling her I had something to say to them. I could hear her mumbling something in the background.

"Go ahead, sweetheart. We're both here," my dad finally said.

"I just got a promotion to chief financial officer," I all but yelled through the phone.

"That's great, baby."

"I thought you were about to say Michael proposed. I don't know why I would think that when he caught you cheating on him last night," my stepmother accused in the background. I rolled my eyes. I have no idea why my dad even put her on the phone. She always found a way to make my accomplishments sound like they were nothing.

"I'm sorry you were misinformed."

"Misinformed? He caught you in the act." For the life of me, I didn't understand why Michael felt the need to tell my aunt everything, including lies.

"Well, Aunt Sonya, he's delusional, just like you are," I spit venomously.

"There's no need to get disrespectful, Charm. Mind your mother," my dad, the peacemaker, said. I didn't know whose judgment was clouded the most, my dad's or Sonya's. I just wanted to hang up the phone without saying goodbye, but my dad deserved better than that. I ended the call respectfully, sending my love.

I closed my eyes, then remembered the piece of paper that Chase had given me. I unfolded it and almost fainted at the number of zeros behind my new yearly salary. I was making way more money than Michael. I took several breaths so that I wouldn't scream. Then I rushed through moving everything from my cubicle to my office and getting it functional. By the time I finished, it was lunchtime. I packed up my things and left for the day, driving right to Autumn.

I pulled into her driveway, and she opened the door before I exited the car. She had been doing that since we were kids. I never understood how she knew I was there. She would tell me I was one of her twins, and it was a part of her telepathy. As I approached her, I knew the first thing she would say. I held up my hand, stopping her.

"You get one minute to get it off your chest. After that, we celebrate." I set the timer on my Apple watch and nodded for her to start.

"You need to leave that good-for-nothing-ass kid you call a man. You know he's a kid because he let his imagination run wild. What were you thinking when you started dating him? Even I know your loyalty runs deep, and you would never cheat on him."

My watch beeped, and I cut her off. "Now that that's over, do you have wine so we can celebrate? We will talk about Michael another day. Today, I want to celebrate this." I held the paper up showing her my new salary, and she screamed, jumping up and down, and hugging me.

"I'm so happy for you that I don't know what to say." She stared at the paper.

"Don't say anything. Let's drink."

We got our glasses of wine and went into the sitting room. I told her all the events that happened today, from me spilling coffee on Chase this morning to him offering me the job of a lifetime. Autumn was just as shocked as I was to discover that Chase was now my boss.

"Do you think you and Chase will have a hot, steamy work romance?" She smiled big and wiggled her eyebrows.

"You need to find a man and stop reading all those romance novels. You're beginning to think real life is like the books."

"I don't think that way. I know that you deserve better than Michael. You might not see it, but I do. I'm just afraid of what will happen when you notice he's not what you need. Your man's eyes should light up every time he sees you. He should tell you you're beautiful every day because you are. He should uplift you and be happy when you accomplish small and big goals. Not down you because you are a size sixteen instead of a six."

Tears came to my eyes as she spoke. I knew Michael was an asshole 80 percent of the time, but the other 20 percent, when he showed me affection, I knew he loved me.

"You don't understand," I told her with my head hung low.

"I understand that Michael looks good on paper, and that's the reason you are holding on so tight. I understand that, for some reason, you don't feel worthy of having all that you deserve out of relationships. What I *don't* understand is why you have buried who you really are. Where is the confident woman who loved all of her curves and didn't care who didn't?"

"She's long gone," I whispered. Autumn used her index finger to lift my tear-stained face.

"I'm willing to help you get her back, whatever it takes. If it takes me getting up and going to the gym with you or having to sit through a church service, I'm here."

"Today, we are supposed to be celebrating me," I told her, wiping my face with a paper towel.

"We are celebrating you finding yourself."

Her saying those words spoke volumes to me. It was like something shifted in the atmosphere and made me feel something big was about to happen. Maybe Michael would finally begin to love me as I am, but I didn't want to spend too much time thinking about it.

By seven that evening, I was so drunk I knew I wasn't driving anywhere. I handed Autumn the keys to my car so she could drop it off to me sometime tomorrow. We stood in the doorway singing, waiting for my Uber to pull up.

"I love you, Char. Have a good night."

"I love you too, Autumn. See you tomorrow."

I hugged her, got into the car, and rested my head against the window. I would have to take some aspirin before I went to bed, or I would wake up with one hell of a hangover. It seemed as soon as I closed my eyes, we were pulling up to my apartment. I staggered out of the car and thanked the driver before walking into my building.

I walked into the home with my eyes practically closed. All I wanted was to get in bed.

"You can open your eyes anytime now."

My eyes popped open to see Michael standing in front of me. *Why couldn't he just give me tonight without being here talking crazy?* I rolled my eyes. I wanted to ask him to leave, but that would be rude of me.

"I stopped by your office today to take you to lunch and noticed that the man I thought you were cheating on me with is your boss. I owe you an apology, honey. I just get so jealous when I think of you with another man. I love you, babe."

"Love you too," I slurred, then stumbled to my room to find gifts on my bed.

I was too intoxicated for this. From the smile on his face, I knew he wanted me to fawn over everything he had gotten me. This was his way of saying he was sorry for everything he had done over the last twenty-four hours. The more expensive the gift, the more he had messed up. Michael thrived from showing off the things he could buy me. People would look at me and feel like I was loved and well taken care of. He loved that image. It was everything to him. If I were completely honest with myself, I can say that he ensures I have the best of everything. It's just other parts of this relationship that are lacking something significant.

I sat on the bed, kicking off my heels, and picked up the biggest box on the bed. I gazed up at Michael. He genuinely smiled as he waited for me to open the neatly wrapped box. Ripping the paper from the box, I opened it, and there was a purple Chanel patent double-flap bag and purple velvet Chanel pumps.

"I thought you might want something new for your new journey at work."

This gift was so him. The shoes and purse were pretty, and as expensive as they were, they lacked value for me. There was no thought put into it. I got the same gift from him when he felt bad about something he had done or said something wrong. I moved over to the next box, which was likely jewelry. When I opened the box, there was a gold and diamond heart pendant on a thick snake gold chain. He was so predictable that these things didn't excite me anymore. I placed a smile on my face and played the role I had been playing for years.

"Thank you, babe. I appreciate it."

"So, what type of benefits do you get from becoming CFO? I know it will be more work, but is the pay worth it?"

"The best benefit overall is that I'm finally recognized for the work I have been doing for years."

"That's not answering the question, Charm. If we are working on taking our relationship to the next level, we need to know what each other is bringing to the table. I have never hidden anything like money from you. So, don't be ashamed if it's not much, but don't let the company run over you either. If they upgraded your position, you must demand that they upgrade your pay."

I listened attentively as he went on about my company trying to get over on me. I was too drunk to come up with anything clever, so I relented.

"I just got a four hundred thousand-dollar raise." His mouth dropped at my statement. I could see his expression going from shock to anger. Any other man would be happy for their woman, but not Michael.

"I *knew* you were fucking your boss!" he spit out.

"That's not true. I have been doing Mr. Hillard's job for years. I deserve this raise." I finally stood up for myself.

He could talk about many things concerning me to make me feel bad, but I wouldn't let him make me feel incompetent about one of the things that I was sure about. I was sure of myself when it came to numbers and my job. And I was sure I loved Michael even though he made it hard for me to do so 80 percent of the time. As he continued to rant and rave about things he didn't know anything about, I got up on wobbly legs, kissed him, and then walked into the bathroom to shower. As the water ran on me, tears ran down my face. More than anything, I wanted to be the woman that Michael could love. I had changed so much to become the type of woman he wanted that I didn't even know who I was anymore.

Chapter 5

Chase

Charm dragged into my office with a pair of huge dark shades on her face. She stood before me, placing her bag on the floor and setting her laptop on the table. Then she flopped down in the chair, crossing one leg over the other.

"I'm ready whenever you are." She took off her glasses and sipped her coffee, exhaling a breath.

Her long, brown hair swung as she glanced at me over her shoulder. It was so silky that I wanted to run my hands through it. Charm is definitely a true beauty, but I could tell she didn't really know it. She hid behind layers of makeup, expensive jewelry, costly clothes, and shoes. I could tell that the woman I saw before me was only a shell of the woman I knew she could be. I went to sit across from her and took in her beautiful brown eyes. Something was wrong with her. I debated whether I should ask her about it or begin our workday. I sat and stared at her for a while. I could tell she was becoming nervous under my gaze because she started to fidget with the things in front of her. I cocked my head at her, and she made a sudden move, knocking everything in front of her on the floor, including her laptop.

"Damn it," she fumed as she tried to pick up her notepad and pens. Everything seemed to keep slipping from her hands. I got up to help her retrieve her things. As soon as I bent down, her head came up, hitting me in the face. I groaned from the pain. A horrified expression crossed her face as she rubbed the back of her head.

"I'm so sorry," she continuously repeated.

"It's okay. I'm fine, I promise," I told her, removing my hand from my face to show her.

All of the blood drained from Charm's face, and within seconds, she broke out in a sweat. Then her body dropped and hit the floor with a thud. *What the hell?* I thought to myself. Next, I felt something wet coming down my face and turned to the mirror. Blood was coming from my nose. I looked down at my hand, and it was covered in blood too. I went to the sink in the room, wet a paper towel, wiped off my face, and washed my hands. Then I quickly put a cold towel on Charm's forehead and across my nose, throwing my head back. My nose stopped bleeding within seconds. I scooped up Charm, carried her over to the couch in the room, and placed another towel across her head. She began to stir a little. Her eyes fluttered open, and a small smile crossed her face.

"What happened?" she asked, rubbing the back of her head again.

"Are you hurting anywhere?" I let my eyes roam over her body, and she shivered under my gaze. Her breathing was becoming more erratic, causing her full breasts to heave up and down.

"The back of my head hurts a little, but what happened?" she asked again, trying to sit up, but I gave her a light push back.

"No, lie still for a minute, and let me get you some water." I grabbed a bottle of water from the mini-fridge, handing it to her. She took a couple of small sips, then sat up.

"You fainted," I told her before she could ask again.

"I don't faint. The only thing that makes me do that is blood."

She rubbed the back of her head again, then looked at her things scattered across the floor. Her eyes became as big as saucers before she held her head down in shame. I took my index finger and lifted her head.

"Accidents happen. Never feel ashamed about it."

Our eyes connected, and our souls intertwined. At that moment, I could see and feel all the hurt and pain she had been through. I could see how insecure she felt about herself. Her mind and heart were an open book to me. I wanted nothing more than to cure and encourage her about everything she felt was wrong with her. I could tell exactly when she closed herself off to me. She cleared her throat and folded her arms across her chest, causing me to look down at her ample breasts.

"Are you ready to work now?"

She stood up on her four-inch black stilettos and began picking up her things from the floor. I stood back, enjoying the view she was giving me of her delectable ass. When she sat in her chair, I walked to the other side of the table once more, hoping she missed the hard-on that had grown down my leg.

"I told you yesterday that I am here to see what or who is draining this company's money dry. Although I have gotten rid of Mr. Hillard, there are still some underlying problems going on. I am known for doing my background on the company that hires me and their employees, but I can't figure out who or what is causing the problem. The money that Hillard was taking was chump change compared to what's still being taken. This is where you come in. Being Hillard's assistant, you know more than you think you do. Also, you're extremely smart, and I know, with your help, I'll have the job done in no time."

I watched her biting the top of her pen in such a sexy way that my dick grew harder. I would've thought that was impossible if it wasn't doing it. Working with Charm was going to exhaust all my willpower. I wanted nothing more than to bend her over right now. I could tell when she realized I was watching her mouth work the pen she was holding. She dropped it to the table, but the expression she gave me was even sexier than her biting the pen.

"I have no problem helping you in any way I can. I had told Mr. Hillard for several years that the numbers weren't adding up, but he would always wave me off. I love working for Forest, so I will do anything to help," she replied earnestly.

"I know you have other tasks to complete and get used to your new job title after becoming the head of the department, but don't worry about that. I have split most of your work up evenly in your department. They will email both you and me at the end of the day with their assignments. Since you will also be working with me, I will give you a bonus after our work is done here." She nodded, letting me know she was fine with the arrangement.

"Let's get started. The first paper I need you to sign states that everything we do here is confidential. Nothing we speak of concerning Forest leaves this room. Next, this paper states that I will compensate you for your work with me at the end of the business deal. You will earn 10 percent of the money that I'm making to restructure the company."

When Charm's eyes landed on the amount of money she would make at the end of the deal, she almost fell from her seat.

"This is too much." She shook her head while picking up her pen to draw a line through the figures. I placed a hand on hers, stopping her.

"No. I promise, you will earn every bit of the money on that sheet." She pulled her hand from under mine as if I had burned her.

"Okay," she whispered.

"I need you to pull all the numbers from five years ago. I want to know everything shipped, paid for, and bought, from the lightbulb to the paper in the copier. Also, I need you to pull the company's bank statements for that year." I continued to tell her what I needed from her, as if I hadn't felt the electricity that jolted through me when I touched her hand.

As we worked and went over the first two months of paperwork, I had to remind myself she had a man. Charm was as sharp as a whip regarding numbers and her job. She could do almost anything concerning a number in her head. While we worked, I took in everything she did when she was thinking about something. Her favorite thing to do was bite on things . . . the pen top or the nail on her middle finger. My favorite thing that she liked to bite was her lip. On several occasions, I had to stop myself from leaning over the table and grabbing her lip between my teeth to nibble on it myself. I closed my eyes to clear my head of all the freaky things I wanted to do to her.

It was after office hours, and we had worked all day without lunch. I wanted to keep working a bit longer just to be in her presence, but I knew we had to bring this day to an end. I got up, stretched, and kicked my legs out to regain the feeling.

"You okay?" Charm asked while she assessed my moves.

"I'm fine, just a little stiff."

She looked down at her watch, and her mouth dropped open. "Oh my gosh, it's after seven. I'm supposed to be at my parents' house by seven thirty for dinner." She picked up her bag, stuffing all of her things into it. She was halfway out the door before she turned to look at me.

"Is it okay if we pick up where we left off tomorrow?" she asked, grinning sheepishly. I let a smile spread across my face and nodded at her.

"Have a nice dinner," I told her retreating back. She threw her hand up as a goodbye while she continued to the elevator.

I took my time packing up to leave. I had no plans for the night except to go to my empty home. I enjoyed the short walk home, but I knew I wouldn't go inside my penthouse once I got in front of the building. Instead, I went to the garage, got into my truck, and took a short ride to PetSmart. It made no sense for me to be lonely in this big penthouse. I might as well make some animal's day by giving them a home to call their own. I went through the store and picked out everything they said I needed for my new German shepherd pup. I wasn't sparing any expense when it came to him. When I left the store, I was over fifteen hundred dollars less rich, but this would be the best money I could spend. I hadn't thought of his name yet, but when I walked into the back of the store and saw him there, I knew he had a background I may never know about, just like Charm. When he jumped in my arms as soon as they opened the kennel, I knew I could change his future for the better, and he would change mine.

Chapter 6

Charm

The one thing that my father hated was us being late for dinner. Here I was, fifteen minutes late and walking through the door of my childhood home. Everyone was sitting at the table, including Michael. *Lord, can I have just one day without having to look him in his face?* I rolled my eyes, then placed the biggest smile I could on my face. Having dinner with my family was already challenging because of my aunt Sonya's smart mouth. It was different when Michael came to dinner because everything was about him and our relationship. If this dinner weren't to celebrate my promotion, I would have turned around when I saw him sitting at the table.

"Hey, everyone," I spoke and kissed my dad on the cheek.

"Hey, baby, you're late," he pointed out like I hadn't noticed.

"I know. I lost track of time at work," I replied as I gave my baby brother a playful punch in the shoulder, and out of formality, I kissed Aunt Sonya on the cheek. I sat next to Michael, planting a light kiss on his plush lips.

"Don't let them work you too hard at that job, baby," my father spoke.

I made my plate and noticed that all of Michael's favorite foods were made. I rolled my eyes because my family thought he was a saint, but he was far from that. If only they knew the things I had to go through with him daily, if they knew what he actually thought of me . . . I bowed my head and waited for my father to say grace before digging into my plate. I was starving, and the steak, potatoes, asparagus, shrimp, and lobster tasted like heaven.

"Maybe you should slow down, baby," Michael commented as I devoured my meal.

"Not right now, Michael. I haven't eaten all day, and I'm starving."

"It's okay for you to miss a meal or two. It won't hurt you," my aunt tossed out. I dropped my fork on the plate, standing up.

"Don't leave, honey. You just got here," my father interjected.

"You know how your mother gets at times. She doesn't mean anything by it. She just wants you to be healthy." My mouth dropped open. I wanted to put so much out on the table so he could know that she meant *everything* she said.

"Don't be silly, honey. Sit and finish your meal," Michael said as he continued to eat his food. Of course, this was nothing to him because he had said worse to me on different occasions. I took a deep breath and sat down again.

"You know, honey, I was thinking that maybe you should quit your job, and we can start working on having a little family of our own. Of course, you would have to move out of your condo and live with me, but what do you think about that?"

I spit tea out of my mouth, and it landed all over Donovan. He *would* do this to me. He would bring something like this up in front of my family. He hadn't said one word to me about this. He only did it in front of them, thinking I wouldn't say no. My dad was clapping his hands, and Sonya had her hand over her chest like this was the sweetest thing she ever heard. I wanted to kick him under the table, but knowing Michael, he would make a big deal out of that.

I busied myself cleaning up the mess I had made, hoping to get away without answering his question. There was no way on God's green earth I was quitting my job to play housewife with him. He was out of his damn mind.

"I think it would be good if you finally settled down and had some children. You're not getting any younger. You'll be 27 on your birthday."

"My age has nothing to do with what Michael is proposing, Aunt Sonya."

"Pretty soon, Donovan will be leaving for college, and your father and I would love to have grandchildren running around the house." I rolled my eyes. She always found a way to make everything about her. She would throw my father in so that it wouldn't sound so selfish.

"I have just got my foot in the door to having the best career I have ever wanted. I'm finally beginning to see everything I worked so hard for sitting at my feet, and now, you all want me to give it up to sit in a house barefoot and pregnant?"

"We're not asking you to give up your life, sweetheart. We just want you to be taken care of if something happens to us," my dad piped in, trying to caress my feelings and get me to calm down. This dinner was supposed to be about my promotion and my making a better life for myself with this opportunity. Instead, I was beginning to feel ambushed into being at Michael's every beck and call. I wanted to be able to give Michael kids one day, but not at the expense of losing the only part of myself that I was still holding on to.

"I gave up my dreams and became an instant mother when your mother left-I mean died. I wanted to find a career and make things happen for myself, but you needed me. I didn't question your father when he asked me to stay home and raise you. It was one of the best things that has ever happened to me. Are you saying you're better than me?"

I closed my eyes because this was getting out of control. I was ready to burst at the seams. There has never been a time that she didn't try to use the fact that she raised me as a ploy to get what she wants. I turned to look at my father, who was holding his head down. Michael was sitting with a smug expression plastered across his face, and Donovan let his eyes gaze at everything *except* me. This is how it always went. Everyone would make me out to be the bitch instead of my dear stepmother.

"I appreciate everything you have done for me, but no two women are alike. You made the choice not to make more of your life. You made the choice to take your sister's place in raising your niece, and you made the choice not to continue your education afterward. Those were *your* life's choices, *not* mine. I chose *not* to put my life on hold just to say I have a man. I choose to continue my career so my children will know they can do whatever they put their minds to. I choose to become a better person so that if I have a daughter, I will never want to treat her like you have treated me. It is 2019. Women have healthy children and happy marriages, all while clocking nine to five. Some women don't even have men supporting them. Yet, they still take care of their children. I refuse to let a man—or woman—run me away from my dreams." I picked up my purse and headed to the door.

"Michael, the answer is no. I don't feel like company tonight. Since my stepmother is always dickriding you, maybe she has room for you in their bed."

My heart pumped triple time as I walked out of the house. I tuned out whatever was being said to my back as I left. This night was a disaster, and it was only eight fifteen. I hadn't even made it an hour before everything kicked off. Although I was kind of upset about the language I used, I was proud of standing up for myself. Autumn would be proud of me, but did my family really deserve my disrespect? I sat in the car with my eyes closed before someone tapped on my window. I opened my eyes and wanted to pull off when I stared into Michael's eyes. His expression said it all. He disapproved of what happened in the house, but for the first time in my life, I think I really didn't care. I cracked the driver's window a little.

"What?"

"You embarrassed me in there."

Was he serious? I *embarrassed* him? If this weren't my life, I would think this was some type of twisted comedy.

"Michael, I really don't want to do this with you right now. We can talk about this after I have calmed down."

"I think *I* should be the one making that statement. *I'm* the one who needs to calm down. I am ready to change our lives for the better, and instead of you just agreeing to what I want, you have to make a scene in front of your family. You know I'm the perfect man for you, and with how you look and act, no one would want you *but* me. At this point, I don't even know why I want you. I do my best to make you into the woman I wouldn't be ashamed to hold your hand while walking down the street, and *this* is the thanks I get? There are plenty of women who would kill to take your place. Yet, I have to beg you just to eat healthier for your own good. If you don't begin to see things my way, this relationship is over."

Yes, his words hurt me, but they didn't cut as deep as the last time he went on a rampage. I politely put my car in reverse.

"They don't have to kill to be in my shoes. They can have them."

I hit the gas, turning my steering wheel so hard that I burned rubber on the way out of the driveway. I made a mental note to have my locks changed in the morning. I needed space to clear my head and think if the love that Michael was willing to give me was the type of love I wanted.

I checked the time, and it was still kind of early. I had enough time to go to the bar and have a couple of drinks. I wish today were Friday so I could drink up the entire bar. As I sat in the Lion's Den at the bar on my third shot of vodka, I reflected on my life and realized I had been through a life of pain since my mother left. Only for the pain to amplify and deepen once I found out about her death. Life was given so I could live, not just exist. And with the life I led, I only existed in a world where I sacrificed myself for others' happiness. I wanted to be happy right along with everyone else. I wanted to be loved the way I saw my dad love my mom and aunt. He never held back from showing them love and affection. I deserved to be happy in this lifetime. I work so hard, so I should be able to play even harder.

I took a napkin from the holder, pulled out my pen, and made plans. When my work with Chase was over, I would put in for a long overdue vacation. I wrote down a few places I always wanted to visit and made a note on the side to check the prices.

"Is this chair taken?"

"No," I answered, not looking up at the person I was talking to. A hand came in front of me, taking the napkin I had been writing on. "What the fuck do you think you're doing?" I questioned, gazing right into Chase's eyes.

He was unfazed by my tone and continued to read what I had written down.

"Dubai, Greece, Paris, Jamaica, and the Bahamas. All of these places are beautiful. You should do your research on them before you choose one."

"I'm not choosing one. I will visit all of them. The only thing I need to choose is which place I will go to first." I was on my sixth shot, and my words had begun to slur. Usually, I would be embarrassed to be seen by my boss this drunk, but after the day I had, I didn't give a damn.

"What are we celebrating?" Chase casually asked as he ordered a drink for himself.

"I'm here to forget. What's your excuse?" I managed to say after a couple of times trying.

"I'm celebrating a new addition to my family."

"It figures a man as fine as you wouldn't be single, but I want to know why you tried to talk to me last week if you have a wife. You and your guys must've made a bet like Autumn and me, or were you just trying to get a taste of Black girl magic before you got married? You must've thought I would be easy because of how I look. I knew you were too good to be true." I laughed a little and took my next shot. Chase slammed his glass on the counter, giving me an appalled expression.

Chapter 7

Chase

I couldn't believe what I had just heard from her mouth. She couldn't be serious. Charm is one of the most beautiful women I have had the chance to meet. She could work on her confidence, take away most of the makeup, and let go of the heels she wore daily that I was sure were murdering her feet. Her hair was almost to her butt and bone straight. I knew women from all races who would pay good money to get that type of hair put into their heads. Her eyes had a nice slant to them, and her complexion was that of an exotic beauty.

"What do you mean by that?" I asked curtly. The one thing I hated most was for people to be unsure of themselves.

"I mean exactly what I said. You saw a woman who was overweight and self-conscious and thought I would be an easy mark for you to get something you may have always wanted before you tied the knot," she repeated.

I took a moment to look into her eyes. This wasn't just drunk talk. She really felt that she was unworthy to be looked at by a man with lust in his eyes. If she wasn't in a relationship and if she wasn't my employee, I would show her how much of a lie she was. There was nothing sexier than a woman with brains and the curves to match. I wanted to be the man who kissed away her worries and changed her mind about all these things, but I knew I couldn't. I did the next best thing I could think of.

"Charm, you are more beautiful than you think. My attraction to you wasn't just to have sex. I was and still am attracted to your gorgeous face and curves. I love how you walk around in those heels with your head held high, like the world will bow at your feet. After working with you only for one day, I know you are smart and could be a very successful woman if you stop letting people run over you. One thing I don't like is all that makeup covering up such beautiful skin. Also, I can tell your man isn't taking care of you right because you wouldn't be here drinking away your sorrows if he were on his job. You would be home letting him kiss away any pain or self-conscious-ness you are feeling."

I saw a shiver as my words caressed her ear as I spoke to her. I could see the lust in her eyes and how she wished I was doing what I said. She wanted me to kiss away the pain she was feeling. I would have obliged her if she wasn't tied down to someone and if she were sober. I would have put my career on the line to give her everything she needed, but in my heart, I knew she would return to what was more familiar to her. I cocked my head, staring at her. Her eyes were glazed over with tears, and I saw a tear run down her cheek. My heart broke to see a woman who seemed so strong on the outside, ready to crumble in a bar around people she knew nothing about.

I hadn't known Charm for long, but I knew what I saw in her. I knew the day she tripped up the stairs going to the stage that she would be special to me. When she ran into me, spilling coffee all over me, it was like a magnetic charge pulling us together so close that nothing could come between us. I had never believed in fate, but this had to be it. I never believed in love at first sight, but I fell for her the day she tripped over thin air. There was something between us that I couldn't explain. It feels like we have spent a whole lifetime together, yet it has barely been a week. I picked up a napkin and wiped the tears and mascara running down her face. She quickly turned her back to me, getting up from her chair and stumbling a little.

"I got you." I stood up from my stool, grabbing her hand, then her arm. For some reason, the words I spoke felt like they had more meaning than me just giving her a helping hand.

"Thank you," she slurred her reply.

She stumbled halfway through the bar before she decided to kick off her heels. I wasted no time scooping her up in my arms. She wrapped her arms around my neck tight, holding on.

"I'm not going to drop you. I told you I got you."

She relaxed a little, then placed her head in the crook of my neck. I could hear her sniffling a little as she held on to me. She was still crying, and I had no idea why.

"What's wrong, Charm?" I finally asked once we crossed the threshold into the nightly summer breeze. She didn't answer. She tried jumping down from my arms, but I held her tight. She pulled her key fob from her purse, hitting the locks. When I saw the lights from a Volkswagen flash, I walked over, setting her on the car's hood. From the parking lot's dim lighting reflecting off the shiny black car, I noticed her personalized plates with her name across them and a four-leaf clover in the center.

"I just want to go home," she stated.

I placed my hands on each side of her before speaking. "I'm sorry. You can't drive like this, but I do have a couple of options for you. I can take you home and make sure you get there safely, or I can get you an Uber."

"I want an Uber," she replied quickly.

"Then we have a problem. Your car will get towed if it's left here overnight."

She folded her arms over her chest and groaned. "Why does my life have to be so complicated and full of people who want to tell me what to do? Everyone acts like I can't make one choice without people interfering. All I want to do is drive myself home, and here you are, telling me what I need to do. I know what I need to do." She slid down the car, pushing me out of her way. She made a beeline to the driver's seat. I blocked her and snatched the keys from her hands.

"Here's what we are *not* about to do, Charm. I won't argue with you about your safety when you can barely walk. I'm not going to let you hurt yourself or anyone else because you feel like you don't have your life together. You are a grown woman, and no one can make you do anything you don't want. No one can control you unless you allow them to, so don't take your frustrations about your life out on me. I won't let you take them out on an innocent person trying to make it home tonight, either. Your pain and the liquor are making you misjudge shit that is common sense. If you never listen to anything I tell you in your life, listen to me now. It's time that you take all the strength that I know you have inside of yourself and shit or get off the pot. You will never be happy trying to make everyone around you happy. Trust me, I know. Now, what's your address?"

She gave me her address and got in the car on the passenger side. The first five minutes of the ride were silent. I thought she had fallen asleep until she opened her mouth and began speaking.

"Have you ever felt like you were so boxed in and any way you turned, it would be a bad outcome?"

I took my eyes off the road to gaze at her. She seemed to be in deep thought.

"No," I answered honestly.

"Then you would never understand where I'm coming from."

"It's not that I wouldn't understand or haven't felt like that before. The difference is in the way that we would handle it. I tend to do what's best for me with little thought about what everyone around me wants. Whatever has you feeling this way, Charm, doesn't have you secluded on an island with no one around. You have to choose what makes you happy. It's up to you to build your raft and find civilization. If you prefer to sit and wait for a boat to appear and take you to safety, you will always feel boxed in. Who cares what everyone else wants? This is *your* life. Live it the way that *you* want. Life is way too short to be unhappy, even if it's only for one day."

"Thanks for bringing me home," Charm said as we pulled into her parking space.

"There's no thanks needed. Are you going to make it up okay?" I asked, getting out of the car.

"I'll be fine. See you in the morning."

"No, you take a personal day tomorrow. When you return, I expect to see the Charm I first met at the bar."

She gave me a drunken smirk before we got on the elevator. I got off at the ground level and waited for my Uber.

"Sit, Shep," I told the unruly puppy with the most enormous ears I have ever seen. He tripped over his big paws, instantly reminding me of Charm. I had spent most of the morning thinking about her and wondering if she had decided about whatever was on her mind.

"I come in late for the second time in five years and find a German shepherd replacing me."

Charm walked into my office with a new purpose and what looked to be a new purse and heels. I was sure she would have a bad hangover and wouldn't be able to make it. She sat in the chair on the opposite side of the desk. Shep ran over to her, sniffing her, and she picked him up, cuddling him to her chest. He made himself at home on her lap, curling up and going to sleep. Charm continued to pull out her laptop like he wasn't even there. Lucky dog! I grabbed the papers where we stopped the day before, and we began to talk about numbers.

"I'm going to order in lunch. What do you want?"

Charm glanced up at me from the paperwork. Her hair fell in front of her face when she looked back down. She circled something on the paper, then slid her glasses up her head to hold back her hair. Then she set Shep down on the floor next to her, standing up to stretch, causing her blouse to rise and show off the perfect brown skin I was tempted to touch. My dick slowly grew down my thigh, wanting a nice, wet cove to make itself a home in.

"I would like a grilled chicken salad."

"What was that?" I shook my head to clear my mind of all the hot and steamy thoughts of doing so many things to her.

"I would like a grilled chicken salad," she repeated.

I placed the call, putting in our order while she took Shep outside to relieve himself.

When our food came, we put everything to the side so we could eat.

"Sit, Shep," Charm said to the pup, trying to climb back into her lap. The pup took no time sitting right at her feet.

"I have been trying to get him to do that all morning. How did you do that?" I asked.

"It's all about the tone. You must show him you are alpha, or he will run all over you."

Not only was she taking my heart and could have me at her beck and call, but my dog was also crazy about her too. How could this woman have this much control over everything around me? I sat back, watching her take small forkfuls of her food and carefully chew her lettuce. Everything about her turned me on. I couldn't understand why she feels the way she does about herself.

"Do you want to talk about last night?"

Charm placed her fork on a napkin and raised her hand, slightly covering her mouth. When she finished chewing her food, she threw her head to the side, letting her eyes roam over me.

"Thank you for making sure I made it home safe."

I waited for her to continue talking, but she didn't. "I hope any decent person would not have let you drive last night, but that's not what I'm referring to."

She placed both hands on the desk, blowing out a breath that made her hair fly up and fall back in place.

"Can you just forget what happened last night? I'm trying to."

"I can't do that. I know I don't know you well, but I'm willing to listen if you want to open up about anything. This is a judgment-free zone."

"Why would I want to talk to you about my personal life? So you can act like you're so concerned now, then go tell your corporate buddies how you had to save the poor Black woman from herself."

"First, there's nothing poor about the Black woman sitting before me. You walk around here in all of your expensive shit like you have it all together. If your close friends and family can't see you drowning and ask about it, I will. I have a close friend who lost it all, and the first thing he did was drown his sorrows in a bottle. It took my friends and me months to get him back on the right track. When I tell you you can talk to me, it's not because I think you're incapable or incompetent. I think you are keeping everything bottled in and are about to lose your leverage. I don't have to be the one you open up to, but you need someone, and I'm letting you know I'm available."

She sat in the chair with tears in her eyes. I guess Shep felt the tension in the room and whined for Charm to pick him up. When she did, he gave her puppy dog eyes and licked her face. He turned to me whimpering, looking from Charm to me.

"It's okay, boy," Charm told him, rubbing his head.

Afterward, she closed her salad container, moving it to the side. She didn't say a word as she continued to do her work.

Chapter 8

Charm

"Today is a good day," I told myself, staring in the mirror.

Chase and I had been working together for a few months. Everything at work has been going well so far. We figured out where the company was falling short of some money. We still had a lot more digging to do, but things were looking up. I took Chase's advice and found someone to talk to, and he was right. When we sat and discussed what I was going through, he kept his judgment-free attitude. I really feel like he's in the wrong business. He would make a fortune being a therapist.

Michael and I agreed to move in together in the future. I guess our time apart was good for both of us because he was sweet like he was the first year we were together. My aunt and I did the usual . . . acted like nothing happened, and I apologized to my dad for being disrespectful in his house. Things were looking up for me for the first time in my life.

"Today is a good day," I repeated in the mirror before making sure my edges were lying down.

In the last few months, I have been reflecting and discovering that Michael has had a hold on me since we started dating. Things he felt would make me a great woman weren't always what I wanted for myself, but I did as I was asked—or told—to keep him happy. I still wore heels most days because I loved them, but I added some sneakers occasionally. I also didn't wear as much makeup anymore. Chase helped me discover that all of that wasn't needed to make me beautiful.

"Good morning, birthday girl!" Chase shouted as I walked through the conference room door.

I had the biggest smile on my face. He remembered today was the big day. Today, I turned 27. Chase opened the side door, and Shep came running to me with balloons tied to his collar and a card attached to it. Tears came to my eyes. As I bent down to get the balloons, Shep gave me a good lick on the cheek. I rubbed his head. Then he got up and trotted over to Chase, waiting for his treat. Chase delivered, and he returned to me, trying to get into my lap.

"Shep, you are too big for that now. Sit." He sat down at my feet, waiting for his next command.

I opened the card to read it. Money and gift cards fell on the table.

"I can't accept this." I was more than surprised and appreciative, but it was too much.

"This is from your department. They wanted to thank you for saving their asses last month."

My smile had to be from ear to ear because my cheeks started hurting. Last month, the computers in the finance department crashed and caused an uproar with the company. It took us two days to get everything back online, but I stopped my work with Chase to help them with the important papers that needed to be out by the end of the week. During the crash, some of the company's accounts were hacked. We're still trying to find out how it happened, but with me thinking quickly on my feet, it stopped my entire department from being fired.

"I need to go thank everyone for being so generous."

As I stood to leave the room, Shep was on my heels, following me to the elevator. Everyone at the company loved him and deemed him my personal bodyguard, and I couldn't agree more. He went everywhere with me during work hours, and when it was time to go home, he would whimper all the way to my car until I pulled off.

Since today was my birthday and Friday, Chase decided we would work a regular shift. I was ecstatic because that gave me more time to prepare for my night out with Autumn. I said my goodbyes to everyone at work and got home with plenty of time to chill out. I set my work bag on the table, and it fell over. As I bent down to pick up my things, an envelope with my name across it caught my eye. I picked it up, and a small box was taped to it. I pulled the letter out and began to read it with a smile forming on my face.

Dear Charm,
I knew if I gave this to you, you wouldn't accept it from me. I had to be clever enough to get you to take this home. You are a beautiful woman inside and out, and like any beautiful woman, you deserve beautiful things. I hope you like the gift. After all, they are a girl's best friend.
Happy Birthday
Love
From Chase.

I quickly dropped the letter, opening the box, and my mouth dropped open as 2-carat diamond studs with the clarity of a bottle of water greeted me.

"Holy shit."

I put down the top of the box, ran into the bathroom, took out my small heart earrings, and replaced them with the huge diamonds. He doesn't know me that well, but I never turn down diamonds. After spending minutes in the mirror looking at the rocks in my ears, I decided to take a short nap.

I woke to my alarm going off. I turned, looking at the clock, and jumped out of bed. I was supposed to be up an hour ago. I rushed to shower. What usually takes about thirty minutes took me fifteen minutes. Although we were going downtown, I dressed in clothing I could move in. I was going to make the most of this birthday and planned to be on the dance floor all night. I went to my closet, pulled out some ripped, black, high-waist jeans, and pulled off the ridiculous high-priced tag. I picked up a sheer blouse and a black cami. Then I got dressed, went to my shoe rack, and grabbed my black lace heels. There was no need for a purse because I didn't want the responsibility of keeping up with it. I picked up my small wallet that held my ID and credit card.

When I got downstairs, my Uber was waiting at the front door. During my ride to the bar Autumn told me to meet her at, I took the time to shoot Michael a text. I hadn't heard from him all day. When we pulled up to the bar, I checked my phone one last time, and there was still nothing. Autumn was standing at the door, waving for me to come on. As I walked up to her, my phone pinged. It was Michael. He sent the okay emoji. I stuffed my phone in my back pocket and decided to begin my night on a good note.

I held on to Autumn's hand as we moved through the thick crowd of people dancing on the floor. We walked up several stairs when I saw him sitting next to his friend. I pushed my hair behind my ears, hoping his eyes would catch the bling in my ears. It worked like a charm because his smile spread wider across his face.

"Hey, beautiful." With those two words, Chase made my body heat up several degrees.

"I didn't know you would be here." I gave him a one-arm hug as he kissed me on the cheek.

"I wouldn't have missed this for the world," he replied.

Our eyes locked on each other, and his eyes went from hazel brown to a deep green as we held eye contact. We have been attracted to each other for a long time. Sometimes, I can feel him staring at me when we're working. Other times, I stare at him, watching the faces he makes when he's frustrated or thinking about things. While at work, we try to keep our attraction under wraps, but outside of the job is a totally different thing. Being in this space with him has woken up something I can't explain.

"You remember Dylan, right?" Autumn broke the connection Chase and I had.

"Yes, I remember him, although we weren't formally introduced."

Dylan held out a hand to me. I took it, keeping a smile on my face while side-eyeing Autumn. She didn't tell me that they kept in contact. Dylan was a nice-looking man. I'm sure if Autumn brought him to meet me, there was more to this story than she let on. I wasn't going to pressure her about it tonight. Tonight is all about having fun.

"Michael should be here shortly," Autumn informed me. I was surprised that she invited him. They hated each other. It was so crazy too because they both said the same thing about each other. Autumn felt I let Michael control me, and he felt the same about her. I personally thought both of them were crazy.

"That's fine. I was wondering why he hadn't called me today. Maybe he wanted to surprise me with you two working together for a change."

"I wouldn't say all that, but let's toast, then dance until he gets here." I gave her a solid nod, and Dylan picked up a bottle of Dom Pérignon Rose, filling our glasses.

"Happy twenty-seventh birthday! Nothing but the best for you tonight," Chase yelled.

We could hear the clinking of our glasses before we all put them up to our mouths, sipping the champagne. Two glasses of champagne in, and I was ready to hit the dance floor. Michael had yet to appear, so I pulled Chase out of his seat and went to the center of the crowd. We danced three songs straight before they slowed down the music. Chase grabbed my hand and twirled me into his arms. As they wrapped around me, I began to feel like I was right where I was supposed to be. I lay my head on his chest and listened as he sang to me while we swayed to the music. I could live just like this in his arms forever.

When the song ended, Chase leaned down to me with his eyes closed. I wasted no time meeting him the rest of the way. When our lips met, I felt like the earth trembled beneath my feet. He swiped the tip of his tongue across my lips, and my body shuttered. I opened my mouth to let him enter. He pulled back a little, using the tip of his tongue to outline my lips before slipping his tongue gently into my mouth. Our tongues intertwined and locked together perfectly. He flicked his tongue in my mouth, and I moaned as my body went into an overdrive of emotions and lust-filled thoughts. He pulled back a little, and I gently bit down on his lip, getting a groan out of him that made me want to kiss him forever.

Once we pulled away from each other, I felt eyes burning the back of my head. I slowly turned around, feeling a fist to the gut. My eyes landed on Autumn with a silly grin on her face. I sighed in relief, knowing I didn't get caught with my hand in the cookie jar. I pulled Chase off the floor, going back to our VIP section. I was a jittery mess. I have never felt so exhilarated, free, and ashamed in my life.

"As great as that was, it can never happen again."

"Why not?" All the joy left his face.

"What do you mean, why not? I have a boyfriend, and you are my boss. I feel like that's reason enough."

"Okay, you're fired. Now, I'm no longer your boss."

I took in his expression. He was as serious as a heart attack. I crossed my arms over my chest, and his eyes diverted directly to my breasts. He had a smug smile on his face that I wanted to wipe off with the heels of my shoes.

"You can't fire me just to be with me. That's illegal. And it still doesn't change the fact that I have a man."

"Where is your man, Charm? You have been looking at your phone all day today. I guess you were waiting for a text or call? As a matter of fact, we've been here for over two hours, and the bar will close in forty-five minutes. Where is he now? I don't get it. How can you sit and be loyal to a man who hasn't even reached out to you on your birthday? I swear if I hadn't met him a few months back, I would think he was a figment of your imagination."

I sat staring Chase in his eyes, mad at his truths, mad that everything he said was hitting so close to home for me. *Where is Michael?* Why wouldn't he show up to support me on my day? Anything he has ever asked me to be there for him, I have: his CEO anniversary party, their annual company party, all of his family events. But he couldn't be here for this one thing and still hadn't wished me happy birthday. It's now a new day, almost two in the morning, and I haven't received a text.

"Fuck you, Chase!" I got up and left the bar without saying goodbye to Autumn. I didn't want to ruin her night. This was the first time in a long time she was out dancing and laughing. Although I was going home, I wanted her to continue to enjoy herself. I stood in front of the bar watching my Uber app, which showed that the driver was five minutes away.

"Don't leave like this. I'm sorry."

Chase pulled me to him by my arm, then embraced me so close that I could smell the mixture of mint and champagne on his breath. I closed my eyes, laying my head on his chest, and taking a deep breath of his cologne. I relaxed in his arms for once, letting another man other than my father be the comfort I needed.

"Do you forgive me?" he kissed my ear and whispered.

I nodded, not saying a word. I wanted to live in this moment of tranquility. At this precise moment, I felt I had a man by my side who would do everything under the sun to keep me happy. Chase lifted my head to look me in the eyes. I could see nothing but lust and passion in his beautiful eyes. My heart skipped a beat because this was the first time a man had looked at me like he couldn't wait to undress me. My mouth went dry, and I diverted my eyes because his gaze had penetrated my soul. Chase leaned a little so he could look me directly in my eyes.

"Come home with me." His words came out soft but demanding. I nodded again, too afraid to speak.

"I need to hear the words come out of your mouth, Charm." I leaned back, taking him in, his light blue shirt with no tie and the first three buttons unbuttoned for a more relaxed look. He wore black slacks and leather loaferlike shoes that I was sure cost a fortune. I cleared my throat.

"Yes," I whispered and nodded at the same time. He gave me a blinding smile before his full lips came crashing down on mine.

Chapter 9

Chase

"Yes," Charm whispered.

Her words echoed in my ears as I pulled out my phone and texted Dylan, letting him know that Charm was safe and to relay the message to Autumn. Her Uber arrived, and I opened the door, letting her slide into the backseat. Once I got in, I changed the address in the app. When I asked Charm to come home with me, I never expected her to say yes. I had gotten my ego ready to be broken. Now that she had given in and was ready to see what being with a real man was like, I wouldn't let her down. I know it's absolutely wrong to want something or someone another man has, but it was different with her.

Her man had a great, smart, intelligent woman willing to give all of herself to keep him satisfied—only for him to try to tear her down. She had talked to me about him a few times while working. She didn't disclose much about him, but she told me enough to know he wasn't worthy of her. I was going to show her differently. Charm needed a man to build her up and worship the ground she walked on. I know I couldn't make all of this happen in one night, but tonight would be the start of what I needed. As we took the short ride to my penthouse, I kept Charm hugged to my side. I needed to feel her next to me to know she was real. Since we have been working together,

I continued to imagine this day. Every day we parted ways, I envisioned her coming home with Shep and me, making our small family whole.

We pulled up to my building in less than fifteen minutes. I opened the door, giving Charm my hand as she slid across the backseat.

"Do you have a change of heart before we enter the building?"

Charm leaned into me, kissing me with her perfect, plump lips. That was all I needed to guide her into the building to the elevator. I held her hand until we stepped into my house. She let her eyes roam over everything in her sight before smiling, letting go of my hand, and walking to the ceiling-to-floor windows.

"I love the view."

"Me too," I replied, taking in her curves and ass. I couldn't keep my eyes off her. She was the most beautiful woman I had ever met. I strolled over to her as she kept her back to me, snaking my arm around her waist. By how she inhaled, I knew she felt my dick hardening on her round, plump behind. I wanted her more than she could ever know. She turned in my arms, and I backed her against the window, taking her bottom lip into my mouth and sucking on it. She moaned out in pleasure and flicked her tongue over my lips. I wanted to take her right there in the window. I wanted to let everyone see her in the throes of passion. I scooped her up in my arms, and she threw her arms tightly around my neck with a look of terror in her eyes.

"I don't want you to drop me. Please, put me down."

"What makes you think that I would let all of your sexiness hit the floor?" Her frightened expression never changed as she cast her eyes down to my chest.

"I'm too heavy," she replied.

"Baby, I will never let you fall, trust me. Just hold on to me, and I got you." She stared at me. I could see a worrisome look in the depths of her eyes. I kissed her lips and headed to the bedroom, using my elbow to turn on the lights as I walked over the threshold. Finally, I stood her on her feet and took a few steps back just to take in everything about her. I was going to make tonight a night we would both remember. I reached out my arms, pulling her to me. The chemistry between us told me this was long overdue and to have my way with her. I knew I had to give her everything I had tonight. I knew I had to give her something that she'd probably never had before: passion.

When my lips touched hers, I kissed her slowly, letting my tongue hit every part of her mouth that she would allow me to reach. Her mouth was delectable, and I wanted to devour all of her. She returned every lick and flick I gave her. I trailed butterfly kisses from her mouth down her cheek and jawbone to her neck. She moaned, softly rubbing at the nape of my neck, sliding her hands down my back while I planted kisses on every part of her skin that wasn't covered. Then I began to unbutton the blouse she wore. I needed her clothes off.

"Turn out the lights," she said softly, placing a soft hand over mine, stopping me from going any further.

"Why?" I asked, taking a step back from her.

"I would feel more comfortable with them off."

I went toward the door, about to give in to her demands, but stopped and turned to her.

"No." This was more than about comfort. She diverted her eyes to the floor, then turned her back to me. I didn't know what was running through her mind until her blouse hit the floor. My steps were quick as I walked behind her, spinning her to face me.

"I want to be the one to undress you. Why are you trying to keep me from your perfection?"

"Because I'm not so perfect," she whispered so low that I could barely make out her words.

I kissed her lips, then went into my walk-in closet. Getting my full-length mirror, I placed it against the wall closest to the bed. I put her in front of it, standing behind her. I pulled her camisole slowly over her head, revealing a black lace bra. I rubbed my hands over her breasts, then down her stomach.

"Look in the mirror, baby," I whispered in her ear. She slightly lifted her head, gazing at the mirror. I moved in behind her, pulling her closer to me, using my body to straighten her slumped shoulders. Once she stood straight, I lifted her head so she could see herself. I rubbed over the upper part of her body again, making slow circles around her nipples through her bra. Her breathing increased, and she closed her eyes.

"Open your eyes, babe. I want you to see every inch of the beauty I see in you daily."

She slowly opened her eyes, watching every move I made through the mirror as I let my hands roam over her upper body. I knelt before her, removing her heels from her feet as she held on to my shoulders to support her balance. I unbuttoned her jeans, which seemed like they were painted onto her thick thighs. She wiggled as I pulled the jeans down over her ample ass and hips. Now, she stood before me in nothing but a black lace matching panty and bra set. I took my time in front of her, taking in her vanilla and cocoa scent. I could smell the wetness of her pussy, and it made my mouth water. I wanted nothing more than to lick her juices until I was satisfied and she was screaming with pleasure. I kissed the small piece of material that covered her most prized possession. She exhaled a breath, and I smiled.

"In due time," I told her as I ripped the little covering right from her body. I placed another kiss on her freshly waxed skin before flicking my tongue between her folds. She put her hand on my hair, pulling me closer to her. I stood to my feet, circling her like a predator does its prey. Then I unclasped her bra and let her breasts hang free. Charm was heavy-chested, but her girls sat perfectly. She stared in the mirror at me and placed her hands over herself. I gently pulled them down to her sides.

"What is it that you find so bad about your body that you feel you need to hide from me?"

Charm arched a brow at me like she didn't understand my question. I lifted both of her arms, placing them around my neck. There was no way for her to hide now. She looked down at her feet and began to fidget. I let my hand lightly roam the side of her body, causing her to shiver. I kissed her cheek.

"Tell me," I demanded.

"I have love handles."

"They are called that for a reason, baby. I love them." I bent over, kissing each side of her stomach.

"What else?" I whispered.

"My thighs are way too big." I wiggled my eyebrows at her before kneeling and taking my time kissing her thighs.

"Open your eyes, Charm. I want you to see all of the magic your body holds." Her eyes popped open, looking into the mirror.

"Talk to me, baby."

"I have stretch marks on my hips and stomach."

"Those are just guiding me to exactly where I want to be." I kissed and licked her stomach and hips as she moaned and threw her head back.

"Tell me more, baby."

"My breasts are way too big." Her reply brought a smile to my face. I stood up and kissed and sucked her breasts, showing them both equal attention as she squirmed in my arms. When I stopped my assault on her, she stared at me through the mirror, and her pupils dilated with desire.

"Don't look at me, Charm. Pay attention to yourself. Pay attention to how beautiful every inch of your body is. I love everything about you, from the follicles of your hair down to your perfect toes. But none of that shit matters if you can't love yourself more than I do. I need you to see yourself how I see you. You are a queen, baby, and nothing less than that. When you begin to believe that, then nothing anyone says about you will matter because you will love every curve and piece of imperfection, knowing it's perfect. And you are perfect, baby."

She stared in the mirror as I rubbed my hands over her body, cuffing the different parts of her body that she was not happy with. As she took in her appearance in the mirror, I stepped back, stripping out of my clothes. When I stepped back up to her, my penis was as hard as steel and ready to go inside of her. Her eyes widened when she realized my dick was unclothed and sitting in the crack of her perfect ass.

"I like the look of this—of us." I moved her hair to the front of her. It hung low, covering one of her breasts. I trailed kisses from the nape of her neck down her spine, going lower, and kissed both of her ass cheeks. I wanted her in the worst way, and I was about to get exactly what I wanted.

Chapter 10

Charm

I stared at Chase and me in the mirror as he whispered about how perfect I was while he trailed kisses down my spine. The softness of his warm lips hitting the coolness of my body made me shiver with desire. When he bent down and kissed my ass, I was done for. I wanted to push him onto the bed and do things I had never done with Michael. Chase lifted me in his arms and wrapped my legs around his waist. This time, I wasn't scared when he walked across the dark, hardwood floors to his huge California king-size bed. I held his gaze as he softly placed me in the middle of it.

"I want to worship you and do things to you that no man has ever done to you before," he told me, placing a kiss on my lips.

Doing things no man hasn't done to me wouldn't be hard. Michael's and my sex life was just like our relationship: basic. There was no foreplay, always the same position, and no oral sex at all. Michael felt like oral sex was for whores, and if I was going to be his wife, that was something I couldn't explore. Another thing was that when we had sex, I had to keep my shirt on. I have been in the house with Chase for an hour, and he has shown me beauty that I haven't seen in myself in years.

"Do as you please," I told him, lying in bed, trying not to cover myself up. Off instinct, I put my hands over my breasts.

"Do that again, Charm, and I'm going to tie you down," Chase said sternly.

"I'm sorry," I told him, feeling remorseful.

"Don't be; just don't do it again. You are perfect." He kissed each of my ankles and rubbed his hand up my legs. As he moved up my body, kissing every inch of me, I placed my hands over my stomach. Chase stopped what he was doing. Waving his index finger at me, he got off the bed and entered his closet. He returned with four pairs of leather handcuffs. I watched him walk with his usual swag over to the bed. The cuffs were connected to a long chain, then a regular metal cuff.

"I told you not to cover up." He placed the leather part of the cuffs on my ankles. Then he tied them down to the frame of the bed. Next, he moved around the bed, doing the same to my hands. "Now, you have no choice but to let me see all of you."

His voice came out hoarse, and my body tingled with excitement about what was to come. If I had on panties, they would be soaked with my juices from wanting him so badly. Chase didn't hesitate to take his place back between my legs, finishing his assault on my thighs. He licked, kissed, and sucked on my inner thighs, causing me to squirm and pull on the chains that held me down. By the time he moved to my pussy, my clit was throbbing with anticipation of having his mouth there. Chase licked between my folds, and I didn't recognize the moan that came from me. He looked up at me with a devious smile, and I knew I could do nothing to stop him from taking me any way he wanted.

He took his time licking and sucking every crevice of my pussy. When he hummed on my clit, I realized what an orgasm was as my body began to shake. I screamed his name at the top of my lungs. He didn't stop. He continued to pleasure me, causing *another* orgasm to shake throughout my body. Chase kept devouring me until he was satisfied and had my juices running down his chin. When he had enough, he trailed kisses up my stomach while I tried to turn and pull at the cuffs.

"Are you ready for the main course?" he asked, kissing my lips with each word.

I was still in the euphoria of passion. All I could do was nod.

"Say the words," he demanded.

"Yes, I'm ready," I replied weakly.

He uncuffed my hands and feet. "I want to feel your body wrapped around mine as I make you come over and over again." I wasn't sure how much more I could take, but I would make it happen for him.

He made sure to protect us, then placed his incredibly long, thick penis at my center. I opened my legs wider, anticipating the fullness of him connecting with me. He entered me slowly, putting a little of himself in and pulling back. I was in agony, waiting for him to fill me up.

"Hold on to me, baby," he said through gritted teeth.

I wrapped my legs and arms around him. He kissed my lips, then pushed slowly inside of me to the hilt. We both exhaled as he waited for me to adjust to his size and girth.

"Aah," we both said simultaneously.

Beads of sweat began to dart his forehead as he moved in and out of me, slowly rolling his hips into me. My eyes rolled to the back of my head at the pleasure he was giving. Chase was all about giving me what I wanted and needed. Soon, an orgasm was rocking through my body so hard I felt like I had stopped breathing. This man was doing more than rocking my world. He was spinning my world around. I had no idea if I was shaking or gravitating from all the lovemaking. As my next orgasm was building, Chase began to speed up. I knew that the ecstasy was coming to an end.

"I'm coming, baby. Damn, this is too good," Chase said between breaths.

We came at the same time, yelling out each other's names. Finally, Chase crashed down on top of me.

"I'm sorry, babe. I know I'm heavy."

"You're fine. I like feeling you on top of me," I told him honestly.

Chase slowly pulled himself out of me, then turned over on his side, pulling me close to him. All of this was so new to me being sexually sated, then cuddled, feeling like I'm the only one that matters and is being worshiped. There's only one way to put this. I felt like a woman. I fell asleep wrapped in Chase's arms without a care in the world. I woke several hours later to Chase wiping me down with a towel.

"What are you doing?" I asked, trying to close my legs.

"The cuffs are still attached to the bed," he said, dipping the towel in a bowl of warm water. I instantly closed my eyes so I could relax. "Atta girl. Just lie here and let me take care of you. I promise I won't hurt you." He stared me in the eyes with a hidden meaning to his words. Instead of responding and ruining our beautiful night, I let him continue. When he finished, he went to empty the bowl, got in the bed, and pulled me close.

"I would be lying to myself if I thought you would stay here with me forever, but since I'm a realist, I know exactly what this is. I'm glad you gave me tonight to show you how a beautiful woman like yourself should be treated. I can't promise you every day will be this great, but I can promise you better days than you have now. I won't beg you to leave right now, but you will have to choose soon. I'll give you time to decide, but I won't be a patient man when it comes to you, and I won't play fair to get what I want." He kissed the nape of my neck and went silent.

He was right about one thing. I had to choose between what I knew for the unknown. Having his words heavy on my mind, I thought I wouldn't get a good night's rest, but to my surprise, I was sound asleep in no time.

I woke up in a daze, confused by my surroundings. I sat up, looked around, and realized where I was. I moved my hand to the other side of the bed, only to feel a cool space. I rolled over to my side, closing my eyes, remembering my legs and arms wrapped around Chase as he made love to me early this morning. My body began to shiver at the memories, and I wanted to live in the moment. Once I left the comfort of his penthouse, all of this would be a distant memory. I had to return to my real world—a world where this type of love doesn't exist. When I heard the front door open and close, I sat straight up in the bed, covering my nude body with the sheet. After several minutes of hearing nothing, I attempted to stand up to go to the bathroom.

I took one step . . . and the sheet I was wrapped in caught my feet. I was tumbling over. I tried to use my hands to brace my fall, but the pain of my foot twisting made me reach down to grab my ankle. Everything went in slow motion as I plummeted to the hardwood floor, screaming out in pain. Shep began to howl, and I heard footsteps running into the room. I closed my eyes and let the tears roll back into my hair. Shep came and stood over me, licking my tears and whining.

Chase ran into the room, sliding across the hardwood floor like he was running for the home plate. If I weren't in so much pain, I would have called out, "Safe!" opening my arms wide like they do in the baseball games.

"Are you okay?"

"I'm fine." I closed my eyes to the pain that was radi-
ating through my leg. I was sure that my clumsiness had
finally cost me a bone. Chase began to untangle me from
the sheet. When he got to my right leg, I cringed in pain.
My eyes began to water, and tears rolled down the sides
of my face into my ears. I wanted to be embarrassed, but
I was so aware of the pain that my emotions had to be put
on the back burner.

"You are not fine. I know this hurts." I opened my
eyes, taking a deep breath before letting my eyes divert
to where Chase was kneeling. He scooped me in his
arms, placing me back on the bed. My ankle had already
begun to swell. Was this my punishment for cheating on
Michael? The guilt of last night started to weigh on me.
Everything had been so good, so perfect . . . until now.

"I'm fine," I lied, turning and softly placing my feet on
the floor, only to crumble down from the pain. Chase
wasted no time helping and putting me back on the bed.

"Don't move," he told me with a stern expression. Then
he left the room. Within minutes, he was back with an ice
pack, placing it on my ankle as I flinched from the cold
and pain.

"Thank you," I spoke in a soft voice.

"You need to get this looked at. It could be broken."

I nodded my head at his words. A visit to the hospital
was inevitable, but I wasn't ready to leave him. I took a
deep breath as Chase helped me into a jogging suit and
sneakers he had purchased while he was out. He didn't
even attempt to put the shoe on my right foot.

As I sat in the room waiting to hear the verdict about
my ankle, I sent Michael several texts that went unan-
swered. Chase patiently sat with me, talking to me about
any and everything. I stared at him, looking at how his

mouth moved when he spoke and how his eyes brightened when he talked about the things and people he loved. He told me about his goddaughter, London, and I could tell he adored her. He spoke about me meeting his friends Brenton, Dennis, and their significant others. I had already met Dylan, but he talked about him as well. I could tell he had a bond with his friends that made them more like brothers. I could hear the love he had for them in his voice.

"Charm," the doctor walked in, looking down at his chart.

"Yes," I responded, hopeful.

"My name is Dr. Stein. I'm an orthopedic surgeon." My smile fell. He saw my expression and quickly began to speak.

"Oh, you don't have to have surgery. I just wanted to come to speak with you about your ankle." I relaxed a little and waited for him to riffle through the papers before he continued.

"Your ankle is not broken, but you have a nasty sprain. So, we will put a cast on you for four weeks and go from there. The nurse will be in here shortly. After that, we will give you pain meds, and you will be discharged." I was in total shock. How was I supposed to live life with a cast on my right foot? I would need people to help me with everything, from driving me around to helping me with house chores.

"Don't worry, Charm. I will do whatever I can to help you." Chase's voice broke through the thoughts that were plaguing my mind.

"I can't ask you to do that for me. I'll find a way to work through this," I responded.

"You didn't ask for my help; I offered it. I would be less of a man to watch you struggle through this alone when it probably wouldn't have happened if you weren't at my house."

I nodded and sent another text to Michael. This text didn't go through. It turned green. He had blocked my number.

Chase and I left the hospital, and he refused to drop me off at home alone. We went back to his house, and I wasted no time calling Autumn to come pick me up. I appreciated everything Chase had done for me thus far, but I had to get away from him to think. As long as he was around, all I would think about was how he treated me like I deserved to be next to him. Being in his space would only cloud my judgment about things.

The doorbell rang, and I knew it was Autumn. I pulled my leg off the pillows that had it elevated, putting my feet on the floor. I picked up the crutches next to me and stood up. Shep stood up on the side of me. Chase and Autumn spoke in a low tone as they approached the living room.

"I told you that you would hurt yourself one day," Autumn said, shaking her head at me.

"No. If I remember correctly, you said I would break my damn neck."

"Neck, ankle, is there really a difference?" We both laughed as she walked over to me, hugging me. Autumn always found a way to make me laugh through embarrassment, which made me love her even more. She was truly the best friend anyone would love to have, but I was glad she was mine.

"I got you enough clothes for the next couple of weeks."

I frowned, and she rolled her eyes.

"You must have forgotten I leave for my trip tomorrow."

I had. Autumn had been planning this trip for months. I couldn't ask her to give up her vacation to help me because I couldn't keep my feet planted on the floor. I plopped back down on the couch, closing my eyes to think of any solution besides staying with Chase.

"Before you rack your brain trying to figure things out, I called your dad. He says he won't be able to help because he has to work and make sure your brother gets to and from school because the witch is out of town for the next couple of weeks. I tried to contact Michael, but his phone went straight to voicemail. We are out of options, Charm."

I opened my eyes, staring at Autumn. *I can't stay here.* I shook my head, not saying a word to her. As usual, she read my eyes and mind. *Why?* She questioned with her eyes and body language. Chase watched us converse without words.

"I'm going to take Shep for his afternoon walk and give you ladies some privacy." Chase clicked his tongue, and Shep looked between Autumn and me. He gave me a quick lick on the hand before trotting off, wagging his tail. When the front door closed, Autumn sat down next to me.

"What's going on?"

I closed my eyes and exhaled a long breath. If no one else would understand me, Autumn would. She was my best friend, and we had been through everything together.

"I feel horrible about cheating on Michael, and the longer I'm here with Chase, the worse I will feel," I told her honestly.

Autumn gazed at me questioningly. She took her time before she spoke. "Let's talk about last night."

"What about last night?" I questioned, unable to keep the silly smirk off my face.

"You have this glow about you that I haven't seen since your mom died. It's like this one night with Chase has put life back into you. What happened?"

I took my time before responding. How could I tell her that in *one night*, Chase fed my soul by speaking life into me? How could I tell her that it took *one night* for him to show me everything he sees in me? It took *one night* for him to show me that the right man could show me more love than the man I had been with for years. I closed my eyes, thinking of him kissing and licking every inch of my body. He told me I was beautiful with so much conviction that I had no choice but to believe him.

"Chase is an amazing man who deserves more than what I can give him." I opened my eyes when I felt Autumn's eyes on me.

"Okay, the sex was good then?"

"It's not just the sex, Autumn. It's everything about him." I huffed because I couldn't explain everything that I was feeling. It was like I couldn't put it into words because I didn't understand what was happening. I felt like I was at a crossroads between the known and the unknown. With Michael, I knew what I was getting. On the other hand, Chase showed me that everything could be different and better.

"So, what's the problem, Charm?"

"I don't know him. I don't know if he will do a 360-degree turn on me and become worse than what I have now." There it was. I had put everything on the table. Autumn rolled her eyes.

"No one is worse than Michael except a serial killer. Your problem is that you have been put on the back burner emotionally for so long that you feel like you don't deserve anything better. You have instincts, so use them, Charm. Chase will never do the things Michael does, even on his *worst* day. This situation is so cut and dry to me. Chase loves you. I saw it in his eyes when you entered the bar last night. His eyes were locked on you as soon as he saw you coming in the door. You both get that sparkle in your eyes when you look at each other, and he was man enough to come after you and admit he was wrong. Michael has been missing in action for damn near a week and hasn't talked to you in two days. You're sitting in this house sulking about not having any help when Chase is at your beck and call. You have some choices to make; to me, it's so simple. Love the man who loves the hell out of you. Fuck Michael. I've never liked him. I dealt with him because that's what you wanted and what great friends do." She had given me more than enough to think about and made some very valid points.

"Now that you have that off your chest, what's up with you and Dylan? I didn't know that you guys kept in touch." I wiggled my eyebrows at her. I would love for Autumn to have a good man in her corner, especially since she took on the mom role three years ago. At first, it was hard for her to lose her identical triplet sister, but she got custody of her deaf nephew afterward. Storm is the reason she made it through this ordeal. She had someone to take care of. I couldn't say the same thing for her sister, Summer, though. All three of the sisters were close, but Summer and Winter had a connection so deep that Summer almost lost her mind over her sister's death.

"Dylan and I are building a friendship."

I rolled my eyes at her. "I'm your friend. You need a man."

"That's the thing. You are my only friend here. Dylan travels with his job, but he always takes the time out of his day to see how I'm doing. We talk about almost everything except my sisters. You are so busy most of the time, which I'm not downing you for, but it feels good to have a listening ear. Or just to hear about what's happening in someone else's life. My world revolves around Storm, and I needed something else to take my mind off everything."

"I don't want you to get so wrapped up in everyone else's life that you forget what you need. You are a great woman, and you have womanly needs that must be attended to."

"I hear you, Charm. Maybe I can find someone to help me with my womanly needs while on vacation."

"It's not just that part of it. I want you to find love and be truly happy. If no one else deserves it, you do."

Autumn took my hand in hers, squeezing it while she smiled at me.

"You deserve the same thing and more," she replied.

Soon after, the door opened back up, and Shep jumped on the couch, laying his big body across both of us.

"This is my cue to go. I'll see you soon, Charm." Autumn stood up, hugged me, and rubbed her hand across Shep's head.

"See you later, Chase, and take care of my girl." He smiled at her, giving her a loose hug.

"I will. Have fun on your trip." Autumn walked out the door, leaving me with the man who set my body on fire.

Chase walked over to me, giving me a light kiss on the lips. Something as small as that kiss had me warm all over, and my body wanted more.

"Hungry?" he asked, and I nodded. I was hungry, but I wanted more than food. I wanted to eat this man alive.

My phone vibrated as I sat with my mind on things I wanted to do to him.

Michael: There was an emergency at work, and I'm out of town for a few weeks. My phone will be off while I'm here, but I'll call you when possible.

I stared at the text, thinking about everything Autumn had said earlier. I had been feeling like my accident was a curse for me sleeping with Chase, but it just might be a blessing in disguise. I would take this time to get to know Chase better.

Chapter 11

Chase

A week flew by quickly as Charm and I settled into
sharing a space. Our only problem was that I wanted her
to work from home to stay off her feet. She let me talk her
into it for two days. After that, she didn't want to hear
my thoughts on her being home. I put up as much of a
fight as possible before she started fighting back, telling
me she was going stir-crazy from sitting in the house. So,
instead of me driving to work every day, I decided to rent
a car and have a driver drop us off. Charm wouldn't let
having a cast on her foot hold her back from doing most
of the things she wanted to do.

She worked from home for the first two days, and
dinner was ready when I stepped in the door. Since we're
both back at work now, we come home and cook together
unless we stay late. Every night, I help her in the bath
or shower, and when I'm done, I help myself to her as
dessert. For the life of me, I don't understand how such
an intelligent, funny, beautiful woman could end up
with a man who doesn't want to love all over her. I guess
what they said about one person's trash being another
person's treasure is true because I feel like I hit the
jackpot with her. Technically, she wasn't mine to keep,
but I will do everything I can to have her by my side. Hell,
it even crossed my mind to abduct her and elope. If I had

thought she would go along with it, we would have been on the first plane to Vegas.

"Why do you have that goofy look on your face?" Charm asked with mischief in her eyes.

"Oh, nothing really," I replied, watching her get off the couch and limping over to me.

She moved slowly but with purpose. I cocked my head, trying to figure out what she was about to do.

"I need something from you."

"Love, I will give you my last breath if it makes you happy," I stated without thinking, causing her to stop. I thought I had scared her off until I looked into her eyes and saw tears filling them. She stepped in front of me and kissed my lips. Then she dropped the pillow to the floor, which I didn't know she had in her hand, and carefully got on her knees.

"I've been thinking about doing this for a while." She unzipped my slacks, pulled my dick out, and placed it into her plump, juicy mouth with a slurp.

"Oh my God . . ."

My eyes rolled to the back of my head as I closed them from the pleasure of her warm, wet mouth. She wasted no time bobbing her head up and down, using her tongue to make circles around the tip of my pole. What the hell was she trying to do to me? I opened my eyes and watched her work magic with her hand and mouth. It was like she knew I was looking at her because she began to give me the performance of a lifetime. People would pay good money to watch her do this. I was stuck between the ecstasy of having the best blow job in my life and watching how she could have easily become a porn star when she made all ten inches of my length and girth disappear like her name was Houdini.

I couldn't take it anymore. I pulled myself from her mouth, lifted her from the floor, and bent her over my cherrywood desk. I lifted her skirt and pushed my chair under the knee she wore the cast on. I didn't hesitate to plunge right into her, feeling her warm honey coat my dick and hug it like a glove. I quickly moved my hips, thrusting in and out of her with no remorse. Hearing her low moans turned me on even more. It made me want to find a way to go deeper so everyone in the building could hear her cry out my name as she came. Her juices began to rush out of her like warm water. Her pussy gripped my dick and held it prisoner. She was trying to milk me of every fiber of my being . . . and that's when I realized we were unprotected. I pulled out of her, and her moans abruptly stopped. She turned to look at me with confusion in her eyes.

"I'm so sorry. I didn't mean to," I stuttered when she finally looked down at my unsheathed dick.

"I'm clean, Chase; no worries. I have never slept with Michael without a condom," she stated as I looked into her eyes, seeing her truth.

"What about pregnancies?" he asked.

"My aunt put me on birth control at 11, and I continued the practice," she answered.

"Who the hell would put a child on birth control at that age?" I questioned.

"It's a long story for another time," she responded.

I pulled her close to me, wrapping my arms around her. This woman was amazing. Even when I did things without thought, she had the solution.

"Let's go home," I told her, ready to fully finish what she started. The things I wanted to do to her couldn't be done here.

"What about this?" She pointed to where our things were sitting.

"We'll always have tomorrow," I told her, willing to say anything to have my way.

She smiled at me and nodded, giving me an okay while fixing her clothes. Just as we got everything together, someone knocked on the door. My receptionist walked in with a smirk, rolling her eyes at Charm.

"Is there something I can help you with, Anita?" I asked, irritated by her posture and the attitude that she seemed to have.

"This just came in for Charm." She tried to hand me the manila envelope, and I nodded toward Charm. She turned to Charm, handed the envelope to her, and rolled her eyes.

"Anita, next time you step into my office to address anyone, leave the attitude at the door."

"Yes, sir, Mr. Lancaster," she meekly said, turning on her heels and walking out the door.

"What's her problem?" Charm asked with a frown on her face.

"I don't know, but if she doesn't get it together, she can get her walking papers like everyone else has," I stated truthfully. "What is it?" I asked as Charm looked at the front and back of the envelope.

"It's from a lawyer in Mississippi. That's where my mother and aunt are from. I can't imagine what it could be. My mother has been dead for over twenty years now."

"Open it. It must be important," I urged.

Charm turned the envelope in her hand again, then picked up my letter opener. She pulled some paperwork out and went through it slowly before flopping down in the chair behind her. The papers and envelope fell to the floor as she sat in the chair, stunned. I rushed over to her, and tears were rolling down her face.

"They lied to me," she whispered.

"Who lied to you?"

She didn't say a word, just pointed to the papers on the floor. I picked them up, noticing a check with six zeros behind the coma. Damn. She had become a wealthy woman in a matter of seconds.

"How could they do this to me?" she questioned.

"What's going on, Charm?"

She pointed at the floor again, and I finally picked up the letter, reading the date and the first couple of words.

"Holy fuck!"

Charm and I talked about her boyfriend and her family. I knew that things weren't the best that they could be between them, but who the fuck does this to a child? I didn't know any of these people, but I knew a lot about her and knew that she didn't deserve this. No one deserved to go through this pain.

"I can't read it all. Please read it to me."

I stood in front of her, watching her rock back and forth like she was about to have an emotional breakdown. I grabbed her hand, pulling her over to the couch in the corner of my office. I sat, pulling her down, and she leaned over, placing her head in my lap. I cleared my throat and let the words of the letter flow through me.

June 20th, 2019

My Dearest Charm,

I know getting this letter from me is like getting a letter from a ghost, especially since you were told that I was dead. I'm sorry I couldn't be there to watch you grow into the beautiful woman I know you have become. I know sending a letter is very impersonal, but I didn't want to intrude myself into your life without knowing if you wanted me there. Before I go into why I'm sending you this letter, I want you to know that no words can describe my love for you and how much I have missed you. When you were a little girl, I made the worst mistake of my life by not fighting for you. Your father and aunt were two of the closest and most important people in my life besides you. When I found out they had been sleeping together, the pain cut me so deep that I couldn't breathe the very air that I'm taking into my lungs right now.

The three of you were my everything, and for them to hurt me with their lies and deceit was a stab in my heart. I know that what they had done to me has nothing to do with you, but I had given up my entire life to move to Chicago with William—only for me to be pushed out of your lives like it meant nothing.

The night I left Chicago, I returned to Mississippi with your grandmother. That night, I promised you that I would come back in two weeks, and I did. I don't know if you were in the house, but as soon as I rang the doorbell, Sonya called the police on me. She told them that I was there trying to kidnap her daughter. I tried to prove otherwise, but your father and aunt had created documents showing you were their daughter, not mine.

I got locked up that day and was released five days later with a warning to stay away from you or go to jail for a very long time. That day, I vowed that I would contact you when you were old enough. I know twenty years is a very long time, but I didn't want to stop you from reaching for the stars. I have always kept up with your accomplishments and endeavors. The check I sent you does not make up for lost time. Time is something that we can never get back. Your grandmother left me a large sum of money, and I felt the need to share it with the only woman holding a piece of my heart. My contact information is on the legal documents if you ever want to contact me.

*I would never tell you how to spend the money
I have given you, but I will say watch the people
around you. Having a large sum of money makes
people come out of the woodwork.*
I love you, my lucky Charm!
Sharon Sims

I finished the letter and rubbed my hand soothingly across Charm's hair like my mother had done for me so many times when I was a kid. I knew there was nothing I could say that would take away the heartache she was feeling right now, but I could be here for her. Charm sat up and wiped her face.

"Take me to my dad's house." This was a side of her I had never seen before. Charm was pissed, and I wasn't sure if I should take her there or take her home to my place. She looked at me. "I don't want to hear anything you have to say. Just drive me there, or I will find my own way."

I wasted no time picking up the phone, calling for our car service, and giving them our new destination. All I could do was pray that we didn't end up going to jail because Charm was about to lose her shit.

Chapter 12

Charm

I sat in the Town Car in front of my dad's house for about ten minutes, thinking about the letter Chase read to me. I knew I was the black sheep of my family, but I didn't know that my family hated me so much. My mind was conflicted. On one hand, I had a parent and aunt who lied about my mother's death. On the other hand, I had a mother who kept herself hidden from me for over twenty years. I turned, looking at the house I grew up in, and realized it was all a lie. Everything that I had come to love, things that I decided to overlook, the love that a family was supposed to share . . . was all a façade. If this was all a lie, then do I know who I *really* am?

"You want me to go in with you?" Chase asked.

I nodded because I didn't want to take this black hole of anger out on him. I needed him, though. I don't know if I could do this without him by my side right now.

"Ready when you are." He squeezed my hand slightly, giving me the strength to get out of the car.

I used my crutches to hop up the driveway I had walked up plenty of times. I removed my keys from my bag and let myself inside. My father was sitting in the living room watching TV. When he heard the door slam, he turned around. I took in all the pictures on the walls and end tables. The Linseys had come off as one big happy family. In each photo that was taken, you could see how my smile went from genuine to tight and fake. It was something that only people who really knew me would catch right off the bat. My eyes didn't match my smile from age 12 to our most recent picture. Everyone in the house was so happy about being a Linsey . . . except for me.

Then you had the pictures of my mother on the mantle, some with me in them. Others where I had placed little sticky angel wings and halos on them. As a child, until a little while ago, I swore she was my angel watching over me. Then there was her obituary. I took time to pick the perfect picture frame for it. The picture that I had chosen was the last picture she had taken before she left me. I felt like a fool. My own dad had tricked me into thinking something so horrible just to have the woman who made my life hell.

After I confronted my father, he said, "You know . . ." my father's eyes got as big as saucers. Then he had the nerve to look like he was hurt. "Doing that to you hurt me just as much as it did you." His words were my breaking point. I had never been a violent person, but I wanted nothing more than to inflict the hurt that I had felt growing up on him.

"Yeah, Dad? So, please tell me how it feels to be lied to all your life. As a matter of fact, tell me how it felt to be a little girl and lose your mother at 6 years old. Please tell me how you dealt with an evil-ass stepmother who felt threatened by you for being your child! You all fucking lied to me. You took my mother away from me over a piece of pussy that has been nothing but a pain in my ass. You did this so you could be happy." Spit flew from my mouth. I felt like a rabid dog, vicious and ready to bite anything in my sight.

"I did the best I could giving you a mother."

"No, you were being selfish. What the hell have I ever done to you for you to treat me like this? You were so caught up on being pussy whipped over your wife's sister that you never thought about what all of this would do to me. I spent years being verbally abused and downed so much by Sonya that my self-esteem was as high as an ant. *You* did this to me—no one else but you."

"You never told me any of this before," my father stated.

"Because a bad mother is better than no mother at all. And would you have listened if I did? Even as a child, I saw that you were happier with Sonya than I had seen you with your own wife. As a child, I sacrificed my happiness because I wanted *you* to be happy."

He dropped his head like a disobedient child. "I'm sorry, Charm," he whispered.

"Sorry? Sorry? That's all you could ever be—sorry. Sorry doesn't give me back what I lost—twenty years with my mother, and all my father had to do was keep his dick in his pants and treat his sister-in-law like a sister. In fact, you could've kept that bitch all to yourself and let me go with my mom. Do you know that I felt like my little world ended when I found out my mother wasn't coming back for me? There are so many ways you could have done this besides how you did."

"Well, Sonya wanted us just to have a clean break from Sharon, and due to the circumstances, I agreed. Sonya promised to treat you like her own, and I had no reason not to believe her." I rolled my eyes, ready to hit my father. "You don't understand. She was having trouble conceiving. To begin with, she always doted on you like you were hers. I didn't see any harm in giving my wife everything she wanted."

"So, you gave her someone else's child?" I questioned.

"Not exactly. You are my child too. I deserved to have you full time. Without me, your mother didn't have a pot to piss in or a window to throw it out of."

"And that makes it okay to kill her off and start a new family?" I began to step toward my father in a rage I had never felt before. Chase grabbed my arm, pulling me back to him.

"I'm not explaining it correctly. Wait until your mother gets here, and she will tell you." At the sound of him addressing that bitch as my mother, I swept away everything I could get my hands on to the hardwood floor. Glass went crashing everywhere on the floorboards.

"She's *not* my fucking mother! You know what? At this point, I don't feel I have a father, either. Bye, *William*." I turned, walking to the door, and my father yelled out as if he were in pain.

"No, Charm, I'm sorry."

"That pain you're feeling right now, imagine feeling that five times worse for twenty years. You should've known this was going to come back and bite you in the ass."

I tried to walk away quickly, only to trip on the way out the door. Chase had quick reflexes and pulled me to him, picking me up and carrying me to the car. I kept my head buried in his chest until he put me into the vehicle. My chest was burning with so many emotions that I was holding in. When he closed the car door, I let out an ear-piercing scream before sobbing uncontrollably.

"I got you, Charm. No worries, okay?" Chase pulled me into his arms and held me all the way to his penthouse.

Everything was a blur as Chase helped me into the house and to the bedroom. I sat on the bed for hours, looking between the letter from my mother and the large sum of the check. It amazed me that two pieces of paper had changed my life for the better . . . and worse. Although Michael told me his phone would be off, I texted him. He was my man. Chase was great, but I needed someone familiar to talk to. Everything around me had changed in the blink of an eye.

Me: I need you; my family has lied to me most of my life. My mother is alive.

I held my phone in my hand, looking at the blue message I had sent, hoping for a response. When I saw the bubbles pop up, I was relieved he took the time to respond.

Michael: Even if I were there, what do you want me to do?

I threw my phone across the room into the wall, hitting the floor in pieces. This couldn't be my life. Chase ran into the room, letting his eyes roam across everything until they landed on me.

"I have no one," I whispered through my tears. If my own family didn't love me, how could I expect anyone else to love me?

"You have me." Chase sat on the bed beside me, wiping my face for the thousandth time today.

"Why?" I asked.

"Why what?"

"Why do you like me so much? How can you sit here and say that you will have my back when my own family won't? Even my boyfriend has turned his back on me now. The only person that I can count on is thousands of miles away. My mother didn't love me enough to fight for me, my father didn't love me enough to keep me safe, and Michael . . . Well, he is who he is. If I can't trust my family and boyfriend not to turn on me, how can I trust you not to do the same thing?"

"You can trust me because I'm not them. I have no reason to deceive you. All I have wanted to do since I met you is love you, Charm. Let me." He stared at me like he wanted me to see the truth in his words.

"You want me to give up everything I know for someone I know nothing about? All this 'you will cater to me' shit could be a trick. You want me just to love you. I decided to do that with Michael and look where that got me. At least I know what I will get from him. You, though, I have no idea. Things with Michael are bad, but they could be worse. He may be an asshole, but you and I both know it could be way worse."

"Worse than what you're going through right now with a man who could care less about your well-being and mental state? I'm sure your phone is over there in pieces because of the man you know so well. Let me prove that I'm different and will spend my life breaking every chain your family has tried to tie you down with." His words hit me and penetrated my heart like a Mack truck, but I couldn't do it. I was too broken.

"Take me home, please. I need time to think," I finally told him after several minutes.

"No, you stay here. I'll leave." He got up, grabbed a bag, and packed a few things. "I'll be back in the morning to help you get ready for work."

I had turned my back to him because as much as I wanted to be alone, I couldn't watch him walk out the door. I heard the front door close, and then the water-works started.

Three hours later, I got out of bed and walked around a silent penthouse. I wanted nothing more than to hear Chase laughing about something silly I had said and Shep sitting at my feet. My request to be alone seemed so foolish now that I got my wish. I looked around for my phone and realized it was in the corner in pieces. I wanted to call Chase and tell him to come back home, but I had no way of doing that. I walked around the bedroom until I saw his card on the nightstand and a cordless phone beside it. Even when I was acting a bitch, that man still knew what I needed.

Chapter 13

Chase

"I know it's only been about six months, but I love her."
My parents cautiously stared at me. I should have gone
anywhere else other than here. They wanted to know
who I was dating as soon as I walked in the door. When
I happened to say Charm's name, Dad questioned me
about the girl who could sing from the bar. The first thing
my dad asked about was her boyfriend.

"You loved Allysa too, and you see how that ended," my
mother replied.

"She could never be that bad," I said.

"We just don't want to see you hurt, son," my dad told
me.

"Dad, she won't hurt me. If anything, I'm scared of
hurting her." I slumped in my chair a little. She had
been through so much already that I was scared that I
might do something that would break her more than she
already was.

"Chase, you are a good man. That's the last thing you
need to worry about," my mother told me softly.

"Are you sure about this?" my dad questioned.

"I have never been so sure of anything in my life," I told
him honestly.

My phone rang. I saw it was my home number and
wasted no time answering it. I swiped across my screen,

and there was nothing but silence on the other end. I waited for Charm to say something—anything. I just wanted to hear her voice. She exhaled a deep breath before speaking.

"Chase, come home."

"Okay."

Charm had uttered three words, and I was out of my seat.

"Sorry, I have to go. Charm needs me," I told my parents, frantically searching my pockets for my keys.

"They're here." My mother handed me my keys, looking at me suspiciously. She opened her mouth to say something, and my father shook his head.

"Son, go handle your business."

I ran out the door, ready to be there for my girl.

When I walked into the house, Charm was sitting on the couch watching a chick flick with a glass of wine in her hand.

"Are you okay?" I asked with a concerned look on my face.

"Yes. When I really thought about it, all of my problems can be solved with this." She held up the wineglass, smiling. She was so beautiful. To see her smile after all she's been through today made me love her even more. She was so strong, and I admired that about her. She seemed to think the worst about herself, but I could only see a determined, beautiful woman.

"Wine can help every now and then, but it won't solve your problems, Charm."

"I'm telling you, the answer is at the bottom of this." She held up two empty bottles and nodded at the one sitting on the table. I took them from her hands and removed the other bottle from the table. She had more than enough to drink before I had gotten here. As much as she wanted to find the answer with liquor, it would only help for tonight. Her troubles would still be here in the morning. I returned from the kitchen, and she had tears rolling down her face.

"Why don't they love me?" she asked.

"Babe, they love you. It's just that some people are selfish, and they never think about how their actions will affect the next person. When your father decided to hide your mother from you, he only thought of his happiness. He didn't do it to hurt you intentionally, as much as you think otherwise. I don't think he would do that to you." I rubbed my fingers through her bone-straight hair.

"A real man wouldn't put his child through that."

"Your entire life, your father has taken care of you and provided for his family to the best of his ability. Yes, he has made some bad choices, but he did his best. That's all you can ask of anyone, Charm, no matter what."

She nodded.

"Come on, let's get you in a nice hot bath."

I stood up, walked into my bedroom, and went to the master bathroom. I started the bath, putting lavender and vanilla oil into the water. I helped her into the tub, making sure not to get her cast wet. I took my time washing her hair and massaging her scalp. I washed her from head to toe. I wanted her to feel loved and special. I needed to show her that there was nothing I wouldn't do for her. When she was clean and relaxed, I scooped her up out of the tub and took her to the bed. I oiled her body with the coconut oil she had sitting on the dresser. Then I combed out her mass of curls that sat thick on her shoulders.

"I love your hair like this," I told her as I did my best to twist it like I had seen her do several times. My mission was to help her through what was ailing her.

"I love my curls too, but—" she stopped midsentence.

"But what?"

"Michael doesn't really like my hair in its natural state," she responded.

"Fuck Michael. Charm, what do *you* want?"

"I don't know." She shrugged as she answered.

"I think you're lying. I think Michael has controlled your life so much that you just go along with whatever." She looked down at the floor. "Charm." I lifted her head so she could look into my eyes. "I am not him. I want to know what *you* want. I want to hear *your* opinion on things if I mess up. I want *you* to let me know so that I can get my shit in order. Never let anyone dictate your life. It's yours, and you must live it how *you* want. Now, what do *you* want, Charm? Tell me."

"You."

That was all I needed to hear before pushing her back on the bed and making love to her.

With everything going on, Charm and I had slacked up on work. She had been staying with me for three weeks. We decided to stay in the office, putting in overtime. It was after hours, and Charm and I had decided to get more comfortable. She removed her blouse, leaving her in a black silk camisole. She was sitting across from me with her bare foot on my lap, and the other one was propped up on a pillow on the footstool we bought. Her skirt was above her thighs and showed all of her thickness. I sat in my undershirt with my shirt on the back of my chair. Shep lay right under her chair, looking like a sleeping giant. Absentminded, I used one hand to rub her foot, which was in my lap. We both were in deep concentration, looking at all the documents in front of us.

"Who is Brad Winthrop?" Charm questioned with a frown on her face.

"I believe he is the son-in-law to Mr. Forest or something like that. I stopped searching through my paperwork."

"Look at this." She passed me the papers that she had circled and written all over.

"I need to have someone look into this," I told her as the door was pushed open, and Michael stormed into the room with a scowl. Shep instantly went into protection mode, growling, ready to pounce on command.

"You two look pretty cozy in here," he smirked at both of us. "*This* is what you call *not* sleeping with your boss?"

Charm pulled her leg out of my lap and stood up, leaning on the desk. Michael stomped over to her, and I stood up. Shep jumped in front of Charm, growling deeply, causing Michael to stop within reaching distance.

"This is *not* the place for this conversation," Charm told him.

"I think this is the best place to converse about you fucking another man." He raised his voice at her, making her flinch. "I knew all along that this was going on, but I listened to your stupid, lying ass. I knew there was no way you got that salary without sucking a couple of dicks."

I couldn't believe how he was speaking to her. His tone and body language showed he genuinely thought that low of her.

"I would never sleep my way to the top of anything. I gained this all on my own. As far as Chase goes, we didn't sleep together until the night of my birthday. The night that *you* were supposed to be there for *me*. He's been here for me more in three weeks than you have our entire relationship. So, if you want to blame someone, blame yourself, you selfish son of a—"

Whap!

Michael's hand landed so hard on Charm's face that she fell onto the table. Shep lunged through the air at

Michael's neck while I was going for him. I couldn't believe he hit her.

"Down, Shep," I commanded. Shep hit the floor with a thud before grabbing Michael's pants leg as soon as he turned for the door. Rage pumped through my veins, and I was seeing red by the time my fist landed on the back of Michael's head. He went face forward into the door, crying out, and I jumped on top of him. He had put his hands on the woman I loved and would pay for that.

Charm's screams and her pulling me back broke through the fog that had clouded my mind. I stepped unwillingly away from a bloody Michael, ready to do more to him.

"Get the fuck out of here before I get you arrested."

"She meant nothing to me anyway. She's a disgusting pig. I don't know how I managed to stay with her so long. She's not even attractive." He spit, looking at Charm with so much hatred.

How did she stay with a man like this for so long? I thought.

"Leave if you don't want to be in the hospital getting fed through a tube."

The horror in Michael's eyes gave me so much pleasure. He quickly turned, jogging to the door.

Once he was out of the office, I locked the door and called security to escort him from the building. I pulled Charm close to me, holding onto her. I found an ice pack in my first aid kit, broke the small tube inside, and handed it to Charm to put on her face.

"Your hand," she said softly, pointing to my right hand that had swollen from the impact of repeatedly hitting Michael.

"Don't worry about it," I told her.

That night, after Charm was sleeping, I called my father.

"Dad, I need you to find some information for me."

"Whatever you need, son," he told me, and I gave him the information I had.

My father called me back five minutes later with the information. Then I made one more call. I stayed up most of the night packing Charm's and my suitcases. Where I needed to go, I could kill two birds with one stone, and I would take pleasure in all of it.

Chapter 14

Charm

Welcome to San Antonio, Texas. I stared at the signs as I walked through the airport. This morning had been busy. I woke up thinking we would get my cast taken off and go to work. Chase had other plans, though. We had to go to Texas for a business meeting. When we arrived, a man stood by the conveyor belt with Chase's name on a large card.

"This way." Chase held my hand so I wouldn't get lost in the thickness of the crowds. He maneuvered me through the people with expertise until we got into a waiting limousine. Our flight here was quiet, sitting in first class, sipping champagne. Our ride from the airport was a short one. My mouth dropped when we stopped in front of a massive house that I was sure had its own zip code.

"This is all of Mr. Forest's property?" I asked, amazed by everything I had seen.

"Yes, everything you have seen for the last ten minutes is his."

"Wow." It was a beautiful green oasis of land as far as your eyes could see.

"Wait until you see the rest of it," Chase said, grabbing my hand and leading me up the stairs to the massive door. The door opened, and an old man stepped outside with a welcoming smile.

"Chase, Charm, I presume."

"Yes," I smiled, walking to the door.

The old man reached for my hand. I extended it, and he pulled it to his lips, kissing it softly.

"Chase didn't tell me how beautiful you were," he stated, watching me blush.

"That's because she is spoken for," Chase replied, giving me a wink.

"Come. Let's go to the sitting room. I'm sure you're hungry. I had Joel fix us lunch. Follow me, please."

We walked into the house, and I was awestruck by the cherrywood floors and the cream décor. This house was massive, and its tasteful elegance could be seen throughout it.

"Please, sit," the old man told us before he came to pull out my chair for me.

"Thank you," I told him, then realized I had been welcomed into this man's home and didn't even know who he was. I turned a confused stare at Chase; it was like he was reading my mind.

"Mr. Forest, thank you for welcoming us to your home on such short notice." I raised a quizzical brow. I had met Mr. Forest before, and this was *not* the man who came to the office quarterly.

"Charm, this is Gerald Forest the Second. He's the grandfather to Philip Forest. He's also the man who hired me." All of this was beginning to make sense. When Chase came to the company, it surprised everyone, even Philip.

"I still hold most of the shares in the company. That is, until they are signed over to my son."

I nodded my head.

"Let's talk business, then have lunch," Mr. Forest said.

Chase pulled out his notes, and I pulled out my laptop, placing it on the table.

"Mr. Forest, when Chase first came to Forest Brands, he discovered that my boss, Mr. Hillard, was taking money from the company. He wouldn't tell us who else was stealing from your company, but we figured the money he was getting was to keep him silent."

"So, Hillard was being bribed by someone else?" Mr. Forest asked, shaking his head.

"Yes, and after further research, we discovered Brad Winthrop was helping him."

"But that's not all that caught my attention," Chase piped in. "He's also using Jaylen Forest's account information to pull funds."

"You mean to tell me that my own great-granddaughter is taking money from her family?" Mr. Forest sat up in his chair.

"No, sir. I think he hacked her account because all of her information changed right before the money began to disappear. Jaylen rarely deals with the company business, and after having someone track the computer's IP address, it led us right to Brad's home computer," Chase finished.

"So, he's making it look like his sister-in-law is stealing funds from the family."

"Yes, sir," Chase answered.

After that discussion, we sat at the table talking over lunch.

"Charm, do you like your new position at Forest?" Mr. Forest asked, digging into his steak.

"Yes, sir," I answered truthfully.

He smiled and continued eating.

Once our lunch was removed from the table, Mr. Forest handed Chase and me an envelope.

"This is a little something to thank you both for figuring this out for me." We accepted the envelopes and walked out the door.

As soon as we got inside the limousine, I opened my envelope. My mouth dropped at the amount of money he had just given me.

"Is it a thing for rich people to just give away money?"

Chase laughed. "No, but when rich people value your work, they will pay you accordingly."

I took in what he had said.

"Are we staying in this house?" I asked as we pulled up to another mansion sitting on acres of lush land. We had driven past horse stables and what looked like a golf course.

"No, we're here so I can introduce you to some friends. You're going to love them."

We walked into the house, and again, we were offered food and drinks.

"I'm so sorry, but we have just eaten lunch. I couldn't possibly eat anything else," I told the man standing before me, whom Chase introduced as Brenton Thomas.

Brenton's wife, Reign, was beautiful and couldn't wait to get me by myself. When I told them I wasn't hungry, Reign pulled me away from the men. I turned back, looking at Chase. He smiled and nodded his head, letting me know it was fine.

"Let's go swimming," Reign suggested, pulling me to a changing area.

"I don't have a suit," I replied as she handed me a Gucci bag.

"Chase had me pick you out a suit before you got on the plane this morning. He told me you would love to chill poolside since you have been in a cast for a month."

I smiled at his thoughtfulness. There was just something about him taking charge of things like this that made me love him even more. How is it that I fell for him without even trying? I shook my head, clearing my thoughts. Then I started removing my clothes and pulled out the two-piece bathing suit.

"I can't put this on. It shows everything," I told her, holding up the suit.

The suit was a purple halter top that was separated in the middle, with a triangle shape showing off my stomach and the word "Gucci" across the bottom portion of it in gold. The bottom was a high-waisted bikini resembling a pair of boy short panties.

"What's wrong with it?" Reign asked me with a perplexed expression.

"There's too much of me to go in there." I pointed at the suit she was holding. She looked down at the suit and back at me, then gave me a soft smile.

"No, it's not. It will fit you perfectly. Just try it on. Chase picked it from the pictures I sent him. You will be fine, trust me," she said, handing the suit back to me.

"I'll need something to cover up with," I told her. She rolled her eyes but smiled at me and pulled out the matching thin cover for the suit.

We walked barefoot to the enormous pool in the back of the house. Instead of getting in the water, we sat poolside.

"How did you and Chase get together?"

I smiled, thinking about the day I tripped going on stage to sing. I told her about everything, and she laughed at some of it.

"You two look so great together. I know you'll be sad when he leaves Chicago after the company is settled," she stated.

"Yeah, it's going to be hard for me." I kept my expression neutral.

I didn't want her to see my heart breaking right before her. He had promised never to hurt me, and hearing information as important as this had ripped me in two. I felt the tears about to fall down my face, but I couldn't let her see them.

"Excuse me," I told her, going to the pool. The water would hide the tears threatening to fall.

"Wait." She grabbed my hand as I tried to walk off. "You didn't know. I'm so sorry." I pulled away from her, diving into the pool.

"Sorry" was a word I never wanted to hear again. That word had been used on me too much within the last three days. Every time I heard it, I heard something that impacted my life in a way I wasn't sure I could recover from. I wanted to take that word and shove it up someone's ass. I dipped my head under the water, doing one lap after another, until I heard a splash right next to me.

"Charm."

The tears started falling between the bass in Chase's tone and the way he pulled me up from the water.

"You told me you would be here for me. You said you wouldn't hurt me," I yelled at him, trying to push him away from me.

"It was a misunderstanding. I'm sorry." The words left his mouth, and my hand came crashing across his face.

"No, you are worse than sorry. You made me love you!" I was done with all of this.

Chase turned and looked at Reign. I saw her mouth move, saying, "I'm sorry" to him. I screamed and swam away from him.

"Charm." He pulled me out of the water a second time. "I'm not going back to Massachusetts unless you are with me. This was all a misunderstanding," he pled with me, and I stopped, turning to him. I felt like a complete idiot, knowing his friends must think I'd lost my mind. "I was planning on talking to you about that once we returned to Chicago." He let me go, and I saw the redness on his cheek from the smack I had given him. I was the one who needed to apologize. I kissed his cheek and whispered in his ear.

"I'm sorry."

He pulled me into his arms, kissing me. We both got out of the water, holding hands.

"I owe you an apology for disrespecting your home." Reign smiled at me. "No worries. It was all my fault. I should've kept my mouth closed." Brenton kissed the top of her head and smiled at me.

"Nice blow you landed back there." He pointed to Chase's reddening cheek, and I felt terrible again. I turned, putting my face on Chase's chest.

"That's what we call a 'Chicago smack,'" Reign said, laughing. I turned around, staring at her.

"You're from Chicago?" I asked. Out of all our talking, that had never come up.

"Yes, born and raised," she told me, grabbing my hand. "Come on. Let's finish talking and let Chase dry off so they can continue their business."

Instead of lounging in the chairs, we decided to get into the pool.

"He loves you," she said as soon as we were settled in the water.

"I love him too. It's just that—" I stopped, not wanting to reveal my deepest thoughts to this woman I had just met. But something about her made me feel like she would help me gain a clearer understanding.

"I'm not here to judge you; whatever you tell me stays between us. I'm sorry about earlier, and it will never happen again."

I thought about what she said. Sometimes, you have to talk to someone who isn't so close to the situation. I told her everything in my heart, about my trust issues, and why I was struggling with the thought of Chase loving me for me.

"I want to tell you a story about myself. I grew up on the West Side of Chicago. My mother was a drug addict who loved me and took care of me to the best of her ability. The day before I was accepted into Harvard, my mother died, leaving me alone. I felt I had no one in this world to have my back until I met Brenton. His family hated me. They wanted him to marry someone born into money and could help out with their businesses. Brenton couldn't care less about what they thought. He saved me; he was there with me at my worst. He nursed me back to health and beat his brother's ass over me. Brenton became my family, and his friends, or should I say, his 'brothers,' Chase, Dennis, and Dylan, became my brothers. Dennis is engaged to my best friend, Amber. They have a little girl named London, who we all spoil rotten. They have made me an aunt and godmother.

"My point in telling you this is because when these men love you, they love hard. I needed a family, and they became that to me. There's nothing I wouldn't do for any of them, and they feel the same about me. I'm not telling you to ditch your family, being a woman who has lost a mother that will never come back. I advise you to try to fix it. If you hand them an olive branch, and they reject it, do what's best for you. Just know with Chase by your side, you have a family here with us."

I took in everything she said and made a few decisions about my life and what I wanted to do with it. It was time that I took control of my life.

Chapter 15

Charm

The three days we spent in San Antonio were nothing short of amazing. After meeting Brenton and Reign, I knew why Chase loved them so much and why he couldn't wait to return to them. When Reign said they were a family, she wasn't lying. They teased each other like brothers and sisters would. Being around them made me long to have that same relationship with my family.

"Are you ready for our next destination?" Chase asked as he sat beside me in the private plane Brenton had let us use. Although we had on our seat belts, he pulled me close to him.

"I thought we were going back home."

"We are, but there's just one more stop we need to make." The hesitance in his words caused me to look up at him.

"Is it more business?"

"No, it's personal." He paused momentarily, looking out the window as the plane ascended.

"I'm taking you to visit your mother." I pulled away from him, turning as much as possible in the seat.

"That's one place I don't want to go. As soon as we can move around, I need you to tell the pilot to take us home."

I know he felt he was doing the right thing, but this was a decision I needed to make on my own. He had no right to take control of my life when it concerned my mother. Sharon was a problem I had to deal with on my own, and right now, I just wanted to forget about her. The check she sent me sat on the kitchen counter at Chase's house for so long that he put it in his safe to secure it. I felt she was trying to buy my time, and I wasn't for sale.

"Hear me out." Chase clasped my hand in his, tugging it a little until I turned to him.

"During our time together, I have seen you go through a lot dealing with people who are supposed to love and protect you. These last few weeks, you have gone through hell. Most of this stems from a time you don't know anything about. You talked to your father and heard his side of what happened. You gave him a chance to tell you his side of the story, and it was a piece of shit truth. Yet, you gave him a face-to-face before you decided to leave his home. From what the letter says, your mother didn't want this for you. She didn't put herself in a grave to have her way. Your father did that for her and you. Both of you are victims, and she deserves to see you in person. Even if it's only this one time, she deserves to see your beautiful face and know you are okay."

"But she didn't fight for me."

He kissed our joined hands. "You won't know that until you get the entire story." I frowned. "I won't force you to do anything you don't want to do, but if you think of this as something for your benefit, then it won't be such a hard decision."

I sat and thought about his words the entire flight. I became nervous when the seat belt light came on, signifying we would land. What would I say to her? Will she look like the same woman I saw twenty-one years ago?

We walked through the airport to a restaurant off to the side.

"I can't eat right now, Chase. My stomach is in knots," I told him as he continued to usher me through the small crowd.

"I called her yesterday, and she agreed to meet us here," he said.

We got to the back, and she stood at the table waiting for us. I took one step . . . and tripped over my feet. Chase's quick reflexes kept me from plunging face-first into the woman.

"I see some things never change," she said with a gentle smile. She took a few steps toward me with open arms, but I stepped out of her reach. "I'm sorry." She stepped back with her hand up so we could shake hands.

When her hand touched mine, I couldn't believe it. It was like I was seeing and touching a ghost. There had been so many nights I cried for this touch, knowing I would never have it again, but here she was. Her hands were warm and soft. She still had that glow about her skin that I had never forgotten. The scent of cocoa butter was all over her, and she had aged gracefully. She looked just like she did the day she left, except for a few strands of gray hair. If she dyed her hair, she could easily pass as my sister. We looked just alike except for the few genes my father passed down to me. My mother was beautiful.

I covered the space between us and hugged her. I let my hands touch the ends of her hair that hung down her back just as long as mine. I made sure to take a deep breath, so I could remember her scent, which I thought I had forgotten until now. She rubbed my back to soothe me as I broke down crying in her arms. My mother was here. I was touching her, hugging her, and for the first time in a long time, I felt that comfort that only a mother could give.

"It's okay, Lucky Charm." When she said those words, I broke down even more. I never knew that you could miss something as simple as four words. I had gotten something that many people never get . . . a second chance.

"I missed you so much. You don't understand what I went through," I told her once I got myself together.

"I missed you too," she told me as we sat at the table. People had begun to stare at us, but I couldn't care less. If they only knew that I had buried this woman a long time ago, and now, she was standing in front of me . . .

"Why didn't you come back for me?" The words left my mouth before I knew it.

"I did come for you, Charm, but your father and Sonya were on some shady shit. I beat down the door to get into the house the day I returned for you. Sonya called the police on me and told them I was lurking around the house trying to kidnap her daughter. I did everything I could to prove that I was your mother and not her, but she and William had forged a birth certificate that said you were their child. There was nothing I could do. The police said if I came back, I would go to jail. I couldn't let that happen because your grandmother needed me here to help her. The week I got back here, I found out that your grandmother had breast cancer. Since Sonya was too busy stealing my husband, I knew she wouldn't dare return here to help Mama, so I did everything your father wanted me to do, including signing over all parental rights for you. I had no idea they told you I was dead until about seven years later."

"How did you find out about that?"

"My nephew, your brother, came here with Sonya for a week to meet Mama, and when he saw me, you could've sworn he thought I had stepped from the grave. He was so scared that I had come back to haunt him for being bad."

I laughed. "I always used to tell him if he was mean to me or was a bad boy, my mother would come back from the grave to get him." We both laughed at that.

"Well, it worked, and he told me that I was the lady in the picture with the wings." When she told me that, my mouth dropped open.

"He told me he saw you on that trip. I thought he was referring to a picture since they stayed at Grandma's house," I told her with a shocked expression. "What happened the night you left the house?"

Chase came to the table, setting two cups of coffee down for us. He moved to sit at the table across from us, and I motioned him to sit beside me.

"They never told you?" my mother questioned.

"No. They continued with life like you were never there."

She shook her head, and I could see the sadness in her eyes. "I'm so sorry you had to go through that."

"That wasn't the half of it. Your sister turned out to be a complete bitch," I mumbled. Simultaneously, both my mother and Chase grabbed my hands.

"I am truly sorry for everything. I know I can't make up for lost time. Hopefully, we both can start a new chapter in our life together."

I nodded my head before speaking. "The night you left . . ." I slowly took my hand from hers, and I could tell the action hurt her.

"William was my world. We met in college. It was a whirlwind romance. When I fell for your father, I fell hard. A year into college, I was pregnant with you. I never regretted it. We got married, and since William came from a family that was doing well for themselves, he was able to give us a decent life. I gave it all up to become a stay-at-home mother and wife because that's what he wanted from me. I loved that man so much I would have given him anything he asked for.

"Sonya and I were two years apart. We grew up as best friends. We moved away from the family to Chicago. It had always been in the plan for her to follow me. Once she turned 22 years old, Mama finally gave Sonya her blessing to come live with me. Finding out that those two had betrayed me made something inside of me snap.

"That night, when you went to sleep, I decided to go out and get some things from Walmart. I asked both your dad and aunt if they needed anything. They both gave me a short list of things they wanted, and I drove to the twenty-four-hour Walmart. I went through the first couple of aisles before I realized I didn't have my purse. I pushed the cart to the side to check the car, but it wasn't there. I got into the car and returned to the house, surprised by the noises I heard coming from my bedroom. I busted in the door, and Sonya was doing things I had never seen before. They were so into what they were doing and making so much noise with the bed and moaning, they didn't even notice I was in the room . . . until I placed a gun to the back of Sonya's head."

My mouth dropped. I couldn't believe she would do something like that.

"I made her leave the house. William and I got into this huge argument. The reason I didn't put a bullet in their heads that night was because of you. I couldn't have you waking up to a crime scene. If I had followed through with my thoughts, you would have had no one to look after you. Once Sonya walked back into the house, I knew I had to leave. There was no way we could all stay there for another night."

"Why didn't you contact me once I turned 18?" This question had been plaguing my mind since I got her letter. Although she stated some of the reasons in the letter, I needed to hear them from her mouth.

"Charm, you were doing so well for yourself, and I knew me stepping back into your life at that time would have done more harm than good. I didn't want you to lash out at the only family you knew at such a crucial time in your life. If I had let everything out then, you would have failed at being successful. You would have questioned everything you've known, down to your very own existence.

"I came to you now because you have grown into a great woman capable of handling things. My popping into your life at this point has caused a rift in your world, but you are handling it. You have a great man by your side; if you can't stand on your own two feet, he will hold you up until you can. You may feel like my approach was too late, but I know it was perfect. If it weren't, you wouldn't be here."

She paused, pushing her hair out of her face. "Do you understand what I'm saying?" she asked, her eyes willed me to see things from her point of view.

"Yes," I answered softly.

As much as I wanted to blame her for everything that happened, I couldn't. She was right about everything. If she had come to me when I was 18, I would have been depressed and devastated. I wouldn't have gone to college and gotten the great job that I have now. I would have resented everyone around me, and most importantly, I wouldn't have met Chase. I wanted to be mad at someone—anyone—but the more I think about everything, the more it's not even worth my energy. My mother and I caught up on as much as we could during our brief time together. We both made promises to visit each other soon.

As we got back on our private plane, I couldn't believe my father would stoop that low to have sex with my aunt in a bed he shared with his wife. I didn't understand. If he was so unhappy, why didn't they just pack up and leave together? Why did they have to make the two innocent people suffer the most?

"Are you okay?" Chase asked with a concerned expression.

As I sat thinking, I realized my brows were furrowed, and I was biting on my thumbnail.

"I'm fine. I just need to talk to my dad and Sonya," I told him honestly.

"Okay, but give it a couple of days. There's something I want to do first." I thought about his request and decided I needed more time to process everything.

"Whatever you want, my love," I told him, watching a smile spread across his face.

I began believing that Chase was the best thing that has happened to me in my life. Although we still had a lot of work to do, I knew that I could trust him even if I couldn't trust anyone else in this world. He had shown me that repeatedly since we met, but I was just now seeing it for myself.

Chapter 16

Chase

This was the most nervous I had been in my life. I was taking Charm to meet my parents. I prayed that my mother behaved herself. She wasn't a mean woman, but she was naturally outspoken, which could sometimes be intimidating. I watched Charm as she got ready for our dinner. She had tried on several outfits, but the cocktail dress she had on was perfect. It was a cream dress wrapped around her body and came a little above her knees. It didn't show too much cleavage, but the opening at the front of the dress gave an appearance of a split. It showed just enough thigh to be sexy and modest at the same time. The dress hugged her curves like a second skin but seemed comfortable enough for her to move around. She was finishing her makeup, which I didn't think she needed, but she wanted to look her best. She took the pin out of her hair and let it drop straight down her back. When she turned around, my breath caught because she was drop-dead gorgeous.

"How do I look?" she asked me.

She was waiting for a reply, but I was choked up. I didn't know she could look any better than she did then. Charm was really in the wrong profession. She could have made a fortune by becoming a plus-sized model. When I saw the worried expression cross her face, my brain had finally connected to my mouth, and the words fell out.

"You look amazing."

She sighed deeply in relief before stepping into a pair of burgundy Manolo Blahniks. She picked up her matching purse, and we were out the door. On the way to Everest, an upscale restaurant in downtown Chicago, I tried calming Charm's and my nerves. This was a big occasion for both of us. I hadn't brought a woman to meet my parents in a long time.

"I know you're nervous, but remember that I love you no matter what happens tonight. Our happiness depends on us, not anyone else. So, no matter what happens tonight, remember, we are going home together." I squeezed her hand slightly, lifting it to my lips and kissing it softly. I did not doubt that they would like her, but my parents are very concerned about my well-being when it comes to it.

"Nice to see you again, Mr. Lancaster. Your party is waiting. Please, follow me." The waitress smiled politely at us, turning on her heels to lead us to our table. As we approached the table, my parents stood up. We embraced one another before I introduced Charm to them.

"Mom and Dad, this is my girlfriend, Charm. Charm, these are my parents, Mr. and Mrs. Lancaster." They both smiled, and each took turns shaking her hand. Although Charm wore a mask of steel, I could still tell she was nervous.

"Please, just call us Collen and Susan," my father stated as we pulled out the chairs for our women, and the small talk began.

"We have heard so much about you, and we couldn't wait to meet the woman who held our son's attention," my mother started. I gave her the eye like, "Don't start this."

"Same here. Your son admires you both, especially the relationship you share." My mother gave her a tight smile. "Yes, it takes dedication to be married for thirty years. What about your parents? Are they still together?" I closed my eyes at my mother's question because of all the recent drama Charm had been through. To my surprise, Charm didn't break.

"My parents separated when I was 6 years old. My father and stepmother raised me."

"How could a woman ever leave her child? I would never do something like that," my mother said, shivering.

I shook my head. This was a very sensitive subject, and it would go left quickly. My father grabbed my mother's hand and squeezed it.

"How about we order drinks?" my father piped in.

I took Charm's hand in mine and kissed the back of it. She didn't have to answer anything that she was uncomfortable with.

"My mother didn't have a choice in raising me for those years, and it wasn't because she was neglectful. She just married the wrong man. Before you decide that I'm not good enough for your son because of my parental background, let me get this off my chest. Your son and I love each other and plan to be together with—or without—your blessing. So, before you judge me, realize we will have children. Due to things from my past, it's not looking too good for my father and stepmother. I would love for us to be one big happy family that can learn to love each other, but I will never let my children be around anyone who will mistreat them or down their parents because of shit they don't understand. For your sake, I'm willing to start this dinner over and act like this conversation has never happened."

I held Charm's hand on the table so my mother could see I would stand by what she said. My mother saw our hands linked together and gave us a curt nod. My father waited until my mother's head was turned and gave Charm a small smile and a wink.

"I'm sorry. I didn't mean to offend you," my mother said.

In a way, I felt like she really didn't mean it. My mother was so used to people coming from two-parent homes. If the people we knew weren't in a two-parent home, they always stayed with their mother. The tension was a little thick at the table. But as soon as the wine hit the table, my father ensured our glasses were full. Charm took a sip of the wine and visibly relaxed.

"We heard you are a very smart young woman," my father stated.

"I wouldn't say that I'm that smart. I just have a love for numbers."

"She's being modest, Dad. Her credentials are better than some billionaires we know." My dad smiled at Charm, blushing.

"If you don't like working for Chase here, I have a friend who would love to get you in the studio," my father told her with a huge smile.

"You sing?" my mother asked, setting her wineglass on the table.

"She has a voice that shouldn't be hidden," my dad answered for Charm.

"No, really, I'm fine working for Forest Brands," Charm stated.

The night went smoothly from there. By the time we left, my mother was setting a date to take Charm to a spa she loved.

This woman was so amazing. And when we got home that night, I showed her just how amazing I thought she was.

***

"I know you prefer I wait a little longer, but I need to speak with my father again."

"Okay, baby. Do you want me to go with you?"

"Please," she said, putting on her sneakers.

Michael's car was in the driveway when we pulled up to her father's house.

"This doesn't surprise me," she said, sighing.

"What?" I asked casually.

I knew exactly what she was referring to. I just didn't let her know. After Michael came into the office and hit Charm, I made sure to find out everything I could about him.

"Michael's here."

She got out of the car, stalking to the front door. I caught up to her and stood in front of her. "You are here to talk to your dad and aunt—nothing else. If Michael says anything to you, let me handle him." She nodded.

We quietly stepped into the house, and Sonya's words smacked us in the face.

"You just couldn't keep your hands to yourself. All you had to do was wait a few months, and that money would have been ours."

"What the fuck?" Charm mouthed to me. I shook my head at her and shushed her. I didn't want her to say anything.

"You should have seen her in that office sitting with her legs all over that man in the shit I bought her. She had me in there looking like a fool."

Charm raised an eyebrow at me.

"When you first started talking to Charm, I had to see you hugged up on her in the clothes that I put on her back. I didn't snap in front of everyone when you were hugged up with her. While you were in that office trying to play the wounded boyfriend, you forgot about one thing . . . You owe me. Don't ever forget. Without me, you wouldn't be where you are now."

Charm grabbed my hand and squeezed it tight. There was silence before anyone else said anything else.

"You might have put in a word for me at my job when you set me up with Charm, but I was the one that put in the work to stay there. Don't forget, I don't need Charm's money. That was all you. I make enough money to carry my own weight *and* your big-ass stepdaughter's."

Chapter 17

Charm

I stood by the front door, listening to everything they were saying. I would say that I was surprised by their words, but I wasn't. I knew something was off with their friendship the first time Sonya came to me with some things Michael and I had discussed. It seemed like the drama would never stop.

"Do you think she suspects that we're having an affair, and that's why she started talking to her boss?" Sonya asked.

"Who gives a damn what she thinks now?" Michael stated.

"I do. If she finds out about us, she's going to tell William. I can't lose the best thing I have in my life. William makes sure I have everything I want and need; he always has."

Find out about them? I thought to myself. This woman just couldn't leave well enough alone. First, she took my dad from my mother, and now this. I wasn't sure of all the emotions that I was feeling, but it was one I was familiar with. I stomped away from Chase before he could grab my arm.

"I guess what they say is true. Once a snake, always a snake." I watched as the shocked expressions crossed both of their faces.

"What are you talking about?" Sonya asked. I could tell she was unsure how much of their conversation I heard.

"I'm talking about me calling my father and telling him how his wife likes to sleep around and how she set up her niece to get robbed blind."

Sonya stood up from her chair, letting her mouth silently open and close. This was the first time that she literally had nothing to say. She was caught red-handed.

"Your father won't believe a word that comes from your mouth. I will make sure of that." Sonya had a smirk on her face that I would have loved to wipe off with my fist and feet, but she wasn't worth my energy.

"Is that how you got him to turn against my mother? How you were able to get him to lie to me about her dying?" Sonya's mouth dropped open for the second time.

"That's right. I know she's alive, and I know how you two forged my birth certificate to get her locked up for coming back for me. I know about my grandmother cutting you off after that, and I know you got my little brother to lie for you to cover your tracks." Sonya sat down in her seat, and Michael turned to me.

"Well, I had nothing to do with any of that," he said.

I turned my furious gaze on him. "Oh, let's not forget about all the psychological shit you have done to me."

"Let's not do this in front of company," Michael said, pointing to Chase. I let out a sinister chuckle that I didn't know I had in me.

"I didn't hear you saying that when you put your hands on me in his office. *Now* you're worried about him?" I rolled my eyes at his suggestion. "I would say that I'm hurt by all this bullshit, but that would be a lie. I'm not even surprised that you two are messing around. What I am surprised about is the fact that you would hurt my father like that after everything you did to have him for yourself. Before you moved in with us, our family was happy and content. Now, look at it. Look at all the confusion you caused over three million dollars."

Both of their eyes grew saucer size at the amount of money I came into. I could see the look of envy in both of their eyes. "I'm going to leave, but please know my father will be the first call I make." I turned on my heels to walk out of the door. I couldn't even look at these two any longer.

"There's no need to call me. I'm right here." I turned to see my father coming into the house from the garage.

We had been going back and forth so much that none of us had heard him come into the house. *How long has he been there?* I wondered. He looked like he had aged about ten years as he stepped toward us. He had dark circles around his eyes, and his pants sagged from his waist. His eyes were red, and I could tell he had been crying. His lips were dry. I wanted to walk across the room to hug my old man, but when I stepped toward him, I thought about all he had done. I stood looking at him, wondering if I could ever forgive him for taking so much from my life. When he looked up at me, I knew then that I would run around the world twice for him.

He took a couple of steps, going to the head of the table, where he placed both his hands on it and cleared his throat.

"Michael, I have treated you like a son since the day I met you. I have brought you into my family and gave my blessings for you to marry my daughter—only for you to sleep with my wife." My dad shook his head, pausing for a minute before his eyes landed on Sonya.

"I have given up so much to be with you, and all that I haven't given up was snatched away because of our lies and manipulation."

"No one made you do any of that. If you weren't so quick to stick your penis in something new, you would

still have it all. So, don't blame your mishaps on me."
Sonya rolled her neck and pointed at my dad as she spoke.

"You are fully to blame. I know I played a huge part in
giving up my wife and losing my daughter. Also, I'm playing a huge part in what happens next." We all turned to
my father; his expression made me think the worst. Is my
father capable of a murder-suicide? He turned, looking
through some of the drawers in the kitchen. I closed my
eyes because I didn't want to see what he would pull out.
I said a silent prayer, hoping he hadn't lost his mind.

"Dad," I called out. He stopped and looked up at me.

"Get the hell out of my house." His gaze went from
Michael to Sonya.

"What?" Sonya's mouth dropped open, and her lips
quivered like she couldn't believe it. My dad had taken
her side of things for so long that she didn't think he
would kick her to the curb.

"You heard me. Get the fuck out!" I had heard him use
a list of curse words before, but this wasn't one of them.

I guess my aunt tended to bring out the worst in all of
us. She stood slowly, looking around at everyone. Her
eyes were pleading for help that no one here would give
her.

"Where am I supposed to go?" she finally asked.

My father shrugged his shoulders.

"Maybe Michael can take you in," I suggested, and I
started to laugh when Michael frowned at me. I leaned
back into Chase, and he wrapped his arms around me
until Michael walked out the door.

"I am so sorry," my dad said, sitting at the table. "I
caused all this to happen, and I am sorry." I walked over
to sit in the chair in front of him.

"Yes, this situation is pretty bad, but we will get through
it together." I grabbed his hands and squeezed them
before getting up to hug him. "I'm going to go. If Sonya

gives you any problems, call the police, Dad," I told him and walked out of the house.

We couldn't mend our relationship overnight, but today was a start.

Two Weeks Later . . .

"Can you see anything?" Chase asked me for the thousandth time. I can't believe I let this man blindfold me with his tie. He helped me out of the car, then uncovered my eyes. I frowned. What was the big deal about being at Michael's job?

"I don't want to go in here. As a matter of fact, why are we here?" I asked with my hands on my hips.

"This is our new business venture."

"We know nothing about oil." I raised a brow at him.

"No, but we know business and numbers. It can't be that hard." Chase was excited about this new venture, but I was worried. Did he know who worked here, or was this just a coincidence? I took a deep breath and followed Chase into the building. He took confident steps, like he was ready to take on the world. On the other hand, I was a little nervous about what might transpire if Michael saw us walking around.

As we took the elevator to the top floor, my stomach plummeted. There was no way we wouldn't be seen. When the doors opened, everything I had thought would happen . . . did.

"What the hell are you two doing here?" Michael asked.

Chase stepped past him without saying a word, so I followed his lead. Michael grabbed my arm, snatching me back.

"Let me go," I told him, pulling away. Chase turned and shoved Michael hard.

"Don't you ever lay a hand on her again," Chase practically growled. I had never seen the menacing expression on his face before.

"When you step into *my* place of business, it's *my* rules that you have to go by, playboy," Michael snarled at Chase, and Chase chuckled at him, shaking his head.

"Do you know who owns this company?" Chase asked, waiting for Michael to respond. Michael gave Chase a look like that's a stupid question before answering.

"Brenton Thomas," he answered, and my mind went into a tailspin.

Brenton Thomas is one of Chase's best friends. This wasn't going to end too well for Michael. I didn't know if I should be happy because karma was knocking on his door quicker than I thought it would or be sad because he was about to lose the job that meant so much to him.

"Wrong, as usual. Brenton sold this portion of his company to me."

Michael was shocked.

"That little thing you did when we walked in the door, that's called assault. You're fired. Pack your things, and I'll have your pink slip waiting. You see, Michael, it never pays to act a fool with people. You never know who they are . . . until it's too late." Chase grabbed my hand and walked off.

"Why did you buy this company?" I asked as we walked through the office. Chase stopped, turning to me. He pushed my hair out of my face and gave me a soft peck on the lips.

"Because no one messes with my queen and thinks there will be no consequences."

Not caring about onlookers, he pulled me close and kissed me deeply.

Epilogue

Charm

One Year Later . . .

We sat on the wraparound porch at my mother's house in Mississippi, enjoying the sun beaming down on the earth. I was sitting in Chase's lap, looking content as my mother told us about wanting to sell the house and move back to Chicago so that we could be closer to each other. Chase rubbed his hands over my baby bump and smiled. I had done well for myself. I had lost sixty pounds in six months, only to pack them back on by getting pregnant. I was upset about the forty pounds of weight I would regain, but I was happy about having a little bundle of joy.

This past year had been nothing short of amazing. I built a relationship with my mother, and my father and I were still working on our trust issues. But what shocked me the most was how forgiving my mother had been to my father. They had agreed to be civil with each other for my sake and their future grandchildren. I think my mother knew that my dad was suffering enough for all the things he had put us through.

No one knew where Sonya went once she left my father's house. She made a fuss about my brother not going with her, but he was firm in saying he was staying with my dad. That was a shocker, considering he's a mama's boy and practically followed Sonya everywhere.

Michael tried to sue the company for wrongful termination, but there were cameras in the elevator that caught everything. The case went nowhere. As soon as his lawyers saw the video, they told him nothing could be done. He didn't stop there, though. He brought up a lawsuit against me, which was also thrown out.

Chase and I were doing more than good. Our child was due in four months, and we decided to stay in Chicago and use the house in Massachusetts as a vacation home for when we visit his friends.

"I think you should keep it," I told my mother, gazing over the land that the house sat on.

"Why? Once I leave, I'll have to have someone to come care for it," she replied.

"This is the house that you grew up in. You have so many great memories here, and you want to leave them behind?" My mother stared at me for a minute.

"It's not the memories of the past that you dwell on. Our goal in life is to create new and better memories as life goes on."

I thought about what she said, letting it sink in. I wanted to do just that, but you never know where you're going unless you know where you have come from.

"I'll buy the house from you," I told her.

Chase kissed the nape of my neck. "Are you sure?" he asked.

"The only other thing I'm more sure about is my love for you." I turned in his lap, kissing him.

Part 2:

Autumn

Chapter 1

Dylan

I watched the fragile fist bang the coffee table in front of him so hard my whiskey sloshed onto the expensive wood. The old man was furious. In some ways, I understood where he was coming from, and in other ways, I didn't.

"You, Dylan, are who I was forty years ago, and it's *not* a good look." I listened to my great-uncle as he spoke to me about my whorish ways. He made it seem like growing older had been harsh to him. I understood he was a couple of years short of knocking on death's door, but he had lived a great life. He had more than most people would see in three lifetimes. He had a big house, an antique car collection, and more expensive cars than he could ever drive. He could maintain all of this and his money because he was never in a serious relationship. He had found the key to wealth—being single. He had never married, and besides my parents, who we never saw or talked to, he had no family except me.

He didn't have to worry about making alimony payments or dealing with lawsuits because he was never with a woman long enough to get to know them. In his monthlong relationships with women, he made sure they signed contracts beforehand, stating that they were only eye candy. If a sexual relationship occurred, it was mutual. This man was the player of all players. He taught me never to settle down, but here he was for the tenth time within the last two years, lecturing me about the opposite.

"Why was this life so good for you but not me?" I asked him the question that I had never asked him during each talk that we had. My uncle was living every man's dream—getting pussy with no attachments. He had many women for whenever the mood hit him, and he never had to have the same woman twice. He was a man of variety and had some of the most beautiful women I had ever seen. I'm not saying I hadn't had my fair share, but my uncle could have women half his age.

"Dylan, as a parent, I was supposed to show you how to become a better man, not how to live the same lifestyle I did. When I got you, I didn't know the first thing about raising a child. I felt that since you were a boy, I didn't have to change, but now that I'm getting up there in age," he paused and sighed, "I've been looking around at all the things I have, and none of this shit matters because I have no one to share it with. I have no one to wake up to in the morning who loves me for me. I have no one who wants to take a nice long drive with me, and we can be happy with each other's company."

Is he serious? All of this is over a long drive on a sunny day?

"With all your money, you can pay someone to ride with you and be happy."

He turned and finally looked at me. "You can't possibly be that shallow." The look on his face told me he was stunned by my words.

I didn't see why he was so shocked. I had said way worse, and he had never looked at me this way.

"This is my fault, Dylan. I have led you to believe that money can buy you happiness."

"No, Pops. You have raised me to believe that I wouldn't need anything or anyone else if I had money and true friends."

"What about love, companionship, loyalty to the woman who will make everything okay with a smile and kind words?" I leaned against the wall, waiting for this conversation to be over. Once it was done, I wouldn't have to worry about it coming back up for another three months. Pop Wilson, or Pops, as I affectionately called him, stopped talking, but his mouth stayed open. He realized I had tuned him out. I saw the wheels turning in his head behind his eyes. When a sinister grin crossed his face, I knew I had fucked up.

"You have three months," he said in a firm tone.

I raised an eyebrow at him in question. "Three months for what?" I asked, unsure of what he was talking about.

"Three months to marry a respectable woman, or you forfeit your trust fund at age 30, and you forfeit your place in my will."

He must have lost his mind! My hands went through my hair, and I tugged at it. I began to pace when I stopped taking in his expression. He had aged gracefully. At 70 years old, he looked about fifteen years younger. He stayed fit by exercising and eating healthy meals. At one time in his life, he used to say the energy from all of the younger women he dated kept him young, but it was something about his eyes. I stared into his warm blue eyes, then took in his skin tone. Something was off. It seemed that 70 years had caught up with him in no time. He was a strong and vibrant man . . . but his eyes looked tired.

"Three months? How am I supposed to find a respectable woman in three months?"

"Buy one," he stated, holding up three withered fingers as he walked through his mansion, chuckling.

"Damn," I cursed and kicked the wall. What the hell was I going to do now?

One Month Later . . .

I leaned on the ship's rails, watching the only woman I had bonded with over the last few months. Autumn Spaulding was more beautiful than words could describe. She had this air about her that spoke femininity. You would think five years in the marines would wash all of that away, but it didn't. She was fit, funny, caring, and, most importantly, the only female I had more than a sexual connection with. I watched as the yellow sundress she had on flared in the wind and dropped back down to her thighs. She rubbed her hands over the short curls on the top of her head. I've never liked women with short hair, but her faded haircut with designs on the sides and the back of her head fit her. She made the style look so feminine, especially with the 1-carat diamond stud earrings she had in her ears every time I saw her.

Her nutmeg-colored skin looked radiant and soft to touch under the sun, and her curves were just right. Her cotton dress lay on her shapely ass, and I could tell she wasn't wearing any panties. My dick jumped in my linen shorts.

"Calm down, big fella," I told myself, looking down at my pants.

Autumn stared down at the water, unaware she was just the type of woman I needed. I had followed her on this trip for a reason, and I was determined to get what I wanted from her before my deadline. Once I put my plan in motion, Autumn would fall. All I had to do was wait for the perfect time to tell her I was here.

The ship had pulled off two hours ago, and I had just found the courage to "accidentally" bump into her. I had it all figured out, and now, it was time to execute the plan I had put together within the month. I was three feet away from her before she spoke.

"It's about time you let me know you were here." She looked down at the water, and I turned, checking my surroundings.

"Yes, I'm talking to you," she said, lifting her head and turning around to look at me. When her jet-black eyes gazed into mine, my heart began to triple beat. She smiled at me, showing perfect white teeth. Her juicy, thick, bow-shaped lips had a gloss to them. She put her hands on her hips, making her dress fit her slim waist. As I stared at her, all I could think about was that she had two identical sisters. I know the boys went crazy over them when they were younger. Autumn was a triplet.

"Are you going to say something or just stare at me like you've lost your mind?"

I cleared my throat. "How did you know I was here?" I finally asked her.

"Once a marine, always a marine," she said with a smile that made my breathing halt.

"Are you ready for some fun in the sun?"

I took in everything about her while I was up close. Her hair was thick but looked soft to the touch. Her skin tone was a mixture of nutmeg, reds, and bronze. What I thought was jet-black hair had a hint of brown in it under the sun.

"What are you doing here? I never told you where I was going. This could be a coincidence, but I don't believe in them. So, explain yourself," she said, getting right to the point instead of answering my question.

I kinda cocked my head. I could tell her exactly what I wanted from her now or beat around the bush. I wasn't sure of how she would take what I had to ask. I thought for a minute as she stared into my eyes like she could tell if I was lying. She crossed her arms, and her eyes narrowed after I took too long to answer her. My eyes went right to her chest, where her breasts were just enough to fit into the palms of my hand. My mouth watered as I thought about putting them in my mouth to suck and lick all over. *Am I supposed to be this sexually attracted to my future play wife?* As she moved her hands to her thick, rounded hips, I answered my own question. *Yes!*

The fury that began to dance in her eyes made me want her even more.

"It must be fate," I told her, watching the right side of her mouth kind of pull up like she was about to smile.

"It must be bullshit," she said, laughing.

"Most women believe in stuff like that."

"Most women haven't been through what I have. Cut the bull. Charm put you up to this, didn't she?" I raised a questioning brow at her.

"Why would you think your best friend would set you up with me?"

"You don't have to cover for her. Before I left, she told me to go out and find a man to have a good time with. Now, here you are on the same cruise as I am, damn near stalking me."

"I assure you neither Charm nor Chase knows anything about me being here, but since we are here together, let's keep each other company. As far as a good time, I'm willing to give you everything you want and need in the bedroom." I winked at her.

I watched her as her body reacted to my words. I could smell the wetness of her pussy over the salty water. Autumn was hot, and watching her lips slightly part made my cock grow down my leg.

"Let's go for a swim." I grabbed her hand, pulling her in the direction of the pool. We needed to cool down before I bent her over the rails and gave the cruise ship a show they would never forget.

Autumn held my hand casually as we walked to the pool area. Other couples smiled at us as they walked past. Something as simple as holding her hand seemed so right. To my surprise, when we got to the pool, it wasn't full of people. Some people sat around on the deck, lounging in their swimsuits, drinking little fruity drinks with umbrellas in them.

When we walked to one of the lounging chairs, Autumn took off her sundress and stood before me in a two-piece swimsuit the same color as her dress. I closed my eyes and opened them again. My dick got harder. This had to be punishment for something I did wrong in another life. I wanted to pull her down in my lap so I could wrap my arms around her and let my hands roam all over her soft skin. She sat in the lounge chair beside me, staring at me.

"Are you going to tell me why you are here?" she asked for the second time.

Chapter 2

Autumn

I watched Dylan's eyes divert from me, like the next thing coming out of his mouth would be a lie. Dylan didn't know me well enough to know that I could spot a liar from a mile away. I watched the pulse in his neck increase just a little. He was nervous for some reason. I didn't know why he was here, but the only thing he had told the truth about so far was that Charm hadn't told him where I was.

"I hate liars, Dylan, and if we are going to be friends, I need you to be honest. I don't care how much it's going to hurt me or how full of shit you are behind it, but honesty will only improve this friendship."

His brown eyes stared into mine, and his bedroom eyes were smoldering. Dylan was a fine man. A few women passed by us, and I knew they were looking at him from the smiles on their faces and the shine in their eyes. Dylan was a beautiful man; you could almost consider him pretty.

He was a little over six feet tall, clean-shaven, with olive skin, light brown eyes, and a toned, muscular body. He wasn't like other men I had met, though. He was down-to-earth and funny, and he loved his friends. The downside of all of this was that Dylan was a player. Raising my nephew, Storm, and trying to help my sister,

Summer, after her emotional and nervous breakdown, games were one thing I didn't have time for. Dylan was great to converse with over the phone, a good dance partner, and an excellent sight for sore eyes, but other things were out of the question.

"I'm here for you," he told the truth.

"Why?" I questioned.

I saw the way he looked at me when he thought I wasn't looking. Dylan wanted to have his way with me. If I had time to waste, I would give him what he wanted, but I couldn't play his little games with everything going on. There was nothing wrong with a night strictly for pleasure, but this was too close. He was too close. Charm and Chase seemed to be getting closer every day, and eventually, they would make things official. We are their best friends, so it wasn't a good look for us to fool around, and it ended badly. I waited for him to answer my question, but it seemed he wouldn't.

He stared into my eyes, and I saw them dilate. My body began to tingle, and heat began to radiate through it. I felt myself become wet with desire when I looked down at his swim shorts. He was as hard as a brick. This sexual chemistry between us was too much, and we would be sharing eight days on this ship together. I closed my eyes, willing myself not to look at him. I couldn't. When I opened my eyes, his brown eyes had become lighter, like tea with a touch of golden honey. It had been so long since I had the pleasure of being with a man, and being around Dylan was sending my body on a rampage.

I have to get away, I thought before standing up, turning on my heels, and diving into the deep end of the pool.

I did a couple of laps, letting the cool water calm my hormones. When I stood up in the water, Dylan was still staring at me from the chair. I took a deep breath, then went back under, and as I swam, I thought about his words. *"I'm here for you."* They echoed in my brain as I stroked through the water. I let myself get lost in swimming for so long that he was gone when I stopped and looked around for Dylan. I let out a relieved breath, got out of the pool, and wrapped a towel around my body. I walked up the stairs to my balcony room, picked up my phone, and went straight to the shower.

I listened to Charm's phone ring several times before she answered with a huff.

"I only picked up to tell you I'm not talking to you."

I laughed because I could tell she was pouting. I had no idea what Chase had done to her, or should I say, *hadn't* done for her, but she had an attitude.

"People who aren't talking to other people don't pick up the phone."

She huffed over the phone.

"What's wrong, Charm?" I asked, laughing a little.

"You left me with a crazy man. He won't let me get up unless I go to the bathroom. He made me stay home from work today too." I had heard it all. She was complaining because this man was trying to take care of her. I wasn't even about to entertain her nonsense.

"Did you and Chase tell Dylan I was taking a cruise to Bermuda?" I asked, holding my breath, waiting for her to answer.

"No, why?" she questioned.

"He's here."

"That should be fun, Autumn." I rolled my eyes at her insinuation. Nothing about wanting this man this much was fun.

"No, it's not fun. He's going to make this trip unbear-able," I told her honestly.

"You're overreacting. A couple of nights ago, you two danced all over the club. You two get along fine, so what's wrong?"

"That's the problem, Charm. He makes me want to do things." I stopped, letting out a breath. I sounded like a teenage girl on her first date with her crush.

"You know," I ended up saying.

"Where you see a problem, I see a solution. You took this trip so you could unwind and have a good time. Now, you have Dylan to do it with."

"This is not going to work," I told her, pausing between each word so she would understand where I was coming from.

"I think it will work like a charm," she stated. But before I could protest, she spoke quickly.

"Take lots of pictures, have fun, and make sure to let Dylan handle your lady parts. Love you." Then the call ended.

I rolled my eyes and stepped into the shower. After bathing, I wanted to call my parents to check on Storm, but they told me I couldn't call them until I was halfway through my trip. That means I had three days left. When my sister Winter died from an asthma attack three years ago, I became an instant mother. Storm was going on 3 years old, and I was on my way home from a five-year enlistment. I had to keep myself together for him, so I did everything possible to make his transition smooth. I think what helped him too was that his mother and I were two of three identical triplets. When Storm looked into Summer's or my face, he saw the exact replica of his mother, except my hair was cut to just a curl on the top of my head. I believe that us being triplets helped him maintain a sense of normalcy.

For me, it wasn't that simple. I felt a void where Winter used to be. Looking in the mirror or being around Summer didn't help me because Winter wasn't like us. She was the optimistic sister who always saw the good in any situation. Seeing her was like walking into a ray of sunshine on a cloudy day. When she left this earth, a piece of Summer and I went with her. Winter was one-third of us that made us whole. I had Storm to keep me grounded, but Summer withdrew from everyone.

She and Winter were best friends as well as sisters, and it didn't help that Summer found Winter after she died. I was on my way to the States, and my last day on the vessel I would never forget because that was the day my sister died.

I sat in my room, thinking about how I wanted to distance myself from them. Growing up being identical wasn't easy—no one thought of us as being our own person. Everyone looked at us as a set. Even though I was a realist, Winter was optimistic, and Summer was far from sunny. Everything was collective when you were born in a set; you were considered one person. I wanted to be looked at as an individual, so I cut my hair off when I was old enough. As soon as my eighteenth birthday hit, I enlisted in the marines. After boot camp, as they saw my sisters at my graduation ceremony, they dubbed me with the nickname "Trip." I carried the name throughout my military career.

I shook my head to clear my mind. This trip was about me and having a good time, not thinking about what I had to return to. One thing for sure . . . I knew I didn't want to be around people. I put on a simple dress to get me something to eat. I needed time to think about what I would do about this Dylan situation. Something was bound to happen during the time that we were here. Today wouldn't be that day, though.

I went to the restaurant, got a burger and some snacks, and returned to my room. I know that being on vacation isn't about sitting in your room, but I needed to strategize today. Tomorrow, I would be ready for whatever Dylan brought my way.

Day 2

I woke up to a knock on the door. I looked around the room and saw the ocean outside my window. I remembered that I was on the ship. I rubbed my eyes and yawned before walking to the door. As I opened the door, Dylan stood in front of me with a smile on his face.

"I see you're up and ready for me."

I took the time to look down at myself.

"Shit!"

I hadn't realized I opened the door completely naked. I pushed the door closed, and Dylan pushed it back open.

"Don't try to hide now," he said, stepping into the room and plopping down in the corner chair.

I picked up my silk robe to cover myself before pulling a dress out of the drawer and entering the bathroom.

"Why are you here so early?" I asked him through the door.

"It's after twelve. I came to see if you wanted to have lunch with me."

I was going to say no, but my stomach growled, saying otherwise.

"Lunch will be fine." I brushed my teeth, washed my face, and stepped out of the bathroom. Dylan was sitting in my room like he belonged there. When he noticed me standing in the doorway staring at him, he gave me a perfect smile.

"Ready?"

I nodded, slipping my feet into a pair of black slip-on shoes. Dylan got up, and we walked out of the door.

As we sat down for lunch, we talked about Dylan being in the real estate business.

"I would love to be able to do what you do."

I had always been interested in real estate, but when I got custody of Storm, I had to be able to work around his schedule. I have enough money saved that I don't have to work for several more years. When I was in the military, I barely had to pay for anything while living on base, so I met with an investor and made some good investments. I paid for my house in full once I came home and bought a more up-to-date car. I had no mortgage or car note, and most of the money left from Winter's insurance policy was in place for Storm's schooling, so we could live off what I had saved for a bit longer.

"If you want, I can help you get into the real estate business." I could see the sincerity in his eyes when he spoke.

"You stay in California. How is that supposed to work?"

He smiled at me. "It's possible. I can come here, or you can come soak up some sun in Cali."

"You're forgetting I have a kid."

"You can homeschool him until you're done." He said it like it was just that simple.

Our food came to the table, and we both went silent as we ate a few bites. Dylan picked up the glass of wine he ordered, putting the glass to his lips.

"It's too early in the day for that."

"It's six in the evening somewhere in the world." He set down his glass, gazing at me, clasped his hands together, and put his elbows on the table. Then he leaned in and rested his chin on top of his hands. I continued to eat my food as he assessed me.

"You need to loosen up. This is a vacation. Step outside of what you normally do. This time is about you and what's going to make *you* happy. It's okay to drink before what you consider the 'proper' time." He handed me his glass, and I just stared at it.

Dylan was right, and we both knew it. This trip was for me to unwind and let down my hair. I didn't have to think like a parent. I only had to worry about myself and what I wanted to do. I took the drink from his hand, sipping the crisp bubbly. It was just right, not too sweet or bitter. He smiled at me before setting down the glass.

"You never told me why you came here for me." I forked some of my salad, putting it into my mouth.

"I wanted to ask you about a business arrangement."

I had no idea what he felt I could do for him, but he had my interest. "What type of arrangement are you referring to?"

Dylan casually leaned back in the chair, stretching out his legs. He paused for a few seconds, keeping his eyes on me before he spoke.

"I need you to marry me."

I began to choke on the juice I had drunk. Dylan got up, slapping me hard on the back as I tried to catch my breath. He had to be out of his cotton-picking mind. Marry him? *Where did this man come from?* I caught my breath after Dylan had beaten me half to death. Finally, I pushed the juice across the table and slowly drank some water. After I cleared my throat and took in his expression and demeanor, I realized . . . *He's serious.*

"Why?" I waited for an answer.

"My uncle wants me to find a respectable wife within the next two months." He used his fingers to quote his uncle.

"But why?" I felt like I was stuck on repeat. He was only giving me a little bit at a time.

"He feels I play the field too much and need to settle down. I feel like he's having a late midlife crisis."

I raised a brow at him. When Dylan and I talked over the phone, he told me about his great-uncle and how he raised him when his parents abandoned him. To my knowledge, the man was up there in age, but I knew he wasn't just picking on him. When Dylan talked about his uncle, he had nothing but good things to say about him. In so many words, he had told me his uncle spoiled him rotten.

"Why?" I asked again.

"Can you say anything else other than 'why'?" He leaned up, speaking through his teeth.

"I keep asking that because I don't understand why he would do something like that to you. Most of all, I don't understand why you'd choose me."

Dylan rolled his eyes, taking a deep breath. "My uncle is feeling like he failed in life. He has played the field all his life, and now he wants some companionship."

"What does that have to do with you?" I quickly replied.

"He feels like I'm following in his footsteps and wants me to find someone to grow old with."

I nodded my head. "Okay. Well, find someone," I told him, raising my shoulders.

"I have," he smiled.

"With all your money, Dylan, you can pay someone to do this for you." My brows furrowed.

"How much do you want?"

I assessed him for a second. "Five million dollars."

He rubbed his hands through his hair and stared at me. Then he put a finger on the side of his face and hummed. It was intriguing to watch him pondering over the amount I quoted. Finally, he gave me a wolfish grin with his eyebrow raised.

"Done," he said without blinking an eye.

Chapter 3

Dylan

I watched Autumn's face go from amused to shocked. Her mouth dropped open, and her eyes got wide. She was so cute with her mouth parted that way.

"Dylan, seriously, I can't do that. I have a kid who needs me. I can't just pop up at my house with a strange man and tell him, 'This is your stepdaddy.'"

I cocked my head to the side. "You know it won't be that way. I can buy a house down the street from yours, and you can slowly introduce me to Storm. I will do my best to fit into your world instead of you fitting into mine. All I'm asking for is four years." I didn't think her mouth could get any wider until I said that.

"Four years, and then what? Leave Storm and act like you never met us? He has been through enough already, losing his mother. Now, you want to step in as a father figure for a short time and leave him too? No. No. Hell no." She folded her arms across her chest, leaning back in her chair.

I got what she was saying. She didn't know me well enough to know that I would never do that to Storm. I would keep up with him like he's my own child. Once we built that type of relationship, it was something that I would cherish with him forever. She had told me how his father left the hospital, never contacting them again when he found out Storm was deaf. I think she said Storm was about 2 or 3 months old. I was left as a child too, so I would never do that to any child I got close to.

"I would never do that to him, Autumn. I need your help. There must be something I can give you to help me."

She didn't say a word; she just stared at me.

"Seven million," I said, seeing if she would change her mind.

"Ten." She just stared at me. When I reached twenty million, she finally opened her mouth, and I thought I was about to hear the words I wanted.

"No amount of money will get me to okay you breaking Storm's heart." She got up to leave, and I stood up, grabbing her hand.

"I would never do that to him or you; trust that. All I'm asking is help from a friend. I need your help." I watched several emotions play across her face, and I held her gaze while she tried to read me.

"Help from a friend is them housesitting for you because you're going out of town for three months. You want me to change all three of our lives forever so you can prove a point to your uncle. You want me to trust that you will do right by my son when his own father left him because he couldn't handle a deaf child? I can't just take your word for it, and again, I ask, why me? I feel that this whole marriage situation is about more than having a lifelong partner. What is *really* going on?"

She placed her hands on her round hips, and I watched her.

"Let's just enjoy today, and we can discuss this again before returning to the States." She stared at me for a minute before she shook her head again.

"I'm not changing my mind," she stated, getting up from her seat and walking away.

I dropped some bills on the table and followed behind her like a lost puppy. I would let her think this was the end of it, but I wouldn't stop until she said yes. Even if I had to abduct her and pay the priest to look the other way during the ceremony, this was *going* to happen. For some reason, I felt she would be the only woman holding up the other end of the deal. When people looked at me, all they saw was money. Women saw shopping sprees and trips to islands they couldn't pronounce. I could see the dollar signs in their eyes when they approached me or I approached them. Marrying one of those women would be the worst thing I could ever do. They wouldn't care about me paying them millions to marry me. Once they had tasted my way of life, they would want more.

Autumn was different. She didn't even budge at the insane amount of money I offered her. She didn't care that I was rich. All she cared about was Storm's happiness. I wouldn't have to worry about that with her, but it's not just about the money. Autumn was simply perfect. I wanted to be around her and get to know her better, and a four-year marriage would give me all the time I needed. I know I'm not the relationship type of man, but that wasn't what I wanted from her. I wanted her mind and body; to be a part of the life she holds so close to her. I wanted someone that I could relax and have fun with. At one point in life, I had Brenton, Chase, and Dennis to go on excursions with, but now they had women in their lives. Our fun nights out had dwindled down to family nights out.

I shook my head, coming out of my thoughts. I had to do something to get her to agree to this.

I followed Autumn into the casino area and rolled my eyes. Out of all the things there was to do here, she wanted to gamble. She sat at one of the machines, and I plopped down on a stool next to her.

"This is what you want to do? They have a lot of things going on this ship, and you want to sit here and chance losing money?"

She raised her brow at me and frowned. "I didn't ask you to follow me here." She folded her arms across her chest.

I opened my mouth to tell her what I thought of gambling away money that could be put to good use somewhere else, and she held up her hand to stop me.

"This is what I want to do right now with the money I have saved for this trip. What you think of as 'chances to lose money,' I look at as 'chances to win.'"

She placed a twenty in the machine and began hitting the button. After about twenty minutes of seeing her lose her money, I left to find something to drink. On the way back, I saw lights flashing and noise coming from the area where I left Autumn. I rushed over, getting closer, when I heard the sound of change crashing and a siren going off. When I got to the machine, Autumn was sitting there with a massive smile. She saw me approaching and stood up, latching onto my elbow.

Day 3

We walked off the ship hand in hand, ready for our visit to Grand Turks. I had arranged for us to utilize all ten hours we had here. Since I couldn't persuade Autumn with money, I would have to rely on my charm. I pulled her close, wrapping an arm around her as we went through the thick crowd of people. She didn't object to the closeness or my hand sitting right at the top of her ass. We settled into a casual pace, taking in the sights around us. I was happy when she agreed to spend the rest of the cruise with me. That meant I had six days to get her to change her mind.

"What are we going to do today?" She took off her shoes to walk along the beach.

"You'll see," I told her with a smile.

When we walked up to the stables, an excited expression came across her face. Her eyes began to shine like a kid in a candy factory. I was glad that she was open to doing this. When I scheduled horseback riding, I wasn't sure she would like it.

"I take it you like horses?"

She nodded.

The instructors took about thirty minutes to review the dos and don'ts of riding in the sand and water. When they finished, we locked up our clothes and saddled up. It was a slow trot down the pink, sandy beach. Each time I gazed at Autumn, she had a silly grin on her face. I hoped that everything I had planned for us would keep that same smile on her face. There was just something about her being carefree that tugged at my heart. We trotted through the water until it covered the horses' backs. Even though I had visited plenty of islands, there was something about seeing the clear blue water from this angle.

The day went by like a breeze as we snorkeled, swam with stingrays, and ate some great food. We ended our day buying souvenirs. Finally, we walked on the ship just as we left—hand in hand.

"Did you have fun?"

She stopped walking, still holding my hand. "Yes, thank you so much. You made this day unforgettable." I couldn't help the smile that spread across my face from her words. I pulled her close, and we continued our walk to the ship.

Day 4

Today, we were too tired to participate in the fun at sea, so we decided to stay in my room and watch TV. I was having dinner with the captain tonight and asked Autumn to be my date. Of course, she agreed. We lay tucked under each other, pretending to pay attention to the movie. I pulled her hand to my lips, placing a kiss on it.

"Are you like this with all the women you talk to?"

I maneuvered our bodies so I would be on top of her. She stared into my eyes, waiting for my response.

"You know, I can tell if you lie to me."

I bent down and gave her a soft peck on her plump lips. "For a woman who doesn't want to marry me, you sure have a lot of questions."

I placed another small kiss on her lips. The room had gotten thick with sexual tension. I wanted her, and I could tell she wanted me. I wanted more than anything to hear her moaning my name. I wanted to be inside of her, giving her exactly what I gave all women.

"This isn't about any other woman. This is about you and me."

She stared deep into my eyes, searching for something inside my soul. I wonder what she would say if I told her that this treatment at this moment was all for her. No other woman has had me so relaxed and cuddled up next to them. They were lucky if I didn't leave once we were both satisfied. I didn't have time for clingy women who wanted to know your every move. I lived a carefree but complicated life when it came to women. Access to the type of money I have was a gift and a curse. I couldn't just open myself up to the possibility of being robbed blind. My family owned Holmes Real Estate, and we were worldwide. My great-grandfather started this company, and my grandfather took it to another level. We find and sell everything from houses to commercial properties. You need contractors? No problem. We have a business for that too. If you put all the wealthy in the United States on a list, I would make the top five. I was a billionaire in my own right.

On top of that, I had trust issues with women. I mean, my mother thought so little of keeping me when I was born. She gave birth to me, and two hours later, she called Pop Wilson to pick me up from the hospital, or she was putting me up for adoption. She told him that I would interfere in her life, and she wouldn't give up doing what she wanted to raise me. I wish I could say she was a drug addict, and giving me up was for the best, but I can't. She and my father are just two selfish people. She returned around seven years later, holding a bouncing baby girl named Julie. The smile on her face was immaculate as she held my little sister in her arms. Both of my parents doted over her. When I asked when she was taking me home with them, she said, "Why would I do a thing like that?" That I was just her baby cousin.

It took Pop Wilson weeks to get me back together. I cried every night because my mother didn't want me. From that day forward, my biological parents became Martha and Stan to me.

I shook my head, clearing it, and Autumn's black eyes looked at me with concern. Damn, she was so gorgeous. I had been with plenty of beautiful women, but it was different with her. It was like her aura shone from the inside out, making her radiant. She was funny and had more energy than anyone I knew. She spoke with passion about things she knew and her loved ones. I couldn't trust any other women in the world to keep their word about anything, but for some reason, I trusted her to keep hers. Maybe it's because we both share secrets with each other. Perhaps it's because I know I will eventually begin to care about her as much as I care about my other friends. Something in me was drawing me to her.

I couldn't understand why she wouldn't give in and become my wife. So many people complimented us on how much of a cute couple we made when we were out yesterday. We got along well. This marriage would be perfect for us.

Autumn lifted up, giving me a light kiss on the lips, causing my dick to harden instantly. She raised her hand softly, rubbing it across my forehead, smoothing out the lines in it.

"What's going on in there?" She placed her hands on each side of my head like it would help her read my mind.

"It's nothing. I'm good."

My hand grazed her nipple, and she took a deep breath. Her eyes turned coal black, and I could tell she was fully aroused. We met halfway in a kiss. Autumn moved over a little more, placing both hands on my face like she was trying to get closer than we were. She wrapped her legs around me, and we became entangled with each other, kissing and panting, wanting more. I repositioned our bodies with me being above her and used my knee, pushing her legs apart. Her white sundress rose up to her waist, and I got between her legs.

I knew she felt everything I had to offer through my linen pants and the small patch of cotton that covered her pussy. She rolled her hips under me, and I moaned, biting down on her lip. Her center was hot, and I wanted to be inside of her, but I knew she wasn't ready. I pushed her dress above her head. She wasn't wearing a bra, and her breasts looked succulent. I pushed her breasts together, taking them into my mouth, moving my head from one side to the other. She arched her back under me, panting and moaning. She rolled her hips, trying to create friction between us. I could smell her wetness and wanted to taste every inch of her body. I lifted up, kissing her swollen lips.

Her cheeks had flushed and were turning red. I smiled at her, kissing her lips once more before kissing my way down her body. Finally, I ripped the little patch of cloth from her body and inhaled her scent. Everything about this woman was intoxicating to me. I kissed the flat part of her freshly waxed love box. She squirmed a little under me. I moved down a little farther and licked her pussy lips before finding her clit. I took one good lick of her wetness and smacked my lips. She tasted delicious. I wanted to make her my favorite meal and eat her when-ever I wanted. She lifted up and rolled her hips, moaning louder. I knew by the time I was finished with her, she would be screaming my name.

"No, Dylan." She pushed my head back a little.

I stopped, looking up at her, but let my finger slide in and out of her.

"No, what?" I used my index finger to rub her G-spot, and she pulsated around my finger.

"Yes," she exhaled breathlessly.

"You sure?" I questioned, still working my finger inside of her.

She nodded, giving me the okay to continue my assault on her body. I bent back down to enjoy my feast. I sucked and licked on her until she released her orgasm on my tongue. Then I fondled her breasts and licked her body down to her toes.

"Marry me. Give me the right to taste you anytime I want." She tasted so fucking sweet she could've been candy. I moved up her body, putting my mouth on what I discovered was my favorite part of her.

"Yes," she moaned out breathlessly.

"I mean, no," she grunted. I laughed at her. I knew what I was doing to her clouded her judgment. I knew, if nothing else, I would be able to fuck this woman into submission. Submission. That would be the word I need her to get used to while we're married. She could do what she wanted outside of the bedroom, but she would follow my rules once we were in the bedroom. Just thinking of all the things I would do with her made it hard for me not to go into her without a condom, but I knew better. I held my hardness in my hand as I slid some protection over my aching pole. Autumn had lust in her eyes as she watched my every move. She was ready.

Her body was screaming for me to enter it. I looked down at her cove, which was wet with my saliva and her juices. It was before our DNA mixed together, making her glisten. She lay with her legs apart, waiting for me to enter her and fill her up until there was no more space left between us. I needed to connect to her and feel her under me as I went in and out of her. I bent down, kissing her privates, then came up and let her taste her honey on my mouth. She moaned into my mouth when I placed my pole at her entrance. I could feel her heat. She was hot, she was wet, and it was all for me.

Suddenly, as I began to guide myself into her opening . . . Someone knocked on the door. I stilled. I had wanted this since the day she came to me to get my number.

"Don't answer it," she whispered, begging me with her eyes to ignore whoever was knocking on my door.

A few more knocks came, and I reluctantly eased myself out of her hot cove.

"Who is it?"

"We have an important call for Autumn Spaulding."

She raised a brow at me. I picked up the linen pants I had just removed, slid them on, and walked to the door.

"I told them that you would be in my room." I shrugged, making sure she covered up before I opened the door. The captain looked between Autumn and me, handed me the phone, and then turned on his heels.

I gazed at her as she lay in the bed with a hand holding the sheet up, covering her chest.

Chapter 4

Autumn

I watched Dylan hold the phone in his hands, coming toward me. His shorts hung low on his hips, and I licked my lips, wanting to taste him more than ever. His manhood is so thick and long I had thought that it wouldn't fit. I had never seen anything as big as he was in my life, and his mouth . . . That man had a motor under his tongue. I wanted him more than I wanted air to breathe right now. I dropped the sheet, letting him look at what he would get once I was off the phone. I pulsated for him. I wanted him and would have everything I wanted while on this trip.

He handed me the phone, and I placed it up to my ear. I flicked my tongue at him, and he smiled at me, full of naughty promises.

"This is Autumn," I stated, listening to the caller on the other end of the line. I heard yelling, and my mother was hysterical. I couldn't determine what she was saying, but I was stuck for words. Just hearing her like this brought back the memory of the night Winter died.

My enlistment was over, I was on my way home, and I couldn't wait to see my family, especially my 3-year-old nephew, Storm. He was born while I was in the military.

I had only seen him three times over the years, and I was ready to build a relationship with him. When I left Chicago, I wanted nothing more than to be away from everyone there. I wanted to find my own way in this world, and I did. Now, it was time for me to get back to what I knew. I was going home to a loving family that didn't shun me because I wanted to be different. I was on the vessel for the last time, heading from overseas to the base in Hawaii. I was sleeping, dreaming about how happy I would be once my feet touched the land as a free woman.

I woke up in the middle of the night short of breath and panicked. Something wasn't right. I felt it in my soul that something was drastically wrong. My hands were sweating, and I was panting hard. My stomach was balled in knots, and all I knew was . . . This wasn't right. My eyes searched the darkness, looking for something, anything that I could focus on to get over this feeling. I sat up in the bed, rocking back and forth. Something was wrong with one of my sisters. They needed me, and I was here. No, no, no, I thought. I felt something pulling at me, pulling at my soul. I closed my eyes and tried to clear my mind, but I couldn't shake this feeling.

Minutes had passed, but it felt like hours before I felt one-third of my soul leave my body. Tears ran down my face as I balled up on the cot. This was not happening to me—not my sisters. We were all that we had, and it took all three of us just to be whole. I had learned that while away, and now that I'm on my way back, this happens. I will never be the same.

"Winter." Her name was a whisper in my mouth.

My commanding officer came into the room, turning on the lights. He saw the tears in my eyes, and I saw the sorrow and sleepiness in his.

"Trip, your family has been calling your phone for over an hour." I heard nothing else that came from his mouth. He handed me a phone, and tears rolled down my face. No one had to tell me anything. I already knew. I knew before they knew, and I was thousands of miles away. I was numb. I couldn't take this pain, and what I couldn't take even more was my mother hysterical in my ears. I couldn't take the screams of Summer I heard in the background, or the baby's cries that I was sure were because he was scared. I couldn't take it. I closed my eyes. When I opened them, the room began to spin. I felt myself waver on my feet. I was light-headed and heartbroken. My soul was in turmoil. All I could hear was the screaming in my ears.

My mom tried to tell me that Winter was gone, and then my pain doubled. I felt Summer's anxiety and pain. I rocked on my feet. The piercing scream that I heard this time wasn't from the phone. It was me. The phone had dropped on the floor. The room was spinning and turning faster than a roller coaster. I couldn't do this. I can't take it. I went down . . . and everything faded to black.

I felt Dylan taking the phone from my hand as I came out of my daze. He had placed the phone on speaker, and I heard my mother's cries fade into the background, and my father's calmer, deep voice boomed over the speaker. I could hear the stress in his voice and visualized the worry lines around his mouth and between his eyebrows.

"Are you there, honey?"

I nodded my head like he was standing in front of me. Dylan gave me a look, and I cleared my throat.

"Yes, Daddy," I answered him in a childlike voice.

Whatever had happened was terrible, but I didn't feel it. It was nothing like how I felt with Winter. My mind went immediately to Summer. I hope she didn't hurt herself. I knew she was withdrawn, and I helped as much as possible. I said a silent prayer, hoping she hadn't taken her own life. After Winter's death, Summer had a bad emotional breakdown. She had told me plenty of times that she wanted to be with Winter. I would sit and talk to her for hours, letting her know that Winter wouldn't want that. I had tried everything I could to get her to understand that I needed her. I knew I couldn't take Winter's place in her life, just like she couldn't replace me with her. I understood how she felt, but I told her that if she left me, I wouldn't make it.

There's just so much that I could take before I folded. Winter was the glue that held Summer and me together. All of our lives, Summer and I bumped heads, but we were there for each other when we needed it. I had learned to be independent without them being around me. Winter learned to stand on her own feet when she had Storm . . . but Summer. The baby of the three of us was codependent and leaned on Winter. I had to collect my thoughts.

"Summer came to get Storm for an outing to the park."

I perked up. She was spending time with her nephew. That was normal for her. She took Storm on outings at least twice a week.

"There's nothing wrong with that." I wanted to know why my mother was going crazy like she had lost her best friend.

"Three days ago," he finished his statement, and I was floored. Three days. Anything could have happened to them within three days. Why didn't they call me sooner? Why would they let this happen? What were they doing about it? I had to go. I wanted to get off this ship. They could give me a boat, and I would row myself to the nearest island. Storm, my baby. I paced the floor.

"We thought we could handle it but couldn't find them anywhere. We didn't want you to have to come back home. This is the first time you were doing something for yourself in three years. We are so sorry." My father's words came out of his mouth fast.

"Did you call the police?"

"Yes, we did that the night they went missing, but we need you home." Did he really think I *wasn't* cutting this trip short? I paced, thinking of a way to get home as fast as possible.

"As soon as we hit land, we'll fly out," Dylan answered for me.

"Okay. Love you, baby."

My father didn't question who the man was listening to our conversation. He hung up the phone. I'm pretty sure he went out of the door, getting in his car, navigating his way through the streets of Chicago with his gun in his lap.

Dylan got up, pulling me into a firm embrace. He ran his hands up and down my back soothingly, and I broke down. This is *not* happening to me again.

"I won't make it, Dylan, if . . . if . . ." I couldn't get my words out. If something happened to them, I would roll over in the grave with them.

"Shh. Nothing is going to happen to them." He was firm in what he was saying, like he knew I would get them back.

"I need to make a few calls so we can get back to the States once we port. Don't worry about anything. I'll take care of everything, and I will find them." I reluctantly left his arms, sitting on the bed, wrapping my hands around my knees. I could see my sister and nephew's faces in front of me, and every vision of them ended in tragedy. I loved Chicago, but it was where bad things happened to good people. Women, men, and children had been shot, killed, and trafficked everywhere in the world. I prayed, hoping they weren't a victim of circumstance. Summer was a beautiful woman. Long, flowing, jet-black hair that came to her butt. She had about five pounds on me, but it was all in the right places. I could honestly say she was a reflection of me. We shared the same face. Storm, he was handsome in his own right. He took all of our Native American features. My mother, Sunflower, is a full-blooded Blackfoot, a beautiful Native American who passed all of her features down to us.

"Yes, Collen," Dylan said into the phone.

"Autumn, I need a picture of Summer and Storm."

I wasted no time picking up my phone, logging into my pictures, and emailing them to him. I gave him a questioning look, but he waved me off, continuing to talk to whoever was on the phone. Finally, he ended that call and started another.

"Hey, Pops. I need you to send the private jet to a private strip in Bermuda. There will be two passengers." He gave a couple of yeses and nos, then ended the call. Once he was finished, he walked right back to me.

"Go to your room and pack all of your things. As soon as the boat ports tomorrow, we're leaving."

I got up and left his room without saying a word.

I walked into my cabin and sat on the bed. This was so surreal. I couldn't believe everything had happened in a matter of four days. I felt so bottled up, like I couldn't leave the city without something happening. Soon, I closed my eyes, taking a deep breath.

"Winter, I know you're watching over us. Please protect our son and sister." Once I got that out, I stood and started packing. It would be a long night because I knew I wouldn't get a wink of sleep.

I sat on the bed, rocking, when someone knocked at my door.

"Who is it?" I asked, getting up to open the door.

"Dylan," he answered. I wasted no time opening the door, and he came in with all his suitcases. He placed them in the corner beside mine and pulled me into his arms on the bed.

"I need you to try to get a little sleep. Tomorrow will be a long day. I have everything you need set up, and a private investigator looking for them as well. Collen is one of the best in the business. He will find them." He held me to his chest as he spoke.

I listened to the calm rhythm of his heart beating in my ear. He rubbed my back in circles and hummed some song. He didn't sound too bad. He was soothing. He was the calm in the middle of this storm I was going through. I relaxed, and sleep came over me like a warm blanket. Cuddling up to him was the perfect way to end a drastic night.

"Everything will be fine. I will be with you every step until we find them." Dylan thought I was asleep as he whispered in my ear.

"I had a dream we found them, and they were okay," I told him with my eyes closed, still lying on his chest.

"Do you trust me?" he asked. I sat and thought about it for a while.

In the short time we've known each other, he never proved himself untrustworthy. I opened my eyes, looking into his.

"Yes," I told him without hesitation.

"It's time to get ready to go. Make sure you wear something comfortable for the flight."

The parts of Bermuda we passed through were beautiful, but I couldn't enjoy taking in the sights. Dylan had taken care of everything. When we hit land, a car was there to pick us up. We went to a private airstrip and got right on the plane. My mind was on Storm's round face, thinking of his cinnamon complexion. Was he hurt? Was he hungry and crying for me? These questions plagued my mind as we flew over the waters we had just sailed. Dylan came over to me, gave me his hand, and held my hand until we fell asleep.

The flight was uneventful, but as soon as my feet hit the ground in Chicago, I wanted to run. I didn't know where to go, but I wanted to search everywhere for my baby and sister. The thought of that was short-lived. Dylan had another car waiting for us and grabbed my hand, leading me to it.

"Where are we going?" I turned from the window, looking at him.

He had his phone out, sending text messages to someone. Once he was finished, he turned to me. "Your parents' house." His phone went off again, and I watched his fingers move swiftly over letters.

"The private investigator, Collen, is Chase's dad. They are going to meet us at your house, along with Charm. I must warn you, though, reporters will be everywhere."

I gasped. "Why?" I was so confused. Reporters meant the worst, and I wasn't prepared for the worst.

"Summer and Storm have been missing for days now, so they also want to know what happened to them. I know you may feel uncomfortable about this, but think of it this way. The more people who know about this, the more chance we have of someone sighting them somewhere. Chicago is a big city, and we can use the extra help." I nodded my head.

We pulled into the driveway, and Dylan was right. Many reporters were outside the house. As soon as the car door was open, the reporters swarmed us. Dylan blocked me in the car with his body.

"Mr. Holmes, can you tell us what connections you have to the family?" The reporters pushed their microphones close to his face, waiting for an answer.

"I am a family friend. I'm here to help in any way I can."

"Does that include putting up a reward for Summer and Storm Spaulding?" one of the reporters asked. I held my breath. I hope it didn't come to that, but if it did, there would be no way I could pay him back. I tried to push past him to get out of the car, but he didn't move, and he didn't turn to look at me. He ignored me and continued to speak.

"If it comes to that, yes," he answered smoothly.

Chase was walking past the car with Charm in his arms. Her cast was bright blue and hanging to the side of them. Another man was behind them. Just glancing at him quickly, I knew right off that he was Chase's dad. I had met Collen months ago at a bar. It was the same day I met Dylan.

"Mr. Lancaster, can we ask you a few questions?"

Chase continued to walk into the house like they hadn't said a thing. Dylan cleared his throat, catching the attention of the reporters.

"We respectfully ask you all to stay on the sidewalk and off the property." When they turned their backs to walk off, Dylan reached a hand in the car, pulling me out. Someone yelled something out, and Dylan scooped me up in his arms taking off to the door. When we got into the house, Chase quickly closed the door.

"Can I get you all something to drink?" my mother asked, looking at the men who took over her living room. I cocked my head at how powerful these men seemed at this point. Apart, they seemed like the average man, but together, they seemed larger than life.

"Mom and Dad, these are my friends, Chase, Dylan, Collen, and, of course, you know Charm. You guys, this is my mother and father, Mr. and Mrs. Spaulding."

"Derrick and Sunflower. It's nice to see you again." I looked between my parents and Collen, giving them a questioning gaze.

"We met last night. He came by to set up some things at the house," my dad answered.

All of the men disbursed, leaving us women in the front room. I could tell from the expression on my mother's face that she felt responsible for what happened, but it wasn't her fault. All we could do was say a silent prayer that they made it home safe. Once I got tired of sitting around, I went to the kitchen. I couldn't just do nothing, so I started making dinner for everyone. Charm and my mother entered the kitchen and began taking out things I needed. Charm pulled out the mixer and things to bake a cake. It was times like this that I was grateful that my parents had gotten a double oven. As I used my hands to knead the dough for some homemade biscuits, I thought of what Dylan told me on the plane.

"You told me you trust me. Let me handle everything for you. I won't tell you not to worry because it would be unfair of me to ask of you. I will tell you that I will do everything in my power to get them home safely. I just need you and your mother to let us work."

He kissed my hand after I gave him a curt nod. I didn't know if he knew how hard it was for me not to be in the center of them. I was a soldier—a marine—and it was my job to help people. I believe in the quote, "Never leave a man behind." It seemed like I was failing at what I had drilled into me.

"Let that man be a man," my mother spoke softly.
"Huh?" I questioned as Charm turned off the blender.

"I said, let that man be a man. I can see from how you're beating that dough that it's taking everything in you not to go in there and take over. If they need your help, they will come to get you."

I rested my hands on top of the dough. I felt tears coming to my eyes, but I held them back. I felt so helpless at the moment. I could do nothing about this situation but what I was doing now. I used my shoulders to wipe the tears from my eyes and kept at my job. I couldn't go out and look for them. I couldn't be in the other room where they were working, but I could cook a meal for the men helping me.

"What's going on with you and Mr. Man, Chase?" my mother's eyes twinkled as she spoke.

"He's okay. He's bossy, but he's a friend."

Charm looked down at her hands, avoiding eye contact with my mother.

"Yeah, with benefits," my mother mumbled under her breath. We all laughed. I looked around the kitchen and realized we hadn't been cooking together since high school. It was so sad that we never came together like this in our happier moments in life.

"I have no idea where these men you brought here came from, but I'm grateful. Those are some caring and good-looking men in there, and they are here because of you two. So, I'm going to tell you both a little something. Both of you are my daughters, and I love you, but if you mess up with these men, I will never talk to either of you again. They are some sexy-ass men too, especially that Dylan. He's the prettiest man I have seen in my life." My mother waved her hand in front of her face to cool herself off.

"You know she's right. Dylan is a very handsome man."

I felt a blush creep up my face.

"We're only friends," I said in a low voice. "And not like Charm and Chase are," I completed my sentence.

Chapter 5

Autumn

"When you find a good man, Autumn, you keep him, and that man in there is one of the good ones." My mother looked between Charm and me. She made a point to both of us and wanted us to understand her.

"He's not so bad, and if he is, he has over a billion reasons for you to test the waters," Charm joked.

My mother's mouth dropped. She was in utter shock as she looked between Charm and me again.

"Come again?" We both laughed at her expression.

"You have a house full of rich folks right now. Hell, even Charm is a millionaire."

My mother turned to Charm, and she gave my mom a shrug and a smile.

We stopped talking, finished the food, and the men walked in just in time. We sat at the table, said grace, and dug into the food we had prepared. Collen's phone began to ring. He looked down at the screen, excused himself, and walked off.

"We need to go now."

We all got up from the table and ran to the front door. One of the men had called for security to come out because our run to the cars went smoothly. We followed behind Collen, not knowing our destination or if they were okay.

I ran into the hospital. My hands and body shook so badly I didn't know what to do. I was happy and nervous, walking up to the desk and asking for Storm Spaulding. I really didn't know what to expect when I saw him, but I wasn't expecting to see the IVs and monitors he was connected to. My heart sank at seeing him, and I would've dropped to my knees if Dylan wasn't there to catch me.

"It's okay. He was dehydrated, and since he had been gone for so long, they wanted to make sure he was okay. It's not as bad as it looks."

I stood up and walked over to the bed. I couldn't describe the emotions going through me all at once. I was overjoyed just to lay my eyes on him. As I stood over him, rubbing his curly hair, I promised myself I would never leave his side again. He opened his dark brown, almond-shaped eyes that looked so much like mine. He gave me the biggest smile ever. Tears filled my eyes as he lifted up. I pulled him into my arms, holding him tight to me. I never wanted to let him go. He wiped my face with his little hands.

"Why are you crying?" his words were jumbled up, but I understood what he was asking. I knew I had to let him go so he could read my lips as I signed to him.

"I'm just happy to see you, baby. Are you okay?"

He smiled at me, reminding me of Winter's mouth curling right before she smiled.

"I'm fine, Mommy. Aunt Summer took me out, and we got lost. She said we would never find our way back," he signed. I closed my eyes, then opened them. This was the first time I ever wanted to lay a hand on my sister. *She got lost, my ass. What is going on with her?* I thought.

"Where's Summer now?" I questioned with my voice tight as I spoke and signed. Storm could tell I was upset, and he shook his head at me, saying no. He finally spotted Dylan standing at the door and leaned over, looking from him to me.

"Who is that?"

I turned, gazing at Dylan, and he smiled a little.

"He's a friend."

Storm leaned over again, this time staring at Dylan.

"Like Aunt Charm?" His eyebrows rose as he signed.

Dylan stepped forward, and my mouth dropped as he lifted his hands and began to sign to Storm. Storm smiled. I could tell just that one gesture had won him over.

"My name is Dylan. I helped your mom find you," Dylan signed to him with a smile.

"But I was never lost. I was with Aunt Summer."

Dylan nodded his head and came a little closer to us.

"How are you feeling?" Dylan asked, and Storm smiled big.

As they talked, I pointed to the door, letting Dylan know I was leaving. I had to get to Summer and find out what was happening with her. She ran off with our nephew, which I would not tolerate. I went to the nurse's station, asking for Summer's information. The nurse smiled at me and gave me what I needed. I walked to the elevator, but Collen cut me off.

"We need to talk, and saying no isn't an option unless you want Summer to go to jail for kidnapping." My heart began to beat uncontrollably.

I was upset with her but didn't want her to go to jail. I stepped to the side, giving Collen my full attention.

"When we initially started looking for your sister, we thought someone had taken them, but that's not true. Your sister intentionally ran off with Storm, making her the abductor. The police have spent much time and money trying to find them. This could go really bad." He spaced out the last five words. I closed my eyes and prayed for the thousandth time in the last few days.

"What do you suggest?"

I leaned against the wall, tapping my foot, hoping he could come up with something valid. Both my sister and son were in the hospital. I didn't want to lie and have the police chasing a lie. I didn't want to blame my parents, saying it was a misunderstanding.

"We tell them the truth."

I cocked my head at him. "I thought that would get her locked up."

"Just hear me out." He pulled me over to the sitting area. I was glad no one was there but Charm and Chase.

"I pulled Summer's health records, and I see she had a nervous breakdown when your sister, Winter, died. Summer has been on meds since then to help her with separation anxiety and the breakdown. If you tell the police that, we can help you get her into a facility that can help her with those issues instead of her going to jail for child endangerment and kidnapping."

This was a lot to deal with. I didn't want my sister to stay in either of those places, but what else could I do?

"How do you know they will charge her with that?"

He took my hand into his like he didn't want to tell me what was coming next. Charm came over and held my other hand.

"My people found them in an abandoned building with drug addicts." Collen let out a breath.

I was in total shock.

"Is my—" I stopped because I couldn't form the words I needed to ask. I took a deep breath, letting it out, trying to calm the storm brewing inside me.

"Is my sister on drugs?" I finally asked.

"I can't say, but once her test results return, we can determine if any is in her system."

I nodded my head. "Charm, can you go in there with Storm?" Charm got up, grabbed her crutches, and went to his room while I waited for the elevator.

When I got to Summer's floor, I halted in my tracks. I had to be buzzed in. They had her in the psych ward.

"God, give me the strength," I whispered as I walked through the halls. When I got to the end of the hall, I heard Summer's voice. She was yelling at the top of her lungs. This ordeal took me back to a time I didn't want to remember. *Inhale through your mouth, exhale through your nose.* I repeated those words to myself before I opened the door.

"*You* did this to me!" Summer screamed as soon as she saw me coming through the door.

I wanted to be mad at her. I wanted to yell and scream about how careless she was. I wanted to tell her how reckless she was with our nephew's life, but I couldn't. The woman I saw before me was the woman I came home to three years ago. I couldn't chastise her for being careless with Storm when she was so lost herself.

"What did *I* do to you, Summer? I let you in my house for a year and cared for you while you were down. I called you every day for the next two years to make sure you took your meds and make sure that you were okay. When you wanted to leave my house, I gave you enough money to ensure you could stand on your own two feet. I helped you get a good-ass job that I could've been working to care for Storm and myself. I did all that because I love you and want to see you happy and healthy. Now, please, tell me what I have done so wrong that you would worry our parents to death. I thought something bad had happened to both of you—only to find out that you have had my son in a fucking crack house!"

I was livid. I wanted to fight her and probably would have smacked the shit out of her if she wasn't strapped to a bed. I turned my back to her. I didn't want her to see me like this. I didn't want to add gasoline to the fire. When I turned to her, she looked at me with malice.

"You have it all, Autumn. You always have. Even when we were kids, you had friends and were more popular. You chose a path without Winter and me because you were more independent. You have everything. You are the favorite daughter who can do no wrong. All I had was Winter and Storm. Winter died, and you took Storm from me too. They were all I had." Summer yelled out a cry that was so painful it wounded my soul.

"Why did she leave me? Why did she leave him with you?" she cried, asking me. Tears rolled down my face. I ached for Summer, but I couldn't get over the fact she took my baby. Summer needed help.

"I never took Storm from you. My doors were open to you anytime you wanted to see him or take him out. You will *not* blame any of this on me. I have been a good sister. As a matter of fact, a *great* sister, and *this* is how you repay me? By taking my son and running away, scaring us half to death. I will give you something to think about while you're here. Winter didn't leave Storm with you because she knew you would do some shit like this. For heaven's sake, you had him in a place where both of you could've been hurt or killed. Winter knew you well enough to know that you would fuck up with raising him. Look around. Do you see where you are? Have you looked in a mirror? You're filthy, and your hair is matted to your head. You are strapped down to a fucking bed. I know I can never replace Winter in your life, but I'm your sister too. We also shared a womb."

Summer raised her head to look at me. My parental expression was telling me to stop my assault of words on her, but she needed to hear all of it. They have protected her for way too long. She had some audacity to call me the favorite. I was just more self-sufficient and had a little more freedom than either Winter or Summer.

"I have had your back all our lives and have your back right now. Yes, you are here because of me, but it was either this or jail. So, if you want me to become the bad sister like you're proclaiming, let me know now, and we can trade those straps for cuffs." My comment stung her. I could see the change in her demeanor right off.

"Why would I go to jail for this?" she asked in a low tone.

"There is a list of charges. Would you like to go through each one?" I knew I was being an asshole, but I couldn't help it right now because I was pissed.

"I'm his aunt. I can take him whenever I want."

"Yes, you had that privilege, but only with our permission."

I made sure to emphasize "had" and "permission." Summer was in some deep shit here, and it was going to take more than me to get her out of it.

"Are you saying I can't see him anymore?"

The words "crack house" echoed in my head, and I wanted so badly to tell her, "No, you can't see him anymore." I knew in my heart that would break her, and she wouldn't live long enough to see him turn 7. I folded my arms over my chest before speaking.

"After all of this is over, you can have *supervised* visits with him. While you're in the facility, no, I will not subject him to that. You can call him or FaceTime anytime if they allow that there."

"Where am I going?" she asked. I could see the concern in her eyes, and I wanted to break down right there. I had to send her away, and it was killing me. Although I stood in front of her, showing little to no emotion, my heart broke inside. I slowly exhaled a breath.

"I don't know." I felt the tears building up in my eyes, so I turned toward the door.

"See you soon, Summer. I have to go fix what you have messed up." I opened the door and walked out, and as soon as I turned the corner, I dropped to my knees, bawling. I felt like I was losing another sister, and it hurt like hell.

When I returned to Storm's room, the doctor was there, requesting to speak to me.

"Hello, Ms. Spaulding. I'm Dr. Benton. I would like to have a few words with you outside." I smiled at Storm and signed that I would be right back and that if he needed anything, ask Charm or Dylan. He signed pizza, and Dylan immediately picked up his phone.

"We'll need to keep Storm here overnight for observation, but there was something else I wanted to speak with you about." He furrowed his eyebrows and looked into my eyes.

"Have you thought about getting Storm a cochlear implant?" I knew immediately what he was talking about, and I had thought about it.

"Yes, I have. I wanted to wait until he was a little older so he could make the choice himself." He tapped his pen in his hand before speaking again.

"To be honest, it's something you should consider doing right now. Once he has the surgery, he will need intensive speech therapy to help with his vocabulary and get used to people talking to him instead of using sign language. Many adults have a hard time adjusting to them. It's just something you should consider."

"Thank you for the advice. I'll see you tomorrow." He walked off, and I went into Storm's room. I already had more than enough stuff on my plate. I was trying to figure out how I would pay for a nice facility for Summer. Now, I had to think about surgery and therapy for Storm. That surgery was damn near fifty grand, and the therapy would probably be another fifty. I folded my arms across my chest and closed my eyes. I know I looked just as tired as I felt. Dylan stood up from his chair.

"Sit here. I'll let everyone know that they can leave." I sat down in the chair he had vacated and watched as he helped Charm up from her chair. I will be forever grateful to all of them. Dylan and his friends went beyond the call of duty for Storm and me. I put my head on Storm's bed and held onto his hand for a minute. After a few minutes, he moved his hand. I knew it was to sign. When I looked up, he was telling Dylan I had fallen asleep. Dylan was carrying a huge pizza in his hand, setting it down at the foot of the bed.

Chapter 6

Dylan

After everything Autumn had been through, I couldn't pressure her to get her to marry me. A woman could only take so much, and I wasn't trying to break her. We talked or FaceTimed at least once a week because Storm wanted to keep in touch. Before I left Chicago, I helped Autumn find Summer an excellent facility in Nevada. Autumn didn't want her that far away, but let's be real. It would be harder for her to heal if she was in Chicago. Her parents and Autumn would hinder her process. I knew where I sent her cost a pretty penny, so I sent them a check to cover the expenses. Autumn would eventually get suspicious enough to put two and two together to know that it was either me or Charm paying the bill.

Although I was happy to help her in any way I could, I was still pressed for a wife, and I only had a week to find one. Time had flown by, and here I was on a date with one of the women from my social status. I listened to her as she went on and on about herself. This date was a waste. I had fucked and left so many women from our social status that no one wanted to give me a chance—let alone a marriage. *So, this is what the next three years of my life will be like? Maybe Pops will hate her and not force me to stay married to her.* My phone vibrated in my pocket. I pulled it out and saw it was Autumn. A smile spread across my face before I slid my finger across the phone to answer.

"That's rude," my date practically shouted.

"I'm sorry. Give me a minute. This call is important," I told her, standing up from the table.

"Are you busy?" Autumn asked.

"No, how are you doing?" I asked her. She was silent. She paused so long, I looked at the phone, wondering if she had hung up.

"Is Storm all right?" She had me worried until I heard her exhale.

"I will do it," she replied softly.

"I'm sorry. You will do what?" I had no idea what she was talking about. I thought I would have to call Chase and tell him to go check on her.

"I will marry you for the amount we discussed." I was ready to jump up and down and do a backflip in the middle of this expensive-ass restaurant.

"Ten million. You have it."

"No—"

She tried to object, but I hung up and walked toward the door. I was at my car before I realized I was on a date. I walked back into the restaurant, putting more than enough money on the table to cover our food.

"I'm so sorry, but I have to go. It's an emergency." I turned, walking off again.

"But we rode together," she yelled across the room. I politely walked back and gave her a hundred-dollar bill.

"Do you mind catching a cab?"

She screeched as I walked back out the door and to my car. I had things to do in Chicago, and dropping her off at home would be a waste of my time. I called the pilot for the private jet and let him know that we would be leaving in two hours. I had to get this done before she changed her mind.

As I was on the flight to Chicago, I pondered why the change of heart. Autumn was so adamant about not bringing Storm into a situation that would cause him heartache. So why now? I stayed lost in my thoughts until I pulled up to her house. I was excited about her agreeing to marry me, but what was it costing her? I had everything to gain from this personally. What was her case?

I knocked on the door, and Autumn opened it. She looked flustered and tired. Whatever she had on her mind had taken a toll on her. She didn't look like the woman I had left months ago. Her wild, uncut, unkempt hair curling at her ears was a dead giveaway. If that weren't the case, the bags and darkness under her eyes would have told me. She stood in front of me in baggy black sweats and a loose black T-shirt that hit right under her breasts and had "Marine" across the front of it. She tugged at her small curls of hair and exhaled deeply.

I stepped up to her, making her take a couple of steps back. I placed my hands on her waist, moving her farther inside the house. Whatever was going on with her, I just wanted to make it right.

"Hey, beautiful. What's wrong?" I asked her softly, dragging my hand through her soft curls.

"I'm not having a good day."

I cocked my head at her. It looked like she hadn't had a good couple of weeks, but I would never tell her that. She flopped down on the couch, resting her head against the cushions. I sat next to her, giving her a moment to collect her thoughts. As I waited for her to open up about what was bothering her, I took in her living room. Pictures of her sisters and her everywhere, and some with her parents too. I stood up to get a closer look. I knew she was one of an identical triplet, but in the younger pictures, I couldn't tell them apart. As the photographs showed them being older, I spotted Autumn out of the set only because of the haircut. Other than that, there was nothing to tell them apart. I could tell what pictures they had taken after Winter died because the light that shined in both Autumn's and Summer's eyes had dimmed. Not only that, but Storm also became the third person in the picture.

I picked up one of Storm's pictures, assessing it. He was a regular, happy child. He had that same shine in his eyes that children have before they find out they live in a cruel world—the look of innocence at its finest.

"Today marks the fourth year that Winter has been gone, and it's hitting me hard. Four years have passed, and I broke down like I haven't done before this week. I had to send Storm to my parents because I didn't want him to see me like this, but I wanted him here because he was the only thing I had left from her. I can't be with the sister I have left because she hates me. She won't even talk to me unless I'm translating over the phone with Storm. It's so shitty that she's doing me like this when I'm going broke paying for her to be in that nice-ass facility. Then I have Storm's surgery to worry about and speech therapy." I stopped her by holding up my hand.

"Calm down. I have handled the bill for Summer, and whatever you need for Storm, I will take care of that too."

She turned to me with her mouth open. "But—"

"No buts." I shook my head as I said it. "I'm assuming that's why you agreed to the marriage."

She covered her face with her hands and nodded. Her chest rose and drew my attention to her hard nipples. I recalled when I was on top of her, nibbling and sucking on them when we were on the ship. My mouth watered for her. She was so fucking beautiful.

"Yes," she finally answered.

"Okay, you're doing this for me, so I will handle whatever you need. Have you eaten yet?"

She sat up straight and gave me an exhausted look. "No."

"Go freshen up. I'll order something to eat, and we can talk about what's to be expected once we tie the knot." She got up from the couch, and when she turned to walk away, my eyes followed her round, plump ass until she closed her room door. The door opened back up, and she stuck her head out of it.

"Thank you." She gave me a small smile. I nodded my head, and she closed the door again. I ordered our food from this little mom-and-pop Italian restaurant that Autumn and I had visited the last time I was here. I called in the order and had to pull some strings to get the food delivered.

Autumn walked out of the room, looking refreshed. Her hair was wet and brushed down on her head, creating waves instead of curls. Her feet were bare, and her pretty toes were polished blush pink. She changed her clothes for a pair of pajama shorts that barely covered her ass and a matching spaghetti string top with no bra. She smelled like lavender and jasmine. I closed my eyes and inhaled her scent. It was like a breath of fresh air compared to the strong perfume my previous date had on. She sat down beside me and crossed her right leg over her left.

"Do you feel better?"

She placed a small smile on her face. "A little," she replied. "I know there's some papers I need to sign. I have no problem signing a prenup." I cocked my head to the side. She was prepared for everything.

"Since this was short notice, my lawyers are putting the papers together now. If there is anything you want to be added to the contract, let me know."

She pulled her legs under her, getting comfortable, then pursed her lips.

"There are a couple of things." She stopped biting down on her lip. "I have thought about this a lot, and not only do I have to protect myself after the four years are up, but I also have to protect Storm as well."

"I would never do anything to harm either of you. You have my word." She held up a hand, stopping me from continuing.

"After the four years are up, you must continue to be in Storm's life. It wouldn't be fair to him when we split up that you stop coming around."

"Done. I love children, have a goddaughter, and go see her every chance I get."

"This will be different. Storm will be a part of your life twenty-four hours a day, seven days a week. He will not be a part-time child. I will be your wife, and since he's my responsibility and my child, he's your child too once we tie the knot. If this is going to be a problem, then maybe we shouldn't do this." She stood up, placing her hand on her hips, but I grabbed her hand, pulling her back down.

"I am not an asshole who mistreats kids, and I take care of the people close to me. So that means that Storm will be taken care of forever. I know how it feels to be the child that's forgotten about. I would never do that to him. Never, but if it makes you more comfortable to have visits and things set up for him in the paperwork, then it's done."

The doorbell rang, and I assumed it was our food. I pulled out my wallet for a tip. I had paid them two hundred dollars just to deliver the food to us, but I knew it was one of Autumn's favorite places to eat. I opened the door, grabbed the bags, thanked the waiter they pulled to drop off the food, and gave him a hefty tip.

"How did you get them to deliver?" Autumn asked, grabbing one of the bags from my hands.

"The power of persuasion," I smirked.

"The power of money," she laughed.

"This was the only thing I knew you really liked."

We dug into our food. Autumn had a healthy appetite, and I loved that about her. The previous women I dated never wanted a real meal. They were always trying a new diet. All of their diets consisted of rabbit food, but not Autumn. She wanted carbs: steak and potatoes, lobster and corn. Although I am a very wealthy man, I feel like I hit the jackpot with her.

When we finished eating, I helped her clear the table.

"There's one more thing I must add to our agreement," she said. I walked up to her, put my arm around her, and pulled her close. I gave her a peck on the lips, and she stepped out of my embrace.

"We can't have sex."

"What do you mean?"

"It means what it means. No sex." I took a few steps back from her. That was the last thing I expected her to say.

"For fuck's sake, you want us to go four years without sex? It's hard enough for me to go four days." She raised a brow at me. *Fuck! That wasn't supposed to come out,* I thought. *How is this supposed to work?* I looked down at my hand, knowing we would have plenty of long nights together.

"But why?" I had to ask.

"Because sex will complicate things, and this situation is already complicated enough."

"But . . ." I rubbed my hands through my hair and pulled at it. This can't be real. She can't really be doing this to me.

"No buts. Take it or leave it." She was staring me down.

"Okay," I relented.

I wanted to fight her on this, but I could tell she wouldn't change her mind right now. But I had four years to persuade her to change her mind. This agreement would be more complicated than she thought it would be. I was going to make sure of that.

"Where do you want to live while we're married?" The expression on her face made me feel obtuse.

"I just assumed that Storm and I would move with you since most of your business is on the West Coast."

"I sell houses; my business is everywhere. I figured you would want to stay close to your family. I don't want you to uproot your life because of me."

"I think the change of scenery will be good for us, at least for a little while." She sat at the table in the kitchen, taking a deep breath. I could tell she was tired and needed some rest, regardless of whether she would agree with me.

"How about I take care of everything, including our living arrangements?"

Her eyes widened, and her mouth opened. "I can figure things out. I just need some time to think about it."

"No, you have a husband now, and it's my job to make things easier for you. Let me take the weight off your shoulders for once. We may not have a normal marriage, but I will take care of you as your husband. Now, go get some sleep, and I'll have our living situation figured out in the morning." She got up from the table and went to her room. I watched the sway of her hips until she disappeared.

Chapter 7

Autumn

I can't believe I'm doing this, I thought as the makeup artist applied a coat of lipstick to my lips. As Dylan promised, he took care of everything. When I woke up the following day, we ate breakfast, and he ran down all his plans. We met with a lawyer to go over the contracts, and as promised, he had them add a clause that he would get Storm every other weekend once we divorced. Also, he would pay for all of Storm's schooling from now until he graduates from college.

Regarding our living situation, we would do the fall and winter in Los Angeles and our spring and summer in Chicago. Since it was the end of the summer, I would be packing up and moving pretty soon. To ease my mind about the situation with Summer, he paid up the fees for the following year. Then he flew us out to Las Vegas since everything was so short notice. I told him I didn't want a lot of commotion behind us getting married, so it was only the three of us. Dylan spared no expense when it came to this wedding. We arrived in Vegas yesterday afternoon and had dinner at a fancy restaurant where Storm ordered chicken nuggets that cost fifty dollars.

I woke up this morning to a beautiful ivory Vera Wang dress. It was a lace, floor-length gown with a court train. It had a V-neck that plunged down to my navel and fitted at the waist, but it flared out at the bottom. Not only that, but he also had Storm a little black Armani tux and matching shoes.

I looked in the mirror, and I looked amazing. My hair was in pin curls with tie-dyed dendrobium orchids pinned on the side. My makeup was minimal, but it enhanced my features. Storm ran into the room. Dylan had taken him for a haircut, and the little guy was so handsome.

"Dylan told me to give this to you," he signed and handed me a bouquet of the same orchids I had in my hair mixed with white.

"Tell him I said thank you." I kissed Storm, and he ran out the door as fast as he entered. The hairdresser and the makeup artist began to fuss over the train to my dress. Shortly after, someone knocked on my door.

"Come in."

The door slowly opened, and it was the wedding planner that Dylan had hired. She gave me a radiant smile.

"It's time."

I took a deep breath and slowly put one foot in front of the other. *Inhale through your nose, exhale through your mouth,* I quoted repeatedly in my head, hoping I didn't trip over my feet. I stood in front of two massive doors, which opened as soon as the music began. I held my breath. Dylan had gone all out for this occasion. Tricolored orchids were everywhere, the stars twinkled in the sky, and the moon was bright and full. Some lights reflected in the pool enhanced the clear blue water. With each step, a light would pop on at my side. I walked on assorted colored orchids with each step. When I looked up, I saw Dylan standing there waiting for me to come down the aisle with a hand around Storm's shoulder. Storm's smile was like a ray of sunshine on this dark night. Dylan never took his eyes off me as I walked closer to him. He was making me feel like the most beautiful woman in the world. When I got to him, he took a thick gold chain off his neck that held the most beautiful cross pendant I had ever seen. Diamonds and rubies covered it. I held my head down for him to put it over my head.

"This is your something borrowed and something old. This chain has been passed down in my family for generations. The orchids are for the blue, and the earrings you have on are something new." I nodded my head because if I spoke, tears would begin to flow down my cheeks.

This wedding is not real. This wedding is not real, I chanted repeatedly in my head. All that was missing was our family and friends, and this would be the perfect wedding. The official began to talk, but I ignored most of it until it was my turn to speak. When my eyes landed on Dylan to do my vows, something in his eyes stirred me. It caused me to become warm from the inside out, and my panties flooded with my wetness. I cleared my throat, removing the ring on my thumb and slipping it on his finger. Then he received his ring from Storm, acting as his best man, and placed it on my finger. When he slipped the ring on, a chill went down my spine. It was then I realized . . . I wanted this to be real.

Before Dylan came along with his proposition, I hadn't had time to think about whether I wanted to get married in the future. Now that I'm standing here falsely professing my love to this man, it made me want more. It made me want the happily ever after that my parents promised my sisters and me when we were growing up. I wanted the love that comes with the marriage and to give Storm some brothers and sisters. I wanted a caring, doting husband who would go home after a long day of work and kiss me as soon as he walked into the house. I wanted the real thing.

When the official said, "You may kiss your bride," Dylan pulled me into his arms, bent me backward, and kissed me so intensely that it caused me to become dizzy with passion for him. Storm stood next to us, clapping his little hands and smiling. My own smile spread across my face when Dylan scooped Storm up in his arms, and we all walked back down the aisle. Dylan grabbed my hand, pulling me close to him as a flash went off. Then several more flashes of us hugging, smiling, and kissing occurred. I was officially a married woman and off the market . . . at least for the next four years.

We walked to the elevator with Storm between us, and we each held his hand. Even though he hadn't known Dylan for long, I could tell he was happy about his new-found friend. We took the elevator up to the penthouse suite in comfortable silence. When the door opened, Dylan picked me up and carried me across the threshold.

"Are you okay?" he asked while I giggled at him. He placed me on my feet when we entered the living area and lifted my head with a finger under my chin. His eyes had a twinkle to them that I hadn't seen before.

"Yes, I'm fine." We held each other's gaze, not breaking contact until Storm patted me on the thigh.

"I'm sleepy. Can I go to my room?" I could see the drowsiness in his eyes. It had been a long day, and we had to leave in the morning. Is this what our life would be like? Always on the jet, going to different places?

"Okay, baby. Make sure to take off your tux and put it on the dresser. I'll be in to tuck you in soon." He turned to walk off and then turned back to us.

"Dylan too?"

"Whatever you want, little man," was Dylan's reply, and I rolled my eyes. Storm was already spoiled, being the only nephew and grandchild in the family. My dad was the real reason behind it. He wanted a son and ended up with three girls. After my mother carried triplets, she said the shop was closed. She didn't want to chance more multiple births, and who could blame her? It was two of them and three of us. My mother said she just about went crazy when we all woke up hungry and needed to be changed.

I walked into the room I was using and looked in the mirror. This was definitely a night to remember. I pulled the flower from my hair and realized I would need help getting out of this dress. I took a deep breath and went into Dylan's room without knocking . . . and the sight before me had me drooling. He had his back to me, and he was naked. I took in his toned calves and ass. I could tell he tanned regularly because his skin was the same color of olive everywhere. My breathing got heavy, and he turned around, not ashamed of anything on his body. The muscles in his stomach were defined like they had been carved into his six-pack. His manhood had more length and girth than I had ever seen before. *Damn him for being this fine.* My eyes were on everything below the belt, and his dick hardened right before my eyes, getting longer and thicker.

Fuck my life!

"Is there anything I can help you with?" He was smirking at me. I closed my mouth and brought my eyes to his face. The smirk never left his mouth.

"Can you unzip this for me, please?" I asked in a voice I barely recognized.

He walked over to me slowly, not taking his eyes off me. I diverted my eyes everywhere except on him. When he approached me, he slid his hands down my shoulders. He kissed the nape of my neck, causing chills down my spine. As he unzipped my dress, he trailed kisses down to my ass. When my dress hit the floor, he fondled my breasts, making me want him more than I have wanted any man in my life.

"Let's consummate our marriage the right way," he whispered. "Let me tie you down and spank that delectable ass of yours."

Spank my ass? Is he serious? Everything coming out of his mouth caused desire to grow deep within me. My mind was telling me to run for the hills at being tied down and spanked, but my body was ready for any kinky game he wanted to play. I turned into his arms and kissed him deeply. Having him this close to me wasn't close enough. I wanted him inside of me. I jumped up into his arms, wrapping my legs around him . . . when there was a knock on the door—saved by the bell.

I jumped out of Dylan's arms, landing on my feet. Dylan handed me a robe and covered himself with a towel. We opened the door, and Storm was standing there in his pajamas.

"What's wrong?" I asked, kneeling in front of him.

"I thought you forgot about me."

"We could never forget about you, sweetheart." I took his hand, walking him back to the room. He got into the bed, and I flipped the cover over him. Dylan walked into the room wearing jogging pants that hung low on his hips. He stood behind me, and Storm smiled up at us.

"Good night," Dylan signed.

"Sleep tight." I kissed him on the cheek and made sure his night-light was on. We closed the door to his room.

"I don't know if I have told you, but thank you for helping me."

If he only knew that he was the one who was helping me. "No need to thank me. You're helping me just as much as I'm helping you." He grabbed my hand, pulling me to him. I dropped my hand from his and took a step back.

"We can't take this any further. We have to stick to the rules. Sex will complicate things too much." I tightened my thighs, trying to make my body resist the passion that it craved from this man.

"It will only complicate things if we allow it to." He held my hand, squeezing it.

"I'm tired. I'm going to bed. We have an early morning." I walked away, leaving him in the sitting area.

I tossed and turned the entire night. My hormones were at an all-time high. I knew the only person who could satisfy this urge was in the next room. Giving up on sleeping, I decided to shower and pack everything. I started with my room and moved throughout the penthouse, picking up toys and clothes. I had packed all of my and Storm's things and still couldn't settle down. I turned toward Dylan's door, opening it, but he wasn't in bed. I picked up my dress off the floor and moved around his room, picking up the clothes he had strewn on the floor.

Then I heard the shower going, and I took small steps, making sure I didn't make any noise. I cracked the door, and there he was in the glass shower, letting water run over his head and down his body. I let my eyes roam over him until they landed on him, fisting and pumping his manhood. His eyes were closed, and his jaw was tight. I crossed my legs, squeezing my thighs together tightly. Just watching him like this was turning me on. I felt my juices coming out of my body onto my panties. I wanted to get in the shower with him, take him into my mouth, and taste his essence. Dylan's head turned toward me, and our eyes connected. He began to pump his fist faster while staring into my eyes.

So much sexual tension was in the air that you could cut it with a knife. I wanted this man so badly I could taste it. He continued to stare, pumping harder and faster. I placed my hand between my thighs, using it to help with the friction. My clit was pulsating and needed some action. Dylan bit down on his lip, and I knew he was close to becoming undone. With my eyes on him, I imagined him using his tongue to pleasure me. He pumped even faster, and the vision of us was playing out right before my eyes. *Holy fuck,* I thought as I flooded my panties with my juices. Dylan groaned, and I opened my eyes in time to see his release come from him and down the drain. My breathing was labored, and I backed away from the door. My legs were like noodles trying to move.

"Autumn." My name on his lips sounded so sensual. I stopped in my tracks but didn't turn to look at him. I couldn't turn around because our agreement would go out the window if I did.

"Yes?"

"It doesn't have to be this way," he said softly.

"Yes, it does," I replied.

Walking out of the room was one of the hardest things I have had to do, but I had to. I couldn't be all wrapped up in a man I had married for money. I am not the kind of girl who does the hit-it-and-quit-it type of thing, but he was that type of guy. If I did have sex with him, as soon as he got bored, he would forget the vows we had taken and find a new flame. I went into my room and, surprisingly, fell into a deep sleep.

One Month Later . . .

We were settling into our new home in Los Angeles. Dylan had gone all out making sure Storm and I had everything we wanted and needed in this house. In my opinion, it was way too big for the three of us. Dylan explained that when people visit, we will have enough room for everyone. This mansion was a smart home with ten bedrooms, thirteen bathrooms, a full-lap swimming pool, a tennis court, and a basketball court. It had a home theater room with plush leather recliner seats and a game room full of games. I decided to rent out my three-bedroom home in Chicago, which wasn't as difficult as I thought. Since Dylan was adamant about us finding a bigger house in Chicago, it made no sense for me not to make any money off it.

The day that we left Vegas, Dylan handed me a Black Card with my name on it. At first, I wouldn't use it. He had already put five of the ten million dollars into my account. I did not need to use his card for anything when I had that much money in my account. Every time I came into the house with a bag, he would check his account, see I didn't use the card, and send me an obscene amount of money. If I came home with fifty dollars' worth of stuff, he would ask for the receipt. Of course, I'd tell him no. Then here comes four or five hundred dollars. After the third time he did this and told me that it was his job to take care of Storm and me, I relented.

We decorated the house to both of our satisfaction. Every room in the house was done, and it only took a month. I placed the last picture on the wall while Storm was with his tutor. That was another thing that had changed. Storm was now homeschooled. Mrs. Smith goes everywhere with us if we stay for more than a week. Dylan calls her a tutor, but I refer to her as the nanny because she also babysits for us. Dylan and I stayed in two different rooms, and I was satisfied with that arrangement . . . for now. I know once we begin having visitors, I'll have to shack up with him.

"Are you ready for tonight?" Dylan came in the door sweaty from playing basketball and gave me a soft peck on the jaw.

"As ready as I'm going to get."

I shrugged, feeling butterflies in my stomach. I was nervous. Today, I would be meeting my father-in-law or great-uncle. I furrowed my brows at the confusion in my head.

"You're going to love him, I promise."

Dylan walked off to get ready, and I looked down at the 4-carat emerald-cut diamond and another 3 carats of princess-cut diamonds that went along the band. This ring was exquisite, a perfect circle of platinum that bonded us in this façade of marriage. I was more worried about him liking me and not the other way around. This man had the power to make my four years of marriage a living hell. I entered Storm's room, pulling out more presentable clothes for him. I wanted him to look like the precious baby I raised, not the rowdy child Dylan was turning him into. Once I set everything out for him, I went to my room, showered, and changed. I wouldn't have to worry about Storm getting ready. Mrs. Smith would make sure he was together before she left for the day.

I entered my walk-in closet to pull out a blouse and a pair of slacks, but to my surprise, our maid, Malinda, was already in there. She was holding up a pair of jeans and a blouse, trying to decide what to pull out for me.

"I'm fine in here, Malinda. I can pick out my own clothes."

She turned to me with her hand covering her chest. "I'm sorry. It's totally my fault, Mrs. Holmes."

I raised my eyebrow at her, giving her a disapproving look.

She began to stutter. "I mean, Autumn."

I nodded my head, smiling. I wanted to be on a first-name basis with the staff. Just because they worked for me didn't mean I would change my way of thinking. They were working-class people just like me, and all of them were older than I was. My parents raised me to respect my elders, so I treated them as such, always using "ma'am" and "sir" when I spoke to them. This rich-people shit was so crazy to me. They even addressed Storm as "sir," and he was only 6.

"Mr. Holmes asked me to get you something to wear because he knew you would overthink this casual dinner."

I rolled my eyes. I can't say that the man didn't know what he was talking about. I was about to go all out to meet Pop Wilson. I took the clothes from her hand and went into the bedroom to change. I bypassed all the expensive perfume sets Dylan felt were a must-have and went for my favorite Bath & Body Works scent, "Magic in the Air." I used the body butter and spray and sat in front of the antique vanity set I just had to have. I put on very little makeup. Then I parted my hair, swooping one side over my right eye and combing the other side down. I finished off my look with a four-inch stiletto black shoe boot.

"I must say I look damn good," I said to myself before walking out of the room.

When I got downstairs, the old man was sitting on the floor playing race cars with Storm. Storm had the biggest smile on his face. *Maybe I was stressing over nothing.* When Storm saw me, he ran to me, wrapping his arms around my waist.

"Look what Mr. Wilson bought me." Storm's smile was heartwarming. I guess Dylan had also ordered Storm's clothes to be put out because he wore jeans and a T-shirt. The old man got off the floor, tapping Storm on the shoulder.

"That's Pop or Grandpa Wilson to you," he signed, and Storm blushed.

"You are raising a fine young man," he signed to me. Automatically, I signed back a thank-you as I said it.

Dylan came from the bar with a glass of wine for me and maybe whiskey or brandy for his uncle, which he accepted.

"Hello, dear. I'm Wilson Holmes, your father-in-law." He held up an old, fragile hand that I happily accepted. Dylan talked about his dad like he was an old man, but this man in front of me had spunk. I could tell he would give us a run for our money. His hands were aged, but he didn't look a day over 60 when I looked at him. He was fit. He wore a tailored, button-up, blush-colored shirt, jeans that fit him perfectly, and a pair of mesh Nike sneakers.

"Nice to meet you, Mr. Holmes." He threw his hand up, waving me off. "Nonsense. Call me Pop Wilson. We're family now."

I smiled at him as he brought my hand up to his mouth, kissing it. I blushed something terrible. This old man was as charming as they come. I now understand how he could be the player that Dylan described. He had me eating up everything that came from his mouth.

"Dinner is ready." Malinda stepped into the sitting area, making her announcement. It was definitely going to take awhile for me to get used to this. I was used to making meals for Storm and me, so I knew I would quickly become bored with this setup. Last week, Malinda had gotten on me for cleaning up behind myself and Storm.

"How's rich living?" Pop Wilson asked, and I almost rolled my eyes at him.

"It takes a lot of getting used to. I'm very self-sufficient, and having everything done for me is driving me insane. The staff always gets on me about doing their jobs, but I can't help it. I have been a stay-at-home mom for three years. That means I cooked, cleaned, and washed my own laundry. If I pick up a vacuum, the staff will side-eye me like I have lost my mind." He laughed at me, and I huffed.

"My dear, most women would love to be waited on hand and foot." I felt myself beginning to pout when I folded my arms across my chest. Both Dylan and Pop Wilson smirked at me.

"Dylan, how about you find her something to do at the company? I'm sure having such a beautiful woman around would be great for business." He winked at me.

"I'm uncomfortable with our male customers gawking at my wife." Dylan began to frown, and it was my turn to smirk at him.

"I'm sure you have plenty of women fawning over you." I watched the amusement in Pop Wilson's eyes as I made my statement.

"Touché," Dylan countered.

"It's settled then. If Autumn is going to be a part of this family, then it's her right to learn the business. How about we make a little wager to make things a little interesting?" Dylan's ears perked up at that.

"What's that, old man?"

I could see that they were about to have a bet of who had the bigger penis.

"I bet you that she will make more money in three months than you. Here's the thing. You have to teach her the right way to make her sales. I will pay for her classes and her license, and you take her out in the field."

"How much are we in for?" was the only thing Dylan asked. I watched both of them with amusement.

"One million."

My mouth dropped.

"No, that's way too much. What if I'm not good at this?" I stuttered. They both ignored me.

"Done," Dylan shouted louder than he meant to.

"But—"

"No buts, dear. I know you won't let me down, and when we win his million dollars, it's yours." I wasn't one to turn down a challenge, but a million dollars was ridiculous.

"Are you with me?" Pop Wilson asked me, and a smile crept across my face.

"Yes, I am."

"Good. We start tomorrow then, and on second thought, Dylan, *I'll* teach her the ropes."

I looked at Dylan and saw a little defeat in his eyes, but he kept up a good front.

Chapter 8

Dylan

Two Months Later . . .

Today was the day we talked to Storm about his surgery. For a minute, I was worried about what he would think about it. Autumn and I told him that he was perfect the way he was, but we wanted him to make the choice. When we brought up the discussion, he smiled and said he wanted more than anything to hear our voices and be a normal kid. I think it was more so because he had been invited to the party of one of the kids in our area. Of course, we took him, but there was a lot of miscommunication because no one there knew how to sign except us. He played with the other children for a while until someone yelled, "Heads up," and he couldn't hear them. The other children were busy trying to get out of the way. When the birthday boy realized what was happening, he ran to grab Storm, but it was too late. My poor boy had taken a Ping-Pong ball to the eye.

Pop Wilson lost his mind when he found out. He promised Storm a boys' day out with just the three of us to Disneyland in a few weeks. Since that day, Storm had been a little withdrawn. That was something else that Pop Wilson had a problem with. Since he was retired, he made it his business to take Storm out as much as possible. He taught him how to ride a horse and drive the car up the driveway, which Autumn and I didn't agree with, but he reminded me he had taught me at that age. He even pulled Storm from his tutoring session one day and brought him to the real estate company, deeming it "Bring Your Child to Work Day."

Looking at my pops being this happy with Storm brought back old memories of myself from when I was growing up. That old man made sure I had a full and happy childhood. Even if he was the only one out with me having a good time, he made it fun and memorable. He was doing the same thing with Storm, making me love the old man even more. I know that we took Storm away from his only family, and he didn't complain or fuss about it. He was happy with his move as long as he was with Autumn. Their being around over the last few months has changed my life for the better, and I didn't want to think of the time they would leave me.

Autumn was still holding true to her word of no sex, and my dick was more than ready for something warm to slide into. I knew Autumn was frustrated about her situation because she was hell on wheels when I walked into a room. The sexual tension was suffocating, but she wouldn't give in. I wanted nothing more than to bend her over on the bed and spank, then kiss, her ass, but she wouldn't let me close enough to her when people weren't around. I watched her as she stood in the mirror with a dress that I had bought her in front of her. I knew the silver silk dress would fit her sexy frame perfectly.

She would need more ballroom and cocktail gowns since she was an agent now, but this dress, in particular, was for Dennis and Amber's wedding. They had decided against a huge wedding and wanted just close family and friends. We will leave in a couple of weeks. I couldn't wait for her to meet my extended family. I finally walked into the room, setting the box I was holding on her bed.

"What's that?" she asked, looking at me through the mirror.

"It's something to help you with that attitude you've been walking around here with." She smirked at me, going over to the bed.

She opened the black box that held her present and dropped it on the bed.

"Asshole."

I laughed at the frown on her face. "If you need any help with that, just let me know. I'm willing to suffer through it." She picked up the box that held the cordless bullet, hurling it at me. I easily dodged the assault, moving quickly and snaking my arms around her. I made sure I caressed her nipple on contact. She exhaled a breath of pleasure, and I kissed her neck.

"Let me take care of you. I promise I will make it worth your while," I told her, already knowing her answer. I twirled her around, making her fall onto her back on the bed. Then I picked up the bullet I gave her, turned it on, and dragged it slowly up her arm and across her breasts, flicking my tongue on her other nipple through her shirt. She began to squirm under me. When I was sure she was as wet as my dick was hard . . . I got up.

"I'll be gone for a few hours, but I'll see you when I return." I adjusted my manhood in my pants and gave my right leg a little shake.

"You have been gone all week around this time. It's ten at night. Where do you go this late?"

I could've lied and told her something that she wanted to hear. I could tell her the truth, and everything would go to hell. I couldn't tell her what I craved, and she wouldn't be willing to give it to me. So, I told her a half-truth.

"I'm going out."

She rolled her eyes at me.

"I'm your wife. If I ask you a question, you're supposed to be honest with me." She jumped up from the bed.

Are we having our first argument? Nah, this couldn't be it. Several thoughts raced through my mind as I watched her.

"Are you cheating on me? I understand that I don't give you all you need, but I'm suffering through this just as much as you are."

"That's the problem. I shouldn't have to suffer through a marriage from my real wife or fake one." She inhaled a breath like I had hit her in the gut. I felt guilty about my words as soon as they left my mouth.

"I thought we were good." Her voice cracked.

I couldn't stay here and watch her cry, so I turned on my heels and left the house. I pulled off in my Maserati like a bat out of hell. I hadn't gotten five miles away before I noticed my black Bugatti behind me. The way Autumn was driving my car was a complete turn-on. I didn't even know she could drive a stick. When I asked her about a new car, she told me she didn't want anything too fast, but here she was, hitting 120 miles per hour to keep up with me. I knew I would have hell to pay once she got to me. I sped up in the car, trying to lose her, but she was still back there.

Finally, I pulled up to the exclusive nightclub, making sure to leave my car parked where she would notice it. You would never know it was here unless you knew about this place. On the outside, it looked like a regular warehouse. There was nothing special about this building, but you had to be a member to get in. This club was like this because this is where the rich and famous came strictly for pleasure. There was always a bouncer at the door, and there was no need to check your phone in because if it got out from someone on the inside, people would want to know what you were doing there. This place was all about living out your fantasies, things your husband or wife may not be into.

As I walked in the door, I showed a picture of Autumn to the bouncer and told him to let her in. He nodded in agreement, and I walked off into a dark corner to see her as soon as she entered.

I watched everyone around me and wondered what she would think about this setup when she walked in here. When the door opened, and she stepped into the main lobby that was set up with a bowl of condoms, I could see the shocked expression on her face. I could see her trying to take in her surroundings, but the room was too dark. She took slow steps in the opposite direction, and I waited for her to put some distance between us before I began to follow behind her. I wished I could see the expression on her face as she saw a familiar face doing some very naughty things.

I was surprised she hadn't run for the door yet, but she kept her slow pace, walking around the entire first level. I watched as one of the men walking past her grabbed her arm, and she shook him off her. I walked into the light enough for him to see my face and shook my head no. He dropped his hand and continued to walk past her. I dipped back into the doorway so she wouldn't see me.

Chapter 9

Autumn

What in the Christian Grey is going on in here? I asked myself, referring to the scenes in front of me. I swear it was like something from *Fifty Shades of Grey*. The bass from the music pumped in my ears as I watched people being whipped and paddled. I could have sworn I saw the weatherman on his knees with both hands chained to the wall and a ball gag in his mouth. Dylan was nowhere in sight, meaning he must have been in one of these closed-off spaces. I pushed one door open . . . and was sorry I did. A girl was suspended from the air with clamps on every part of her body. I quickly closed that door and went to the next. There was a well-known celebrity in a big-ass diaper with a pacifier in his mouth. I shuddered at the sight of that.

What in the hell is Dylan into? Is this what he does when he comes out at night? Does he know that this is considered being unfaithful? I know I had refused him sex, but did he *really* have to come to the house of horrors for pleasure? I took deep breaths to calm my heart, which was beating out of control. I couldn't find him, and now I was worried about the type of man I had married. I opened the last door on this side of the room, and what I saw didn't disgust me. It actually caused my honeypot to get wetter than it has ever been. The woman who was strapped down to the bed looked into my eyes as the man in front of her gave her pleasure. Her hands and feet were tied to each side of the bed, leaving her open and totally at her partner's mercy.

A hand snaked around my waist, and I stiffened, but the smell of his cologne wrapped itself around me. Then I relaxed in his embrace.

"Is this the type of thing you like?" he whispered in my ear, then dragged his lips across the back of my neck.

I wanted this. I wanted *him.*

"I would love to help you with this. Let's throw the no-sex clause out. Let me take you into my world. I promise you won't be disappointed." He rubbed his hands down my stomach to the apex of my thighs. He used his finger to massage my clit through my jogging pants. A breath escaped me as I leaned back into him, giving him more access to me. The fact that I was watching the woman who was tied to the bed getting pleased, and she was watching me, made me explode. I stepped away from Dylan, turned on, and embarrassed that I had an orgasm in public. *What is he doing to me?* I backed away from him, finding my way to the door and going outside. Dylan was on my heels, and he stepped in front of me.

"Time to go home, Autumn. When you get there, come to my room and bring your bullet."

I nodded and walked to the car with my head full of thoughts. I should've known Dylan was into this type of stuff since he found any reason to spank me on the ass. When he's close to me and blocking me, he usually holds my wrists above my head, and then he kisses me hard. It was all a turn-on. I just didn't know he was like this. I guess it didn't matter now. I had four years with him and was tired of not receiving the pleasure I knew I deserved. I was on fire for this man and deserved to be just as happy as any other married woman.

When I pulled up to the house, Dylan was already there. I walked through the house, flustered and overcome with need. Tonight had been so crazy. I had no idea about what Dylan was into when I married him. Maybe I was so into it because I had been without sex for over three years. I stopped my life when my sister died. Now, I'm being dragged by my fake husband into some things I had never thought about before. *Maybe this is something I would have been into anyway.* Now that I think about it, my previous sexual encounters hadn't been so great, but tonight, I had a feeling I couldn't explain.

I went directly to Dylan's room, ready for whatever he wanted to do. I was game for just about anything as long as the night ended with me having multiple orgasms.

When I walked into the room, Dylan was standing in front of me with no shirt on and jogging pants that hung low on his hips. His hands were behind his back, and his eyebrow was arched as he stared at me with this sexy expression that would forever be imprinted on my brain. He kept one hand behind his back and used the other, gesturing me into the room. I could hear my heart beating as I stepped closer to the bed. Tonight would change this relationship forever. Although this man had my heart when he ended his cruise to make sure I found Storm, tonight would be the night that made us whole and would make it impossible for me to leave him without a broken heart.

I took in a deep breath, walking closer to him. When he looked into my eyes, it intoxicated me. He pulled me into his arms and kissed me roughly, inebriating me with passion. He let me go and made circles around me like a lion, ready to pounce on his prey.

"Take off your clothes," he commanded, letting me know he was in charge. I quickly obeyed. I wanted everything that he was willing to give. I stood before him naked, stripped of everything.

"Beautiful," he stated as he took a hand across my freshly waxed pussy, inserting a finger into me.

"Thank you!" I gasped out.

"Only speak when spoken to," he retorted, removing his fingers from me. I felt empty and wanted more of what he had to give, so I nodded without a word.

"Now, you speak," he demanded, placing two fingers inside of me.

"Yes!"

"Yes, what?" He removed his fingers, causing me to become frustrated.

"Yes, sir," I replied like I had done so many times in the military.

"Good girl." He placed his index and middle finger back into me, then used his thumb to rub my love bud. "Tonight, we will play a little game."

I moaned as he spoke to me. The pleasure that he was giving me had my head clouded. My knees were weakening with each circle of his thumb, and I felt like I would hit the floor soon. I was getting so close to climaxing that my torso was tightening, and I felt my pussy clamping down on his fingers.

"Hold it, baby. Do it for me," he whispered so close to my ear that I felt the warmth of his breath.

"Yes, sir," came out of my mouth between gasps.

"During this game, you can only come on my command. If you do it before that, there *will* be consequences. If you don't do it when I tell you to, there *will* be consequences."

"Yes, sir," slowly came out of my mouth as an orgasm left my body.

"Consequences." The word left his mouth as he dropped his hand to his side. Pieces of thin leather came across my ass and thigh. I felt the sting that hurt me so good, and I was utterly turned on by it. I felt a flood of wetness coming out of me. Another orgasm ripped through me so hard I shook. I looked down, and he was holding a flogger. He pulled his hand back, slapping my ass again with it.

"From the moment I met you, I knew you get off on this. I knew eventually you would be my little kinky bitch."

I would usually be ready to fight over the "bitch" word, but when he said it, it made me want him even more.

He scooped me up, placing me on the bed. For the first time, I noticed that cuffs were already attached to it. He made quick work of cuffing me to the bed just like the woman in the warehouse. I kept my mouth closed as he left the room and returned with the bullet he had given me in his hand. I knew my ass would be stinging for the rest of the night when he held it in front of me, turning it on as high as it could go. He pulled a blindfold out of his pocket. I immediately shook my head to object.

"Do you trust me?" The sound of his voice and the expression on his face made all thoughts of doubt leave my mind. I nodded.

"No. Say it," he demanded.

"I trust you." When the words left my mouth, he latched his lips on mine, but this wasn't like the rough kiss he started with. This kiss was different. It was sensual. It was like he needed to hear those three words from me. I gave in to him and matched his kiss. It was so caring and full of lust. When he pulled away from me, he had transformed back into the man who was making demands. He put the blindfold over my eyes, and the buzzing started back up. He caressed my body with the bullet, rubbing it over my breasts and down my stomach.

"You remember the rules of the game?"

I nodded my head because I couldn't speak.

The vibration of the trail sent a sensation down to my toes. He used it to circle my love bud, then inserted it into me. Not being able to see what was going on made it more enticing. He put his mouth between my thighs, giving it one long lick before circling my clit with his tongue.

"Oh my gosh." The words left my mouth before my body tensed, and a jolt of electricity shot through me. I pulled at the cuffs and screamed bloody murder, trying not to let the floodgates of my body open up. I held on for as long as I could, but I had an orgasm so hard and so long that I thought I would burst a vessel.

When I came without permission, he was true to his words, and there were consequences. He went on giving me pleasure this way for so long that I felt my soul had left my body. Finally, he got up, taking the cuffs off my ankles and wrists, but left the blindfold on.

"Same rules apply, Autumn. Don't come until I say you may." He placed me on my hands and knees, then pushed my chest down to the bed.

"Yes, sir," was my weak reply.

He took his time inserting his dick into me. He was so large I thought my back would cave in once he was in me. I felt my body stretching to accommodate his huge size, but when he began to stroke in and out of my body, all thoughts of pain left me. He took his time pulling out and going back in until my faint moans became louder. He encircled my waist, placing his hand on my love bud and playing with it. My entire body was sensitive to his touch, and I felt myself tightening around his shaft. His moans became louder, and I could picture him biting down on his lip with his eyes closed, trying to push through the pleasure just as I was. The image I envisioned caused my body to go on a downhill spiral as I came around him. He pulled himself from my body with a grunt, then forced his way back in.

"Consequences," he gritted the words through his clenched teeth.

Slap! A hard hand came across my ass, causing my next orgasm. *Who knew that pain would turn me on this much?* I thought before his hand met my tender flesh again, causing the same effect. Dylan plowed into me, smacking my ass, yelling for me to come each time, and I followed his command. I knew our time here was ending when his speed increased even more. He yelled out one last time for me to come before I felt his seed spilling into me. After a few minutes, Dylan stood up and walked into the bathroom. I was so tired I couldn't move if I wanted to, but I didn't have to because he was back with a towel cleaning me off.

I woke up the next day confused about my surroundings, but when Dylan pulled me closer to him, flashes of the previous night entered my mind, and I couldn't stop the moan that left my mouth. Dylan moved down a little and entered me while we were lying on our sides. The breath that escaped my mouth once he was inside of me made him harder.

"This isn't like last night, love. Come as much as you want," he told me, then bit into my shoulder, causing me to shutter. Damn, this man was full of surprises, and I didn't know which side of him I liked better. The dominating one who was willing to give me a little pain with my pleasure, or the one who wanted to please me and make sure I had everything I wanted. I think I loved each part of him equally.

Two Weeks Later . . .

Dylan and I have gotten way closer over the last couple of weeks. Our fake marriage had become almost the real thing, and all it took was that one night. The day after our night of lust and passion, Dylan had Malinda move all of my things into his room. The house was different in a way, and everyone who entered it felt a shift in the atmosphere. Dylan and my relationship had gone to another level. When we left for work, we would kiss each other

goodbye, and the same when we got home. I chuckled
when I thought of the day Pop Wilson came to the house,
staring at our interactions with each other.

"I see you two have been engaging in your nightly
affairs." Storm had read his lips and asked what he meant
by "nightly affairs." Dylan threw his hands up in the air,
stopping Pop Wilson from discussing the birds and bees
with him. Dylan went on to tell me how traumatized he
was when his uncle told him about fucking. Those were
his words, not mine.

Pop Wilson had come over that day to tell me I had
won the bet and to write me a check for one million dollars. We had another two weeks left of the bet, but in his
eyes, there was no way Dylan could catch up. Pop Wilson
had called on all of his wealthy associates, convincing
them they needed new property. I had sold fifteen very
expensive properties to Dylan's six. Each house I sold
was five million or over. It was amazing what smiling
could get you when it came to rich, old men.

I sat at the table, coming out of my daydream. I was
sitting at the most beautiful wedding reception I had ever
attended. Dylan's friends, Dennis and Amber, had called
him a few weeks ago, letting him know they had decided
they didn't want a huge wedding. Their original plan was
to get married a year from now and invite everyone they
knew to watch them join in holy matrimony. I guess they
had a change of heart and just wanted close friends and
family. After a beautiful wedding that brought tears to
my eyes, they had one long table set off to the side where
everyone sat. There couldn't have been more than twen-
ty-five people here, but we made a pretty lively bunch. I
sat between Dylan and Storm, and Pop Wilson was on
Storm's other side.

"Amber, you really made a beautiful bride," Pop Wilson
told her. She gave him a smile that would brighten up any
room.

"Thank you," she replied while watching her two-year-old daughter, London, play in the middle of the dance floor.

"I want to dance too," Storm signed, pointing at London.

"Go ahead. Have fun, kid," Dylan told him, and he took off to the middle of the floor, dancing to the beat in his head.

Once the food came out, everyone enjoyed a catered feast. It was time for the bouquet toss, and Charm pulled me up from my seat onto the floor.

"No, Charm. I don't want to do this."

"Come on," everyone yelled out.

"One . . . two . . ." Amber counted.

"Why would you want a married woman to catch the bouquet?" Pop Wilson questioned. Everyone turned to look at me, then Dylan.

"What?" they yelled at the same time. Dylan and I decided to take our wedding rings off before the wedding. Dylan pulled our rings from his pockets, sliding my ring on my finger, and put his on, pulling me close.

"We wanted to wait to tell you because we didn't want to take the attention from your wedding," Dylan said, shrugging.

I diverted my eyes to the floor, away from Charm's gaze. I could tell from the expression on her face that she was hurt. The looks of shock and hurt that Dylan was getting made him uneasy. I tightened my grip on him. The people in the room were pissed, and with good reason. Everyone in here was close. His friends were like siblings to him. Charm and I were just as close as my sisters and me. Dylan and I had made a wrong decision not telling them about our marriage, and the expressions of hurt that passed over everyone's faces made it clear.

"We'll talk about this after the reception. I need all of the single women to the floor."

Amber shook her head at both Dylan and me after she spoke. She shuffled about fifteen feet from the small crowd of women in her princesslike white dress. It was stunning, with rhinestones and a sprinkle of glitter. Her hair was up in a halo twist, and the back of her lacey white veil hit the floor. Her colors were yellow, silver, and white, which donned every inch of the hall we were in. She tossed her yellow and white rose bouquet right to her friend Tia. Charm came and sat down beside me. She hadn't said a word. I knew she was waiting for me to talk to her, but how could I tell my millionaire friend with the millionaire boyfriend that I married Dylan for money? She wouldn't understand that. She would be livid if I didn't come to her for assistance. Besides Dylan and Storm, she was the only person I owed an explanation in this room.

"I love him," I told her my truth.

"If that's the case, why did you keep it from me? Do your parents even know?" she asked with so much hurt and concern in her eyes.

"Yes, I told them the day after we got married."

"And how long ago was that?" Her voice had gone up a couple of octaves, causing everyone to stop and look at us. I held my breath.

"Let's talk about this later. I understand you're upset, but I don't want to cause a scene," I told her, getting up.

I had hurt my best friend, and, in return, I was hurting. For that, I would give her all the answers she had sought, but not right now. Charm and I had been friends since we were in pre-K. We shared everything growing up, but I can't say we share everything as adults. She never told me how badly her old boyfriend treated her. I sensed the change in her, heard how he spoke to her one day, and figured it out. That was a time in her life when she would quickly tell me to mind my own business instead of being honest with me. I knew I would never do her like that, but I didn't want people to be happy and celebrate a marriage that wouldn't last long. If I told her the truth, she would understand my reasoning, but I couldn't bring myself to say to her that I was being paid a hefty fee to whore myself out for four years.

"Are you okay?" Dylan walked up, wrapping his arms around me from behind, kissing me right under my ear. I leaned my head to the side, giving him more access to my neck.

"I'm fine," I quickly responded, placing my hands over his.

"Don't lie to me."

He turned me in his arms so he could look me in the eyes, but I let my eyes drop to the floor. He used his index finger to lift up my chin, and his warm brown eyes met mine. He looked behind, and I turned to see what had his attention. Everyone was staring at our interaction, so he grabbed me by the hand, pulling me away. We ended up in another room right off the hallway where he had led me down.

"What's wrong, honey?" He used the endearment he had started calling me once we began to share a room.

"Everyone is pissed at us, and that's fine, but what I can't take is the look in Charm's eyes. She's really hurt behind this. She's my best friend, and I . . . I just don't know." I exhaled a breath that it felt like I had been holding since Pops let the cat out of the bag.

Dylan pulled me close to him, kissing me so sweetly.

"I feel like a high-priced hooker," I finally let out what I was feeling. When I agreed to marry Dylan, I had no idea I would feel like this. The feelings didn't surface until I wanted to tell Charm the truth.

"Babe, there's no need to feel that way. We are helping each other. Plus, no hooker in the world can say she was paid ten million dollars with perks to fuck a man with a big dick for four years." That made me laugh.

He gave me another kiss that I felt all the way down to my toes. When the kiss ended, music began on cue. The deep but mellow voice of Ed Sheeran's "Thinking Out Loud" began to take over the room. Dylan walked me out to the middle of the floor with the rest of our friends. He sent me in a twirl and pulled me close to him. We began to sway to the melody. I lay my head on his chest with one arm curved around his neck and with my right hand tapping to the beat over his heart. I was relaxed in his arms, like this was where I belonged, hugged close to him as his body engulfed me.

"And I'm thinking 'bout how people fall in love in mysterious ways. Maybe just the touch of a hand. Oh me, I fall in love with you every single day. And I just wanna tell you I am." I listened as Dylan sang in a low, off-key voice. When I looked up, he was staring down at me, and it was like I had gotten sucked into an alternate world. I was taken in by those brown eyes, and no one else was in the room but us.

"Kiss me under the light of a thousand stars. Place your head on my beating heart." Dylan lifted me off my feet, turning me. Then placing me back on my feet, he dipped me back, and when he pulled me back up to him, one of his hands slowly slid down my back to my ass.

"We found love right where we are." Ed was singing everything I felt for this man. I was so in love with Dylan that I didn't know what to do. When the song was over, and he let go of me, we turned around to everyone in the room staring at us.

Chapter 10

Dylan

The night had slowed down, and we all were sitting in Dennis and Amber's living room having cocktails. The newlyweds had decided to wait a week before their honeymoon to make sure London was settled in with Amber's parents. This nightly session with us was something normal anytime we got together. We had put Storm and London down for the night. Instead of this being our downtime, Autumn and I were sitting in the hot seat. We tried to explain to our friends why we had not told them about our nuptials. Autumn was leaning on the chair I was sitting in because she was too nervous to sit down.

"We just don't understand why you guys would keep this hidden. We are all friends. Dylan, you and these men are like family," Charm stated with a look of disbelief.

"I know, but we didn't do it intentionally. It's just that things happened so fast," Autumn replied.

"So fast that you couldn't invite me to your wedding? I would want to be at my best friend's wedding even if I wasn't *in* it. We have known each other all our lives, and *this* is what you do? I didn't even know you two were dating. One minute, you guys were on a cruise together, and the next minute, you're married."

I could tell Charm was taking this very personally, and after the year she had had with her family, I understood why she felt this way.

"I'm sorry, Charm. At the time, I wasn't thinking about how it would affect you not being there with me." Autumn was taking her words hard, so I pulled her onto my lap. My friends watched me with curious stares. My being like this with a woman was all new to them. I was the bachelor who swore I would never settle down, and here I was, showing public displays of affection. I slowly rubbed up and down Autumn's back to comfort her as they watched me in awe.

"How long have you been married?" Dennis asked with a curious gaze.

"Going on four months." I smiled at him, but his eyes went from calm to an inferno.

"Please tell me you didn't do what I think you did." The words came out of his mouth, and the eyes of everyone in the room landed on me, including Autumn's. She stood up, looking from Dennis to me.

"What is he talking about?"

"It's nothing," I told her, standing up and trying to grab her hands, but she took a couple of steps back. I eyed Dennis, begging him to get me out of the situation he had just put me in.

"It doesn't sound like nothing to me," Chase chimed in.

"What does Dennis know that we don't know?" Brenton asked.

Not only did I have my wife looking at me like she was ready for war, but my brothers were also wondering what else they had been left in the dark about.

"*What is he talking about, Dylan?*" Autumn raised her voice, and it echoed through my head. I closed my eyes because I hadn't told her why I needed a wife. I didn't tell her what *I* stood to gain from all this.

"Let's go to another room and talk about this," I suggested, grabbing her hand, trying to walk out of the room.

"Let's not. Evidently, you're hiding something from everyone, and we *all* would like to know what it is." She snatched her hand from me, moving out of my reach again. I wanted to pull her to me and just hold on to her because I wasn't sure how she would react once she knew why I married her.

"Just spill it," Pop Wilson told me.

I looked directly at Autumn. I couldn't care less who else was in the room. She was my only concern. When she agreed to marry me, she became an open book about why she wanted to do it. I should've told her my plan then, but I didn't expect to care for her like I did. *Who am I trying to fool?* I didn't expect to love her, and when I figured it out, I should have been candid with her.

"I was a fool," I told her and paused. "No matter what I bring to the light right now, I want you to know that I care for you and Storm, and I don't want you to leave me."

She said nothing. She just stared at me, wondering about any betrayal on my part.

"I married you to get my trust fund and inheritance." I saw the tears come to her eyes, and my heart broke when they rolled down her face. I had hurt her.

"You lied to me," she whispered.

"No, I just didn't tell you the entire truth," I told her.

"Not telling the truth is a fucking lie, Dylan." Her words had more impact than I expected. I instantly became angry with her. Her hands weren't as clean as she thought. I had done the same thing to her as she did to me.

"You married me for money too, remember? This is just one hand washing the other." Everyone in the room gasped at my statement.

"Yes, I may have married you for money I needed, but I didn't lie. You made this entire marriage seem like it was something you were doing to show your dying uncle that you weren't the lonely, lying, manipulating, dog-ass man that you are."

Wow, I thought.

Her words hurt like hell, and those words from her mouth cut me more profoundly than I had ever been cut. Her words hurt like my mother's did when she didn't acknowledge the fact that I was her son. I took a few steps back from the blow she had just landed.

"I'm out of here." She ran off in the direction of the room Storm was in, and I turned to go after her.

"No, I got this, asshole." Pop Wilson was behind her on her heels.

"*Shit!*" I let the curse come from my mouth and wash over me like cold water.

"Shit is right," Brenton said.

I turned around, realizing I was still in the room with everyone, and all eyes were on me. All of the women looked at me like they were ready to pounce, and my friends didn't look any less violent.

"Did you not once think that since I was going with her friend, you shouldn't have made this agreement with her? Not once did it cross your mind that this could end badly?" Chase chastised.

"Anyone around the two of you can tell you love each other regardless of how you came to be. We have been friends since we were 18, and we have never seen you so attentive and caring with any of the women you have dated. We can tell that Autumn and Storm mean a lot to you. Don't mess it up being childish over a situation you created."

"He's right, and if you ever treat her like that again, we will kick your ass. Good people are hard to come by, and even though we are just meeting her, we can tell she is a good woman," Amber included.

"You all are right. I messed up," I told them, and everyone frowned at me simultaneously.

"Why the hell are you telling us? Go tell *her,*" Charm shouted.

"And make sure you grovel. Groveling always works," Dennis yelled as I ran through the massive house, trying to figure out which room she had gone to.

"I know he messed up, but I'm to blame for this." I heard Pops telling Autumn as I cracked open the office door.

"You're not the one that lied to me, and even if you did, I'm married to Dylan, not you. He should have been man enough to tell me what was going on. I shouldn't have had to find out this from a man I just met today. It's all just so messed up. I brought my son into this bullshit. How am I going to explain to him that we are no longer a family because his stepfather is a liar?" I could hear the hurt in her voice at the mention of leaving me and telling Storm.

"It doesn't have to go that far. You two can work through this. You can do this, and it will help you forgive him. He loves you."

"He doesn't love me. His only love is money," she told Pops.

"No, sweetie. He loves you, and I know because the same way he looks at you is the same way the love of my life looked at me." I moved closer to the door when he said that. To my knowledge, Pops had never been in love.

"Dylan said you have never been in love with a woman," Autumn spoke my thoughts.

"Dylan only knows what I tell him," he paused. "When I was a young man," he paused again, and I pictured that faraway look in his eyes when he told me about something in the past. "When I was a young man, I fell in love with a woman who I felt was why my heart beat. She was so beautiful with brown hair and brown, doe-shaped eyes like a sea of chocolate. We fell in love very young and promised to love each other forever. We just didn't know that forever would end with her being promised to my brother. Back then, people built business deals off of arranged marriages, and that's what happened to us. I had to watch my brother marry the woman that I loved. All I got a chance to get was that one, and she was promised to someone else. I tried to find a woman to make me feel like she did for a long time, but it never happened to me again. The purpose of me telling you this is that in life, you only get one person that you love like that. You will have plenty of people you like, a couple that you will love, but it will only be one with whom you share that really deep connection and will be in love."

My grandmother and great-uncle were in love with each other? I stood at the door bewildered for a few minutes. Then I found the nerve to knock on the door. My Pops looked up at me when I stepped in, then turned to walk out.

"I hope you got the message," he said so low that only I could hear him when he passed me. I gave him a curt nod and walked over to Autumn. I pulled her into me and hugged her. I held her so tight that when she tried to pull away from me, she couldn't budge.

"I'm sorry," I told her as she fidgeted.

"I am so sorry," I told her again, holding her tighter.

"I'm sure you are, now let me go."

I loosened my arms just a little, and she pulled out of my grasp, backing away. I could see the pain in her eyes.

"I shouldn't have spoken to you that way," I paused, trying to think of the right words to say. The last thing I wanted to do was offend her more than I already had. All of this was just so new to me. I have never had to watch my words or explain my actions to any woman. Now, I'm standing here trying not to fuck up the good thing I have with her. She is the only woman I have cared for with such a strong emotion. Seeing her hurt was like sticking a knife into my gut and twisting it. I just wanted to see the look in her eyes that she had twenty minutes before I opened my big mouth. I wanted to see her smiling and happy. Just seeing her that way made my heart swell.

"You know you are confused. A little while ago, you were crying. You should've told me the truth then, and now, it's that you shouldn't have spoken to me that way. I think you're full of shit, and I have wasted my time with you. We came into this as friends. We were supposed to be honest with each other from the beginning. I would have still taken the plunge with you because we were helping each other. I feel like you brought me all the way to Massachusetts to flaunt me in front of all your rich-ass friends, then embarrass me." Her chest heaved up and down as she raised her voice at me.

"I would never do that to you. You're my wife. I brought you here because I wanted everyone to see the wonderful woman I married. You are beautiful and strong. You took on raising a child that wasn't yours at one of the roughest times in your life. You make sure you take care of the only sister you have left. You plan birthday parties for your friends with boyfriends that you can't stand because it will make your friend happy. You get up earlier than Storm and me to make us breakfast, even though we have people who get paid to do that. You are sacrificing four years of your life to ensure Summer and Storm can get the treatment they need. You are so loving and caring. You take care of everyone around you without blinking an eye. As your husband, I should be doing the same for you, and I failed at doing that tonight." I held my head down in shame because I had been a real asshole to the woman who I admire more than anyone in the world.

"I wanted my friends to meet you so they can learn to love you as much as I do," I told her honestly, watching the tears build up in her eyes.

"You don't have to pretend you love me to get me to stay. I'm not a liar like you. I'm a woman of my word. I gave my word that I would give you four years, and I will do that, but I will do that on my own terms. I will no longer be staying—"

"I won't let you leave me. I'm begging you. Please, don't do this to me." I dropped to my knees in front of her, ready to wrap my arms around her waist to keep her from moving. We haven't been living together long, but I couldn't imagine coming home without them being there. If I had to lock her in the room and have the maid give her three meals daily, she wouldn't leave me. They were my family, and I would never leave my family, so they couldn't leave me. She looked down at me on the floor, shaking her head.

"Like I was saying, I will no longer lie next to a lying-ass man." She stepped around me, walking out of the room. I exhaled a breath of relief.

Autumn is going to kill me. You would think that with us sleeping in separate beds and her barely speaking to me, I would be on my best behavior, but nope. Today, Pops and I took Storm to Disney for our boys' day out. Autumn has been telling me religiously not to give Storm too much junk while we were out. As soon as we entered the park, I got him cotton candy, and it didn't end there. I bought him everything he wanted, from toys to junk food, until we left the park. Now, I have to go into the house and explain to Autumn why he has on an outfit that he didn't leave the house in, and I have to take her Porsche Cayenne truck to get detailed.

"You're never going to hear the end of it," Pops laughed, walking into the house carrying some of the things we had won and bought for Storm. I grabbed Storm from the backseat, lifting his sleeping body to my shoulder. He tightly wrapped his arms around my neck without opening his eyes, and something began tugging at my heart. I turned carefully, taking a few steps into the house and then going directly to his room. I carefully stripped him of his clothes and went into his bathroom, soaping up a towel. I wiped him down twice before following Pops and Autumn's voices to the kitchen. As soon as I arrived, Autumn looked into my face with the first smile I had seen from her in weeks.

"How did it go?"

When I didn't answer her right off, she cocked her head like she does when she's trying to figure something out. I cleared my throat and watched Pops as he gave me a grim smile.

"Well, we had a little 'accident' in the car." I stopped, and her eyes went wide. I shook my head, holding up my hand to stop her.

"I kind of let Storm overindulge with junk food . . . and he threw up in your truck. I'll have Winston take it to be detailed in the morning. I know you told me not to let him eat too much junk, but I thought he would be okay, and I'm sorry. Please, don't be mad." She began shaking her head and laughing at me.

"I knew both of you would do the exact opposite of what I told you. I'm not angry that you two spoil that son of mine rotten. As soon as the words left my mouth, I knew I was wasting my breath. What I *am* angry about is my truck. Winston will not interrupt his day fixing a problem *you* caused. *You* will personally see to it that my Porsche is spotless and doesn't smell of vomit."

I nodded my head.

"Let me get ready . . ." She paused with her mouth open and her eyes glued to the TV.

"I'll be damned," Pop Wilson stated as Autumn hit the volume on the television.

"The playboy billionaire bachelor Dylan Holmes has tied the knot and is off the market, ladies. Yes, you heard me right. Dylan Holmes married his girlfriend, Autumn Spaulding, whom he has only known a short time, a few months ago."

Chapter 11

Autumn

I couldn't take my eyes off the screen as pictures of Dylan, Storm, and I flashed on the TV. They had most of the photos from the day we were married and pictures from the night of Charm's party. In one of the pictures, Dylan and I were on the dance floor, my back to his front. You could tell from the way we were standing that we were dancing. One of his hands was on my hip, and my hands were in the air above my head. My face was turned toward whoever took the picture, and my mouth was parted just a little.

"You have to admit that's a nice picture of you. It's almost like you posed for it," Pop Wilson said as I listened to what they were saying.

"Autumn, a native of Chicago who has custody of her deaf nephew Storm, has taken this billionaire off the market. Sorry, ladies," the anchor said with a smile, but I could see the envy in her eyes through the television. If she only knew what came with this marriage built on lies. I took a deep breath.

"Well, with that being said, I'm going to head to bed." I walked out of the kitchen into my bedroom. Although it was my picture plastered all over the TV and my business they were telling, this situation had nothing to do with me.

After we got back from Massachusetts, Dylan began his late-night outs again. I was bothered by it, but what could I do? I was the one who decided to leave his bed and give other women the opportunity to satisfy his needs. He was a man with a large sexual appetite. If I was honest with myself, I can admit I missed it. I missed him. I missed him pulling me close to him at night and wrapping his arms around me. I missed his soft snores in my ear, and when he thought I was sleeping, I would feel his eyes all over me. He would stare at me until I opened my eyes and smiled at him. More than anything, I miss his hands roaming my body while I was tied down to a bed. He had a way of knowing everything I needed when he was inside of me. Dylan had turned me into someone I didn't know when we were in bed together.

I walked over to my nightstand, pulling out one of my favorite gifts from him. I stripped out of my clothes, got in bed, and turned on the bullet to the highest setting. I imagined Dylan sucking my breasts and his hands roaming over my body, finding different ways of pleasing me. My imagination ran wild with images of us being entangled in each other passionately and his mouth all over me. Just when I was about to reach my peak, someone knocked on the door. I tried to ignore it and finish what I started. It was only Dylan letting me know he was headed out or to bed.

Knock, knock, knock.

This time, it was louder and more hurried. I closed my eyes, needing to finish what I started. Finally, the knocking stopped, and I was grateful I could get back to my fantasies.

"Oh, Dylan, yes!" I cried out, picturing his mouth on me as he worked the bullet inside of me. I was so into what I was doing I could hear him moaning like he was right here with me. The sounds excited me. Then I felt his hand touch my foot, go up my leg, and then my thigh. When I felt his warm, wet mouth touch my center, my eyes flew open. I tried to sit up but was pushed back down onto the bed.

"I—"

"Shh, let me do this," he commanded. I let my body relax and let him take me to the place of euphoria that only he seemed to get me to.

I watched as Dylan and Storm walked into the kitchen with smiles on their faces. Pop Wilson was already sitting at the island, keeping me company as I flipped pancakes onto the three plates on the counter. Once Dylan and Storm sat down, I placed the plates with pancakes, eggs, and bacon in front of them. As usual, they waited until I made my plate before digging into their food.

"You two seem a little more relaxed this morning," Pop Wilson said, and I rolled my eyes at him.

"Do you really have to notice everything?" I asked him while Dylan tried to smile with a mouth full of food.

"It's my job to notice everything about my children and grandchild. If I never paid attention to you three, everything in this house would go to hell. Since we are all here, I think it's time that I tell you both that this shit you two are doing needs to come to an end. Today makes three weeks that you two haven't been talking."

"We talk," I added smugly.

"You're too smart to play dumb, Autumn." His eyes pinned me, and I bit my tongue to hold back my words.

"Autumn, I understand you were hurt behind Dylan's lies and words. Hell, I wanted to kill him when he said what he said, but you two can't live the next four years like this. You sleep in separate rooms, but you can come together to please each other sexually."

I knew he curved his words because Storm was looking right at him. Pop Wilson was the type of man to say what he wanted, when he wanted, and how he wanted, but if Storm was in the room, he watched his language. I looked down at Storm's plate and noticed he had eaten everything on it. I told him to step out of the room so he wouldn't be in the midst of adults talking.

"I'll come get you shortly," I signed to him before he got up from the table. Dylan went to stand.

"Where the hell are you going?" Pop Wilson asked him.

"I thought this conversation was between you and Autumn," he shrugged.

"She's your wife, and this is your fault. Sit your ass back down." Pops raised his voice, and I smirked at Dylan.

"I don't know what to do about you two. I know you both are grown and think you know what you want. It's like the two of you are coparenting while living in the same home. Autumn, I know he hurt you by lying, but trust me when I say it could have been worse. Dylan, you must learn how to control your mouth during temper tantrums. You are not a damn child." Dylan dropped his eyes to the floor.

"Tell him," I added. Pop Wilson's eyes pinned me, and I wanted to run away.

"Let's not start with the stubborn marine who can't seem to let go or forgive. You were all too forgiving when you opened your legs for him last night, though."

I wanted to fall out of my chair and hit the floor with embarrassment. I sat there taking everything the old man was dishing out and realized one thing. He was right.

"I wish I could split you two in half and place you in each other's bodies. I have never been married a day in my life, but I know that opposites attract. I know that although you're pissed off at your spouse, you still take your ass to bed with them every night. You work on your problems together as a team and respect each other's differences. If you two can't make it through this one bump in the road, how will you make it through four years of marriage? Fix this shit. You guys have Storm thinking that you two will break up, and he will never see Dylan again."

Now, this was a shock to me. Storm hadn't said anything to either of us about how he felt. He went through his days with a smile on his face without a care in the world, or so we thought. It was time for me to fix our broken home. It took so much of my energy to act like Dylan didn't live here. I couldn't promise him I would trust everything that came out of his mouth. To be honest, though, I had no reason *not* to trust that he would do everything he declared he would do before we got married.

Even though I was on my independent woman thing and trying to spend my own money, Dylan would still put money into my account. Every Sunday, he took my car to the gas station for my weekly fill-up, and he never turned his back on Storm. He stepped in as the father the boy has never had and doesn't bat an eye when Storm wants extra time. Dylan still gives me a weekly gift, as he has done since we said, "I do." It's not always expensive things. He takes the time to be thoughtful, sending flowers with little notes attached, bringing me lunch at work, sending me to the spa weekly to unwind, and buying me charms for the bracelet he got me.

Once I reflected over the last few weeks that it wasn't Dylan who had changed, it was me, and it was time for me to give it a rest. I knew exactly what to do, but my pride was in the way. I sat listening attentively as Pop Wilson talked to us about how much of an ass we had been. His words, not mine. When he finished his rant, he thanked me for the wonderful breakfast. After going to talk to Storm, he left the house, and Dylan and I went our separate ways.

The doorbell went off throughout the house several times. Malinda fussed as she walked past my office door. I laughed at her words as she mumbled under her breath. A few minutes later, my office phone was ringing. I hit the speaker button on the phone.

"There's a Mark Stewart here to see you, ma'am." I cleared my throat, and she corrected herself, addressing me by my name. What the hell was Storm's father doing here? Last I heard, he was married to a nurse and living without a care in the world. His wife was one of those women who was willing to cripple a man by taking care of them. She was a firm believer in giving her man any and everything he needed, and all he had to do was be happy playing the game at home. When Mark was with Winter, he worked a good job and was at my sister's beck and call until Storm's diagnosis.

I walked into the entrance of the sitting room, standing in front of Mark with my arms folded across my chest. *Why is he here?* The thought kept running through my head. He finally looked up at me with a wolflike smile on his face. I had to admit he looked good since the last time I saw him. He was keeping himself up, but it wasn't his doing. It was his wife's.

"Long time no see."

I nodded my head as he eyed me like I was a piece of candy.

"Yeah, it's been a little over three years." I remember seeing him at Winter's funeral. He sat in the corner, crying his heart out. My sister was the love of his life, so he said. I almost felt sorry for him . . . until he walked past Storm like he didn't know him. How could a man have so much love and affection for his woman but none for his own child? I knew the answer to that question. He felt like Storm was defective. He wanted Winter to put Storm up for adoption because he felt like two people with their genetic makeup shouldn't have to deal with a child that wasn't whole in his eyes. He cried to Winter, telling her they could make another baby that would be better and healthier. I stood in front of him, getting angrier by the second, waiting for him to say why he was here. He just stared at me, not saying a word.

"How can I help you, Mark?" I finally asked. It was like he was in shock. He didn't say anything. I knew it was because I was letting my hair grow back, and I looked more like Winter than he expected. I was always the different one, but after a couple of talks with Summer, she asked me to let my hair grow back in. The air began to get thick as I waited for him to answer me.

"I would like to take Storm out and get to know him." His words were like taking a hammer to my head. After all this time, he has finally come to his senses and is ready to be the father I knew he could be. It has only taken six years, but I guess it's better late than never.

"Have you learned to sign?" I questioned.

"No, but can't he read lips or something?" I cocked my head at him. If he really wanted to be a part of Storm's life, he would have at least learned the basics.

"Well, my answer is no, you can't take him out of the house—" His eyes got big.

"He's my son," he cut me off.

"Don't throw that shit up in my face." I cut him off before he caused a scene. Lord knows I didn't know what Malinda was capable of. Instead of calling Dylan or the police, she might come out of the kitchen with a knife or gun. Although we met only several months ago, Malinda was like a mother hen about the people living in this house.

"You forfeited your rights to be his father when you walked out of the hospital that day. Better yet, when you begged Winter to put him up for adoption and didn't even look his way while you were bawling at his mother's funeral. Now, like I was about to say before you interrupted me, you are welcome to visit with Storm. Here. I will introduce you to him, and you two can sit in this room with his tutor and get more acquainted. Please, have a seat." I turned to get Storm.

"So, I have to have a chaperone?"

I turned back to him. "How do you expect to get to know him if you can't communicate with him? Plus, you may be his father, but he doesn't know who you are."

I waited a beat to see if he would say something else, but he didn't. So I walked to the back of the house, pulling out my cell to call Dylan. For some reason, something was off about this entire ordeal. At first, I was happy about him trying to come back into Storm's life. More than anything, I wanted this for him, especially since Winter was gone. Storm deserved to have at least one of his parents in his life. But I couldn't get over the feeling that Mark had ulterior motives. He wouldn't show his hand now, but his dirty deeds would eventually come to light.

I ran over everything with Dylan, and he wanted to come home. I assured him it wasn't necessary and went off to get Storm. When I found him, he was in the kitchen with Malinda, and she had a wary expression on her face. Storm was sitting at the small table in the corner, eating his lunch. She pulled me to the other corner, looking directly into my eyes.

"I know this is none of my business, Autumn, but I don't trust that man as far as I can throw him. I overheard the conversation you two had." In other words, she was eavesdropping.

"I know what you're feeling. Where's Mrs. Smith? I need her to sit in on their visit."

Malinda stepped back. "I sent her home for the day."

I raised an eyebrow at her, ready to go off. Storm needed to keep up with his studies, and she was sending people home. I closed my eyes because I was ready to explode.

"Why would you do a thing like that?" I questioned her. Malinda didn't give in to my attitude. She just smirked at me.

"If Storm is going to visit with his father, she won't have anything to do for the day. Since you said you wanted to cook tonight, I'll sit with Storm and his dad. Plus, we both know that Lisa is a pushover. You need someone in there who will keep a real eye out for him, and that's me." I smiled at her. I thought she was overstepping her boundaries, but she was just trying to protect her self-claimed grandson.

"Next time, ask me," I told her, laughing. I went to the table to get Storm and told him he had a visitor.

"You know all he wants is money, right?" Malinda blurted out.

I wasn't naïve. I know that Mark wants something out of this. I just couldn't say precisely what it was, but money was high on my list too.

Storm stood in the doorway of the sitting room, holding onto my hand for dear life while staring at Mark. Mark stood up with his arms out like Storm was supposed to run into them. Storm gave me an inquisitive gaze. I took his hand from mine.

"Storm, this is your dad, Mark Stewart. He's come a long way to visit you." Storm's gaze left me, went to Mark, then back to me.

"Dylan's my dad," he signed and turned. My heart pounded with joy at his confession of how he felt, but he was being rude, and I couldn't have that. I grabbed him by the shoulder, turning him around to face me.

"Storm, you will mind your manners. If you want Dylan to be your dad, that's fine, but this is the man who helped bring you into the world. You will be respectful, if nothing else. He wants to get to know you, and I think it would be good for you to know him. You may not think so right now, but later in life, you may learn to appreciate him." Storm was wise beyond his years, and I was paying the price for having an intelligent son.

"Do I have to?" His eyes were sad.

"Yes, Storm. Do it for me."

"What is he saying? He doesn't look so happy," Mark asked, looking at all three of us.

"I'm trying to explain to him why his father is just now wanting to meet him after six years."

"I know you're not telling him the truth," Mark said.

"The truth about what?" Storm asked, letting his eyes roam over Mark and me, raising his brow.

"Mark, do I need to remind you again that he knows how to read lips? Now he's questioning me about a truth you need to tell him. I wasn't there. I only heard about it."

"So, you never told him about me?" Mark questioned.

"Why would I break his heart and make him feel unworthy of love because of his disability? We don't even call it that in our home. We tell him that God made him different because he's special. He deserves to feel just as good as any other child." I made sure to keep my back to Storm as I spoke to him.

"Malinda will stay here as a translator for you. I don't want to stay because I actually want him to get to know you. If I'm around, he will cling to me. Mark, make this time with Storm count. You can stay as long as you like today."

Malinda took Storm's hand, and I returned to my office, exhaling a breath. Getting Storm to come around might be more complicated than I thought. That boy can be as stubborn as me when he wants. I sat in the office trying to concentrate on my work but couldn't. Several hours had passed, and things must've been going well. As soon as the thought crossed my mind, I heard Malinda raising her voice.

"Don't you ever in your life touch him like that again! He doesn't know you and doesn't have to do anything you say."

I jumped out of my chair and ran through the hall to the sitting room. When I heard Storm cry out, I picked up my pace and saw Malinda standing toe-to-toe with Mark and Storm safely behind her. I didn't waste any time standing beside Malinda and staring Mark down.

"Get out!"

"She's just the help, and this is my son. You can't tell me what I can and can't do to him," he yelled, looking at me.

"You're wrong. You gave up that right when you deserted him. He's *my* son that I have custody of, and I'm telling you to get out of my house before I call the cops." He stood there like my threat was idle and didn't move an inch.

"How about get the fuck out before I send Storm to his room and have Malinda help me do some bodily harm?" It didn't take him long to turn on his heels and head for the door. He knew better than anyone never to test a mother regarding her child. In this case, I hadn't given birth to Storm, but it didn't make him any less of my son.

When Malinda closed the door behind Mark, I exhaled a breath of relief. I sat on the couch next to Storm, asking him what happened. He told me that Mark wanted him to come and sit next to him, and after he refused three times, Mark snatched him up by the arm.

"I told you that man would be trouble, and trust me when I tell you, this won't be the last time he comes around. I think you and Mr. Holmes need to talk with him," she said as she walked off. "Don't worry about making dinner. I'll take care of that. Make sure our little guy is okay," Malinda stated.

Chapter 12

Autumn

Dylan was unhappy to learn about what happened. It had been a little over a week, and he would still get outraged about how Mark treated Storm. Pop Wilson offered to send some of his unsavory associates to "pay Mark a visit." I had to constantly remind them that the man was Storm's father, and that we couldn't harm him in any way. When I told my parents what happened, they didn't take the news any better. My father threatened to take his shotgun over to his house to "have a talk" with him. My mother had to hide the blasted thing from him because she caught him with it on several occasions, saying he was about to go "human hunting."

I went into the office today because I was tired of working from home. I needed to be around people and socialize.

"Excuse me, are you Autumn Spaulding Holmes?" I turned, eyeing the man in the button-up shirt, nice jeans, and comfortable loafers.

"Yes, I am Autumn. How can I help you?" I asked with a welcoming smile on my face.

"You have been served." The man placed an envelope in my hand, still holding the smile on his face before he walked off.

What the hell? I thought, opening the envelope. When I saw what it was, I stopped breathing, and my heart stopped beating. The room began to spin out of control, and I felt myself stumble. *Breathe, Autumn . . . breathe . . .* I told myself, but my lungs weren't cooperating with my mind, and everything around me began to fade, starting with the outer portions of the room . . . until everything went completely black.

"Are you okay?" I heard Dylan's voice as I came back from my little episode.

My head was pounding, and when I tried to sit up, my head began to swim again.

"Just lie back, baby. The doctors are going to take care of you. When you fell, you hit your head on the desk."

I remembered what had happened and me leaning on the desk, trying to gain my balance. I guess I didn't succeed with that. I rubbed my hand across my forehead and felt the knot that had formed. I winced in pain and lay back on the bed. There was nothing I could do until I was well. All of a sudden, dizziness hit me, and I turned away from Dylan, throwing up on the floor on the opposite side of the bed.

"Well, we know she has a concussion now," Pop Wilson stated with a frown.

I felt like I had been hit in the head with a bat. I turned again, emptying the contents of my stomach while Dylan held my hair back.

"What happened?" Dylan asked, and everything hit me at once.

"Mark is suing us for custody and child support of Storm," I told him with my eyes closed.

"I told you to let me have my friends pay him a visit," Pops said seriously.

"If you had, we wouldn't be going through this now. I guess next time, I need just to follow my first mind," he continued.

"Don't worry about that right now, Autumn. I won't let that happen, I promise. We just need to get you well," Dylan said, smoothing my hair as I lay back with my eyes closed.

I had to stay in the hospital overnight, and Dylan was right by my side the entire time. The next day, I was released, and Dylan had his lawyer meet us at the house. Pop Wilson kept Storm at the house with him overnight and said he would bring him back home the next day. He wanted me to be able to get several days of rest without having to worry about him.

When we arrived at the house, Dylan's lawyer, Tom, was waiting for us in the sitting room. Dylan helped me to the couch, and we sat beside each other.

"I'm sorry we have to officially meet like this. You may know already, but my name is Tom Lever." He reached over to shake my hand. I gave him a small smile.

"I went by the office to get the court order. I must tell you that courts are partial to parents having custody of their children. I am in no way saying that there's nothing that we can do. Since you have legal custody of Storm, and in the law's eyes, you are his mother, you may have to share custody with Mark Stewart."

My eyes widened. I didn't want him anywhere near Storm after their first and, hopefully, last meeting.

"No, Storm doesn't want that, and neither do we. Autumn let Mark into our home to meet Storm last week, and he snatched him up, trying to force him to sit next to him. Storm doesn't even know him, and after last week, he won't *want* to get to know him. I refuse to force my son into doing something he doesn't want to do," Dylan stated.

"Dylan, we know what this is about. This man hasn't been a part of your son's life since birth. Pictures of your family went viral a few weeks ago, showing off your beautiful wife and her deaf son. It was in the newspapers, on TV, and online about how the billionaire has gotten hitched. Then, out of nowhere, Storm's father pops up, wanting a piece of the pie. It doesn't take a rocket scientist to figure it out, but if he brings a good case to the court crying about being denied his rights, this will go left."

I didn't want what he was saying to be true, but I knew in my gut that it was. All of this was my fault for marrying Dylan. If I had stuck to my guns and told him no, this wouldn't be happening. But if I hadn't done it, I wouldn't be able to take care of Summer and pay for Storm's surgery. This was a damned-if-you-do-and-damned-if-you-don't situation. My head began to pound, and I didn't know if it was from the concussion or the stress.

"All we can do is go to court and hope for the best," Tom said, standing up to leave.

Dylan took a couple of weeks off work to help out with me. Malinda told him she could hold down the fort until he got home from the office, but he refused and thanked her. He was just as worried about what would happen with Storm and was trying to spend as much time with him as possible. Storm would be getting his cochlear implants in a few weeks, and he was excited about it and couldn't wait to hear our voices. He asked me the other day if Winter, Summer, and I sound alike. He was overjoyed when I told him that we do. Then he went on about how he would finally be able to hear his mother's voice. I watched his excitement until he turned and asked if he hurt my feelings. I pulled him in for a hug and let him know that he could never do that. As long as he was happy, I would be satisfied.

Today, Dylan had given Malinda the day off. She refused until he told her she would be fired if she didn't. Of course, Dylan would never do that, but she had been waiting hand and foot on everyone in the house since I had gotten a concussion. Although Dylan was by my side trying to take care of me, she would know what I wanted and needed before he did.

Suddenly, the doorbell rang throughout the house, and Dylan ran past me in the hall.

"I got it."

I went to turn back to the stove, but something told me to follow him. When I heard Mark's voice, my back stiffened.

"Hey, playboy billionaire. You know that's what they call you, right?" Dylan cocked his head, taking in the man in front of him.

"Deadbeat dad is what we call you. What are you doing here?" he asked. Mark smirked at Dylan like he could care less what he thought of him.

"Where's my little man?" Mark asked, trying to look around Dylan.

"He's not here. Maybe you should call before coming next time," Dylan lied smoothly.

Mark smirked at him. "Call you before I see my son? That's *not* how it works when he belongs to *me*. I should have full access to him whenever I want."

Dylan started laughing at him. "Not when he lives in *my* house. When you want to see him, call, and *if* he's available, you may see him." Mark laughed like he'd been told the funniest joke in the world.

"I guess we won't have to worry about that too much longer, huh?"

Dylan's back stiffened, but Mark was so busy being an asshole that he hadn't paid attention to the change in Dylan's stance. This would end badly, and one of them, mainly Mark, would end up in the hospital.

"You know, for a couple of million, you can make all of this go away and live happily ever after with your little family."

My mouth dropped, and Dylan's face turned red. The audacity of him coming to our home, trying to use our love for our child as his meal ticket. I wanted to rip him to shreds from limb to limb.

"Get the fuck away from my house," Dylan said through clenched teeth.

"Why are you so hostile about it? You don't want to separate with your money over a half-assed child?" I closed my eyes, hearing him say those things for the first time.

"You will *never* get him," Dylan yelled, causing me to jump.

"That's where you're wrong. My lawyer promised me full custody of Storm with a healthy-ass child support payment to go with it. He said I could get at least fifteen grand a month with the money you have. Since Autumn is married to you, your money is her money. I know she would never go for a complete payout, but you're a businessman. You know how stuff like this goes. If you want a happy life, you have to pay the price."

Dylan inhaled, holding it in before exhaling. "It's a shame you don't want him around just because you love him. He's a really good kid and deserves way better than anything you could offer him."

"I don't give a fuck about him being a good kid. He can't hear, and I don't have time to raise a retard for a son."

Well, that was the last straw. I stomped out of my hiding spot, but before I could get to the door, Dylan had struck Mark so hard I heard his jaw crack. Dylan continued his assault on Mark as he went down to the ground. I ran over, trying to pull Dylan off him, wishing Malinda was here to help me. On second thought, I'm glad she wasn't here because she would be helping Dylan.

"That's enough!" I told Dylan, pulling him back.

"Get the fuck away from my house before I call the police."

Mark tried to get up and fell back to the ground, then tried again, succeeding this time. His jaw was hanging on one side, and I knew it was broken.

"If you want some money, sue me for that," Dylan told him, stepping back.

"First thing in the morning," Mark mumbled, dragging his leg, trying to walk. What Dylan pulled will probably have us tied up in court for a while, but I couldn't have been prouder of him at this moment. He had taken up for our son, and my love for him immediately grew ten times more.

I took his face in my hands, taking a closer look to see if he was hurt. He had a couple of scratches but nothing major. He shook his right hand out. It was swollen. I pulled him to the kitchen to get him an ice pack to put on it.

"Did you hear that?" Dylan asked me with a concerned expression.

"From the moment you opened the door. Today is one of those days I'm glad that Storm is deaf. I don't know if his poor heart would have been able to take hearing that fool say all that stuff."

Somberly, Dylan nodded.

"I never asked you this before, but how did you learn to sign?"

A smile touched his lips, and I could tell from the look in his eyes that his mind had wandered back to another time in his life.

"When I was younger, Pops sent me to this expensive-ass camp for the summer in New York. It would be just camp activities all day for the kids ten to fourteen. After fourteen, we would have something like teenage business classes in the morning. Then we would do regular camp activities. I've already signed up Storm for them. I know he would love it there. Anyway, one of the boys at camp was deaf, and people would mess with him. They would call him dumb because they didn't know how to communicate with him. I felt terrible about how some kids treated him, so I befriended him.

"He taught me how to sign some things over the summer, and I made him promise on the last day of camp that if he returned next year, I would learn to sign throughout the year, and we could bunk together. When I got home, I told Pop what had happened and that I needed a tutor to teach me to sign. He told me he was glad I was willing to expand my horizons and add a new language of study, and he learned with me. Both Brad and I made good on our promises and returned the following year and the years after. We still chat to this day." This man keeps surprising me with everything he does. I stood on my toes, kissing him, and he deepened the kiss. I just knew I made a puddle on the floor.

"I love you." He signed the words to me, making me smile, and tears came to my eyes.

"I love you too." I spoke the words out loud because I wanted to hear my confession of love to this man. I could think it to myself all day, but it didn't mean a thing if I didn't say it out loud or to him. How could I not love a man who loves my son and me so much that he would cause bodily harm to another person just to keep us safe? I'm sure Mark would make good on his word to sue us, but since Dylan wasn't worried about it, I wouldn't worry either.

Chapter 13

Dylan

Autumn's declaration of love for me sent me into overdrive. I picked up my phone texting Malinda, asking her if she could watch Storm for a few hours. Although I gave her the day off, I knew she was staying in her room in the back of the house. When she sent me the okay I was waiting for, I picked up Autumn and took her to our room. This separate room shit would end today, but not until I showed her how much I loved her. Whenever we connected as one, we always played games, but not today. This time, I would make love to her like a man does with his wife. I will take my time, do things slowly, and let the emotions I feel for her flow through my body until we are complete and sated.

When we stepped into the room, I took her lips in mine once more. I felt like I couldn't get enough of the way she tasted. I missed how she tasted and our scent once we were in the throes of passion. I placed her on her feet and slowly helped her remove her clothes. When she stood before me naked, I stood back, taking in every crevice of her toned body. Tonight, I would worship her body because all of this, all of her, belonged to me. She was mine, and I would show her in the only way I knew how. I would place my mark all over her body, letting her know that no man could ever make her feel the way that I do. I will satisfy her yearnings because I never want her to look to anyone else for anything other than friendship. Tonight, I will make her mine forever.

I stripped, then picked up Autumn, placing her in the bed. I started at her feet, kissing every toe, then went up from there, kissing her calves, thighs, and stomach, knowing my child will be growing in her belly one day. I made my way up to her chest, taking one of her breasts in my mouth while playing and toying with the other until I gave it my full attention. I stayed there for so long that she squirmed under me, crying out my name as an orgasm ripped through her body. I took a moment to inhale the womanly scent I created by satisfying her. Then I moved up to her mouth, kissing her slowly and sensually before kissing each one of her fingers and the palms of her hands where she had the power to crush or hold my heart there safely.

I dragged my tongue up her arm back to her pouty, full, soft lips. Finally, I trailed kisses down to the place I really wanted to be, between her thighs. I so anticipated her taste that I licked my lips and moaned before diving into her sweetness. I took my time loving her pussy with my mouth. This was all mine. I would be right here until she screamed my name and gave me all the honey I wanted from her. I stuck my tongue inside of her, and she grabbed at the top of my head, pulling my hair and moaning. Her body tensed from the wave of desire that she was riding on.

"Dylan . . ." she screamed my name while she rode the high wave that I had put her on. Now, it was time for the main course. I lifted one of her legs and slowly stroked her until we both were too weak to move.

"I love you," I told her before my eyes closed.

***

Today was Storm's big day, and everyone came to California to show him a strong support system. Autumn's parents, Derrick and Sunflower Spaulding, her best friend, Charm, and one of my best friends, Chase, came here to show their support. Summer was even released for a few days to be here for him. Pops was right there with us, waiting to hear that our Storm was all right. Finally, the doctor came through the door with a smile.

"Storm's surgery went great, and he's in recovery, sleeping now. You and your sister are welcome to go back with him, but everyone else must give him an hour."

"Thank you so much, Dr. Wong."

Autumn and I updated the family and went to the back to sit with Storm. About an hour and a half passed before Storm was placed in his room, and everyone came in.

"Are you okay, baby?" His grandmother signed to him, and he smiled big, letting everyone know he was fine.

"Why can't I hear?" he asked, looking around at all of us.

"Because they have to wait until everything heals before they turn it on, buddy," I said with a smile. He smiled back at me, saying he understood.

"He's my fucking son. I should be in there with him. I have every right to be there."

Everyone's eyes flew to the door upon hearing Mark on the other side. I rolled my eyes. How did he even find out we were here? I stood up, ready to handle the situation, when Mark burst through the door with a glint of hatred in his eyes. I smiled, seeing the metal wiring across his teeth. Autumn grabbed my hand, stopping me from walking up to him. Storm had a look of terror in his eyes that broke my heart when I saw it.

"How can we help you?" I finally asked, blocking his path from getting to Storm's bed.

"I want to see my son," he said through his wired teeth.

"He doesn't want to see you," I told him curtly.

"He should *want* to see me. He's finally a real kid now."

I rolled my eyes, glad they hadn't turned the cochlear on.

"He was already a real kid, you prick," I replied, getting irritated with him.

"Son! Son! It's your daddy."

"He can't hear you, Mark, and you're upsetting him. Come with me in the hall so we can catch up," Sunflower told him. If looks could kill, Sunflower would have dropped dead right before us.

"I don't give a fuck about him being upset. He might as well get used to it because he will live with me soon."

That was it. I couldn't take it anymore. Before I knew it, I had punched his other jaw. I heard his bone, and maybe even mine, pop on impact. Chase opened the door, and when he fell back, he was in the hall.

"I swear I'ma sue you again," Mark mumbled, trying to hold his jaw in his hand.

"Another thirty grand won't kill me. It's just pocket change, chump," I told him as Chase closed the door, laughing.

"At least he's already in the hospital."

We all laughed at Chase's antics until I saw the sad look on Storm's face.

"Don't let him take me away."

I took a deep breath, walking over to the bed. I sat on his bed, pulling him into my lap. I needed to hold him close. I just broke the jaw of the man who was the reason I got to hold him like this for the second time. I hadn't really thought about it until now. I didn't know if that would count against us in this custody battle. Yeah, I had a whole lot of money, but I didn't know if it would help me in this situation. The first broken jaw cost me thirty thousand dollars without taking it to court. It was settled between our lawyers since Mark was trespassing on my property. I was sure I would get a slap on the wrist for this one too, but I began to become concerned with how it would look in court.

"I promise I won't," I told him, seriously hoping I could keep my promise.

"How did he even find out about Storm's surgery today?" Autumn wondered aloud.

"Since we had to postpone the court date, his lawyer probably informed him of it. Don't worry about anything, but make sure Storm is okay, babe. I'll take care of everything else," Dylan said.

She nodded okay.

"Chase and Pops, I need to speak with you two. I would ask you to come with us, Derrick, but I need you to stay here with the ladies and Storm in case Mark decides to return." Chase and Pops followed me out of the hospital and off to the side, where we could talk privately

"I need to find a way to keep my promise to Autumn and Storm. I never anticipated Mark to be the pain in my ass that he has been."

"Just pay him off. It's not like you can't afford it," Pop Wilson told me, shrugging his shoulders.

"I can't do that. He's the type of man who will come back with the same shit once he starts to run out of money," I told him honestly.

"What about the videos of him at the house?" Chase asked.

"Tom said I can't use those in court because he didn't know he was being recorded," I sighed.

"We can find out who the judge is and pay them off."

"Pops, everything doesn't always come down to money. Plus, I had thought of that myself until I discovered it was Judge Ryan."

"Damn," both Chase and Pops stated at the same time. This case would have been a slam dunk if it were any other judge, but it just had to be the one who hates Wilson Holmes and everyone with that last name. If Pops could have just kept his dick in his pants. He slept with Judge Ryan's wife over thirty years ago, and that man has never forgiven him. Even if it's in Storm's best interest to stay with us, Ryan will find a reason to give him to Mark. He hated my uncle just that much. I had no idea what I would do about this.

"You know I still mess around with his wife. Maybe I can have her give him something to make him sick that day."

"I guess you hate breathing. You forgot about how that man came to your house with a gun, and Grandpa had to stop him from putting a bullet in your head."

I had been told the story about how he almost lost his life several times when I was growing up. Pop Wilson would always tell me about how his brother saved his life a month before he died. I had to try to figure this out, and for the first time in my life, my uncle couldn't help me. We returned to Storm's room, and I called for several cars to take everyone back to the house. Autumn and I stayed at the hospital with Storm.

Two Months Later . . .

I sat in court behind Autumn with an entire support team. Storm sat next to me, as did Sunflower, Derrick, Summer, and Pop Wilson. They all took up the first bench. Brenton, Wilson Holmes, Chase, Charm, Amber, Dennis, and Collen, Chase's dad, took up the second and third benches. Everyone was here to show a strong family presence. As my uncle would tell me when I was younger, it takes a village. At that time, he was my village to care for and protect me when my parents wouldn't. Everyone on this side of the room was Storm's village, and we would do anything within our power to protect him, even if that meant that our entire village moved to Cuba to keep him safe, and it had been considered several times.

Autumn and I wanted to allow the system to work in our favor. All I could think of was the many children who were given to the wrong parent, and it ended in tragedy. I knew in my heart, though, that if I had to, I would give up my entire fortune to keep my son safe. Yes, he was my son. This year with Autumn and Storm had taught me so much about being a husband, a father, and a man, and I wasn't letting my family get torn apart over something that I could gain back so quickly. Once this was over, I would do the right thing for my family.

Judge Ryan walked into the room, and we all stood, showing respect.

"The case we are bringing before you today is quite simple, Your Honor. My client, Mark Stewart, was wronged by the late Winter Spaulding. She passed away and left sole custody of her then 3-year-old son, Storm Spaulding, to her sister, Autumn Holmes. My client just wants what is rightfully his: custody of his son and a small amount of money for his pain and suffering. He was torn away from his son once his mother died and has been in the dark about his son's well-being for the past four years. Being a father yourself, you can understand the pain of a man having their only child snatched away from them."

Autumn leaned back in her chair. I could tell from her facial expression she was getting heated from the show that the lawyer was putting on. She rolled her eyes, and Tom patted her hand, trying to comfort her. Judge Ryan smirked at her. I hated that this man, a judge, had such a vendetta against my uncle, and Autumn had nothing to do with it. She was guilty purely by association. I knew there was about to be some shit. I felt it in the air.

"Is there anything you would like to say, Mrs. Holmes?" Judge Ryan asked. I closed my eyes, knowing he was baiting her. Tom shook his head at Autumn, telling her not to speak, and she calmed a little.

"No, Your Honor."

"Are you sure?" he asked once more.

Now, Autumn stood to her feet, and I knew the shit was about to hit the fan. Autumn was outspoken, and I knew everything she felt was about to come to light. I just didn't know if it would work in our favor.

"Your Honor, Mark Stewart has lied about everything said so far. I don't know if he told his lawyer those exact words or if they are making things up along the way. It's sad to say they are lying to you. Mark left my sister, Winter, when Storm was 3 months old because he didn't want to have anything to do with a deaf son. In fact, he wanted her to put him up for adoption so they could try again for a better, more efficient child, like he were a car. Mark had years to come and be a part of Storm's life. This lie that he couldn't find him is complete and utter bullshit." She stopped when the judge's eyes widened, and Tom grabbed her hand.

"I'm sorry." She waited a minute, then continued.

"My parents have lived in the same house since my sisters and I were born. Mark grew up with us and went to school with us, and his parents stayed exactly one block up the street from my parents. Mark and Winter had been together since seventh grade until Storm was born. He could have gotten in contact with us. He came to my sister's funeral and didn't even look at Storm four years ago. We had an incident where Storm and my sister Summer were missing for several days, and yet, no word from Mark. An amber alert went out from New York down to Texas. It was broadcast all over the news, and cameras sat outside my parents' house until we found him. Yet, Mark was a no-show. He didn't come to the house and ask how to help. He didn't drive through the neighborhood calling out Storm's name until his voice was hoarse. He did nothing at all."

She took a deep breath, picking up a paper towel to wipe the tears that came down her face.

"A few months ago, the news of who I married was all over the TV and internet. Suddenly, Mark misses the child that was 'snatched out of his grasp.' He came to my house asking to take my child out, but he couldn't communicate with him. After all this time of knowing he has a deaf son, he never took the time to learn how to sign. Even though he's putting us through all of this, I will bet my life he can't even sign 'I love you' to his own son. He doesn't care about Storm. All he wants is money from my husband. He could care less about how Storm is being treated now. He's just looking at dollar signs behind the name Holmes."

"She's lying, Your Honor! They snatched my son from me. I deserve to have a chance to raise him on my own."

Judge Ryan pounded his gavel until Mark sat down from his antics. He was putting on a performance that was fit to earn him an Emmy.

"I'm obligated to do what's best for the child, and who's to say that his father isn't? This man deserves a chance to get to know his child. Mrs. Holmes, you're standing here telling me your side of the story, but who's to say you aren't lying to me?"

I rolled my eyes, knowing who he was and what he held against my family. I knew that this wasn't looking too good for us.

"Your Honor, I have no reason to lie to you. All I have for Storm is the love of a mother. I have nothing to gain from him staying with me but his love and seeing a smile on his face every day. I have a question, sir. If Mark gained custody of Storm, where does that leave me in all this, being his legal guardian?"

Now, we're getting somewhere. Autumn asked the question that was on everyone's mind. We knew the answer to it.

"That will leave you with visitations and paying child support for Storm until he's 18 or until he finishes college," Judge Ryan replied.

Mark smirked, and I wanted to wipe it off his face. Everyone in this courtroom knew this was about money and nothing else.

"Being married to Dylan and combining our finances of what we bring in together, about how much a month would that be?"

Judge Ryan wrote something down on the paper in front of him. Autumn had been making a nice amount of money working for us. When you added money to our accounts and money made in the future, I knew the payments would be high.

"You would be paying about twenty grand a month, and that's more than affordable for the two of you." It was affordable, but what child needed that much money monthly to survive?

"We have to consider that we would want him to keep the same lifestyle he has now. When we add the fact that he would need speech therapy and several doctors' visits for his hearing, twenty thousand dollars is a drop in the bucket for you two."

"What if I leave my husband?" When she asked that, my heart plummeted.

"Your payments would go down substantially because you wouldn't be able to afford to make payments that high," Judge Ryan answered.

"Fine." She turned to me with tears in her eyes. "I want a divorce." I stood up, and she sat in her seat like she hadn't just broken my heart.

"She can't do that! She's only doing this, so I won't get what belongs to me. They owe me this money. He broke my jaw, and I need to get paid for it," Mark yelled through the wire in his mouth. I was sitting in shock at how my marriage just ended right before my eyes. Judge Ryan banged his gavel until the room settled down, bringing me back to the present. Storm pulled at my arm, trying to get my attention. I was the only one still standing in the courtroom.

"If he sends me with him, I'm running away. I don't want to be with someone I don't know and thinks that I'm stupid because I couldn't hear," he signed to me.

"What did he say?" Judge Ryan eyed me as Storm signed.

"He said he would run away if you sent him with Mark. He doesn't want to live with a man who thinks he's stupid because he can't hear," I translated.

"How do we know Dylan isn't lying just to keep custody of him?" Mark yelled, and I rolled my eyes.

"Plus, why would I call my own child stupid?" Mark insisted.

Judge Ryan looked at the translator sitting to his right, and she nodded, letting him know that I was telling the truth.

"Come up here, son, and talk to me." Storm stood up, walking past me, looking nice in his blue button-up shirt and black slacks.

"How can he talk? He can't hear," Mark said smugly.

"Hi, Storm. How are you?" Judge Ryan asked in a softer and nicer voice than he used with everyone else.

"I'm fine. How are you?"

Storm cleared his throat and opened his mouth. His words weren't as clear as they could be, but he did well with his speech sessions. I was a proud father at this moment. Judge Ryan gave Storm a smile that I hadn't ever seen the man give in all my time knowing him.

"I'm good, young man. Can you tell me about the day your daddy called you stupid?" he asked.

"My daddy's name is Dylan Holmes, but I can tell you about it. Mark came to the house and asked if he could see me. I couldn't see what my daddy said, but I saw everything Mark said. I read his lips. He asked my dad to give him money, and then he wouldn't take me away from them. I guess my dad told him no because he said that it would save him from having to live with a retard. My dad hit him in the jaw for that. I may have been deaf, but I'm not stupid."

Storm's soft words broke my heart. Autumn began to cry loudly at his words. We didn't know he was anywhere near the door and saw that.

"That little bastard is lying!" Mark yelled. I had to calm myself because I felt like breaking his neck this time. Judge Ryan had a shocked expression on his face. He beat down the gavel, and Storm covered his ears.

"I'm sorry I hurt your ears. Is there anyone else who saw or heard this transaction?" he asked, and Autumn raised her hand.

"I was in the corner of the sitting room listening to what was being said. I broke up the fight between the two men," she responded. Judge Ryan's expression read, "Yeah, right. You broke up their fight." Autumn read right through it.

"Sir, I served as a marine. I have had to carry men twice my size. I can break up a fight between two men."

I saw the admiration in his eyes for her at that moment.

"Thank you for serving our country," he replied.

"Did anyone else hear or see what happened?"

"No, Your Honor," Autumn answered.

"What about a video?" I asked, and he raised an eyebrow at me.

"Explain," he demanded.

"I have cameras set up throughout the house for security purposes. They have audio too, and I have them here on my phone."

He nodded for me to come up, and I looked at Mark. He had a look of defeat on his face. He knew this was the end of his charade, and we had him by the balls. Storm would be coming home with us. I handed him the phone, and both of the lawyers and I went to the judge's chambers. I showed them the video of the first time Mark came to the house and how he snatched Storm off the couch. Next was the video of him trying to get a payoff. Last, I got a video of him at the hospital.

When we returned to the front, Judge Ryan stared at Mark with a death glare. Mark knew what was about to happen, and he couldn't sit still in his seat.

"You have wasted everyone's time trying to get money you haven't worked for. You have put this child through so much and have only been in his life for a few months. Did you know that he wakes up screaming in the middle of the night because he thinks that you will beat him if he has to go with you? Thank God he has good people in his life who can turn the damage around that you have done. When I came out here this morning, I had all intentions of giving you the son that you cried about being 'snatched away' from you—only to see you in a video abusing him and using him as a pawn in your little sick-ass game. I have a paper right here in front of me that will determine how this day ends for you. These papers state that you will give up all legal rights to Storm Spaulding. If you sign them, you won't go to jail for child abuse. If you do not sign them, my bailiff will take you away."

Mark tried to open his mouth to say something.

"Before you decide to be stupid and say no, let me tell you this. I will email that video of you putting your hands on that boy to myself. Whenever Dylan or Autumn call me and say that you are trying to sue them for *anything*, I will send it to the judge appointed over your case. The choice is yours. Now, please, choose wisely."

Mark's lawyer leaned to the side, whispering in his ear before he signed the papers in front of him.

"Court is adjourned."

We all cheered on our way out of the door.

"Do you still want a divorce?" I asked Autumn later that night while we lay in bed.

"You know why I did that. I couldn't let Mark take one part of your fortune because of me."

I closed my eyes, taking in her words. Then I slowly turned her to face me so she could look into my eyes. "None of this would mean a thing to me if you weren't here to share it with me," I told her honestly. I needed her to understand that I couldn't breathe without her.

"I have something I want you to see," I told her, getting out of bed and going into my dresser drawer.

"What is this?" she asked before looking at the papers.

"See for yourself."

She opened the papers, and tears came to her eyes.

"You want to adopt Storm?" she said between her sobs.

"Yes. I want to make our son a Holmes. If we have other children, I don't want him to feel like an outsider. He's a part of this family, and if you are legally his mom, I want to be his dad legally," I told her.

"I love you so much, Dylan Holmes." She kissed me between each word.

"And I love you too, Mrs. Holmes."

Autumn

Five Years Later . . .

We all had come together for our annual vacation. Life has been good to all of us, and what better way to celebrate it than with each other? Since most of us stayed in different states, we decided to gather for one month every year in a place of our choosing. This year, we were at the Grand Turks, Dylan's and my choice. This was one of the places where we began noticing each other. We all sat on the deck of the huge house we rented, laughing at each other's antics. We all have come a long way, and everything we have been through has made us closer. I watched as a 9-year-old London followed behind Storm as he was trying to find somewhere to hide from the toddlers in the house. Our families had grown quite a lot, and we soon would run out of space to put the kids.

There were some changes along the way too. Like Chase's mom and dad had gotten a divorce. As they say, one woman's trash is another woman's treasure. As a favor to Dylan and me, he let her work for him when Summer was released from the rehabilitation center. Evidently, what we thought was "work" ended up being all play because she and Collen were now happily married. Believe it or not, Collen was what she really needed. Summer was a totally different person now. They have been married for four years and have a little 2-year-old girl they named Winter. Their happiness doesn't end there. Summer is currently expecting, and I'm hoping for multiple births.

Brenton and Reign are what dreams are made of. They have a solid relationship. Brenton continues to bend at her every beck and call, but their little one has both of them wrapped around her tiny finger. Royal is 4 years old and runs their household. She's a very hyper baby but as cute as any baby could be. Just looking at her doll-like features would give any woman baby fever. Reign and Amber never gave up on their dreams of becoming lawyers. They actually ran their own firm in Massachusetts and were a great tag team in the courtroom. We are incredibly proud of them, and when Charm and I were in town, we went in to help them in any way we could.

Amber and Dennis have another addition to their family. Preston is 5 years old today and looks just like his father with his mother's eyes. We are all so proud of Dennis. He extended his bar and grill to Los Angeles and Chicago. He also has plans to expand to Miami. Personally, I can't wait for that opening. Their daughter, London, is still the spitting image of her mother and more than a force to be reckoned with on the soccer field.

Charm and Chase have plans to have a football team of children. I guess since they make enough money to have them, that's good for them. They are the happy parents of three children: their twin boys, Colton and Cole, which was a surprise, and little Casey. She's about to turn 3. Chase said he wanted as many children as Charm would give him. On the business side of things, they are doing good for themselves. They work together as a team and dominate any company they set their sights on. Her mother and father had gotten back together and were doing good as husband and wife.

Dylan and I have a 2-year-old baby that we named Rain. She is surrounded by men, so she is spoiled rotten. Pop Wilson finally let me talk him into selling his house and moving in with us. Sometimes, I feel I shouldn't have ever crossed the line; other times, I'm proud that we made that choice. My parents moved to California a few years ago. They split the year between there and Chicago. At times, it can be a hassle with everyone under the same roof, but it's well worth it. I was given my own office to run at our family real estate company, and competition between Dylan and me is always at an all-time high. I'm glad the love of my life isn't a sore loser.

"What are you over here thinking about?" Dylan came and sat behind me on the lounge chair, pulling me close to him. He pulled my hair out of the way, knotting it on the top of my head. Since I've had Rain, he's been trying to get a handle on doing hair.

"Just thinking about our family and how far we all have come." I leaned to the side to kiss his lips.

"Yeah, we have grown a lot." He smiled, letting his eyes roam over everyone out here.

"Who would have thought I would be sitting here holding my wife in my arms and having two kids? Until you came into my life, I didn't want any of that, and now, look at me. I feel like I always need all three of you around me." I knew the feeling. I rushed home from work every night so that I could hug them. Dylan propositioning me to be his wife was the best thing that has ever happened to me. It has given me more family and love than I could ask for and has made all my dreams come true. I gazed into Dylan's eyes.

"I love you, Mr. Holmes."

"I love you more, Mrs. Holmes."